DEMON KISSED

www.DemonKissed.com

Join over 33,000 fans on facebook!
www.facebook.com/DemonKissed

DEMON KISSED

H.M. WARD

Laree Bailey Press

Laree Bailey Press, 4431 Loop 322, Abilene, TX 79602

Printed in the United States of America
First Printing: April 2011
10 9 8 7 6 5 4 3 2 1

Library of Congress Cataloging-in-Publication Data

Ward, H.M.
Demon kissed / H.M. Ward – 1st ed.
  p. cm.
ISBN 978-0615467092

Thank you to my family
For encouraging me to
Unleash my inner-artist.

And thank you to the
Awesome fans who loved
Demon Kissed
From the very beginning.

DEMON KISSED

CHAPTER ONE

"Let me go, Jake. You're not like this." Desperation was in my voice.

"Ivy, you have *no* idea what I'm like." The moon hung high above the trees. It painted shadows across Jake's face, highlighting his perfect contours. My arms felt like lead, useless at my sides. I couldn't tell how he ensnared me. It felt like my wrists and ankles were glued to the ground, but nothing was there. Pulling hard, unable to move, my heart started to race. I hated feeling trapped. Actually *being* trapped made it worse. Moments ago everything was normal. We were laughing, rolling around on the grass.

"I thought... I thought you wanted a kiss?" I asked.

"I *do* want a kiss." Leaning closer, Jake emerged from the patchwork of shadows. The dim moonlight spilled across his face, revealing his eyes. I couldn't look away. My heart hammered as our gazes locked. An ungodly crimson ring surrounded his normally blue eyes, hugging tightly to his irises. It was like fire and blood, burning together. And they were intently focused on one thing.

Me.

Panic shot through my veins. "What's *wrong* with your eyes?" I shivered, repressing the fear that crawled up my throat.

He shifted, hovering above me. Jake's lips spread into a soft grin. "I'm still me. You can trust me, Ivy.

I've wanted to kiss you for so long. My timing was perfect."

"Timing?" I asked. "I wanted you to kiss me since our first date. And you wanted to wait. So we wait, then you bait me out here, and glue me to the ground? What the hell is wrong with you? Let me go!"

He laughed softly, "God Ivy, I wasn't sure about you at first, but I was right… You'll get your kiss."

Terror flooded through me, "What do you want, Jake?"

"I'll show you," he leaned closer, grinning. As his lips touched mine, I cried out, unable to contain the agonizing pain. The feeling of razor wire slid inside me, from my lips to my toes. It snaked through my body. Sharpness tore into me like a million little fishing hooks, all snagging my insides at once.

I tried to scream, but Jake's lips were pressed to mine. His hands clutched my face, holding me still, preventing me from moving and breaking the kiss. Adrenaline pumped into me, making my thoughts splinter off into a dozen different directions, trying to find a way out. The sensation cut deeper, as I writhed beneath him. I desperately tried to think of a way to ease the pain, and did the only thing that would make him stop, without thinking about what would happen next.

Sucking his lip into my mouth, I bit down—hard. Jake pulled away screaming, as tangy warmth filled my mouth. A warm trail spilled over my cheek. I spit out a mouth full of his blood. Swearing, he moved away from me, cradling his lip with his palm, trying to stop the flow of crimson.

Trees creaked, snapping my gaze to their massive trunks. My eyes sifted through the shadows hoping that someone was there. But there was no one. We were alone. No one would save me.

Jake returned fuming. "That was stupid, Ivy. I would have been nice, and made it less painful. But not now." He lunged at me. Screaming, I tried to break free. Crushing lips met mine. The razor wire sensation snaked down my throat, filling my body. It hooked into every inch of flesh and muscle, spreading deep into my bones. Then he pulled the invisible razors. Hard.

The intense pain tore through me, and I was unable to stop him. My tensed muscles tried to endure the agony, as spots formed and my vision flickered. Frantically, my mind tried to figure out what was happening. Logic didn't have an answer, but my body knew exactly what was happening. My soul, my very being that was locked deep within me—he was ripping it out. It didn't slide away, loose like a ribbon, tied in a pretty bow. It was attached to me, in an inseparable kind of way. Inseparable things—I learned—could be separated, but it hurt like hell.

Releasing me from his kiss, Jake paused just before I passed out. *Oh God, he wants me awake.* Drowsiness pulled at me, making it difficult to think. Pain spindled in my muscles as they twitched uncontrollably. Jake wiped the back of his hand across his bloodstained mouth and smiled down at me, delighted.

I spit out more of his blood onto the ground. It tasted wrong. It had a weird tang that made me gag. I knew his blood covered my lips and washed across my face, but I couldn't wipe it away.

Hysterical sobs bubbled up from my stomach, but I swallowed them whole, not wanting him to see my terror. Trembling, a single word formed in my mind, and spilled over my bloody lips, "Why?"

His greedy smile vanished and his face contorted. His beautiful features were skewed, showing no trace of the guy I knew. Veins bulging, he spit, just missing my face. He snarled, "You're one of *them*. Why else would I hunt you? Following you around for months, listening to you and your insignificant life. Why would I waste my time with someone like *you*?"

Hatred flashed across my face. "Why'd you wait? Why not just suck out my soul three months ago?" The words felt odd to say, but I knew they were true.

"I had to wait for this to appear." Flicking a curl away from my face, his fingers touched the skin above my brow. "That's interesting. Your mark is more...." He paused, sitting back, dabbing at his lip, "It doesn't matter anyway, because you're all the same. An angel-kissed, blue bastard. It's your seventeenth birthday, and *this* happened. Just like all the others." He leaned back laughing at me. "The first twenty-four hours are a bitch. You have no idea what you are, what you're capable of, or why this happened to you." The corners of his mouth pulled into a tight grin. "It's the perfect time to kill you. That's why I waited. And I'm usually kind of nice about it. But you bit me, you little whore. So, I'm going to make sure it hurts much *more* than usual." He leered at me with a satanic smile, "I'm going to rip out your soul so fast that it cracks your bones."

Bloodstained teeth beamed, as he moved toward me. Screaming wildly, I belted the sound through the trees, shattering the still night. Jake's eyes burned in the darkness as he inched nearer. My roaring heartbeat drowned out all other noises. Stiffening in anticipation, tears ran down my cheeks. I couldn't bear it. Not again.

Dripping with satisfaction, he hovered over me. "Are you afraid, Ivy?" His face slid toward me, slowly. His lips curled, as he sensed my terror. "Of course you are. I'm your mortal enemy. Well, *immortal* enemy. You would have been around for a while—if you'd never met me."

The ring of fire around his eyes flashed and pooled solid crimson with only a single spec of black remaining. A wicked smile pulled at his lips, as his hand slammed the ground next to my head. Jake lowered his body on top of mine, crushing me, as he came closer for the last kiss.

"No! Jake don't!" Terror shot through me. Bloody lips smashed down on mine. Slicing razors flooded my body, for the third time, searching for my remaining scrap of soul.

The last fragment of my spirit came into contact with his deadly kiss. Tiny hooks snagged it, and started ripping it away from my bones. My body shuddered one last time before it became limp, and my soul loosened. It floated freely, as it traveled from within me toward Jake's lips.

Inky haze distorted my vision, as I realized death was trying to take me. Barely aware of Jake's mouth on mine, the pain dulled as my consciousness fought to live, but my body surrendered. Strands of life slowly spilled out of me. I could see them leave my body, and spill onto the ground—like liquid gold. There was one strand left—only one bit of my soul remained.

As the last golden strand of life left me, Jake was violently torn away. My body reacted without my consent, and I shot up gagging. It felt as if the razor wire was ripped from my throat in one sharp pull. My head wobbled on my neck, as my body crumpled, and fell to the ground. Hands caught me before my head smashed into the dirt. It all occurred so fast that I wasn't sure what happened.

Death was still trying to take me, even though Jake was gone. My chest felt like it was beneath a pile of boulders. My breaths were so shallow that I wanted to stop breathing. Just for a minute. It was so heavy and I was so weak.

As my consciousness was fading, I felt warm arms wrapped around me. A voice whispered, but I couldn't understand the words. My muscles still vividly remembered the pain. I tried to focus on the voice, to allow it pull me away from the blackness that was taking me, but I couldn't. Everything sounded far away, echoing hollowly in my head. It was impossible to take another breath.

The whispers of the stranger's voice sounded farther away when I felt warmth spread across my head, with a gentle touch. Softness brushed across my lips. Feeling a surge of life, I sucked in air, and the blackness receded as quickly as it came. The haze lingered, making my body feel like I'd awoken from a dream too quickly. I swallowed, soothing the burning sensation in my throat.

Suddenly aware of the warm arms holding me, my eyes fluttered open. The moon seemed brighter than I remembered, outlining a masculine shape. The trees above me were blurred in jagged shafts of shadows and light. Attempting to focus, I looked up into a hazy face with sorrowful eyes; he said nothing.

Sleep pawed at me, making my eyes flicker, and feel heavier. Staring, I couldn't make out more than a pair of eyes, and pale flesh. Carefully, his warm fingers pushed my curls back. An unspoken message brushed inside my mind. *You're safe.*

A weak smile tugged my lips, as I leaned into his chest, and sleep stole me.

CHAPTER TWO

Dread clawed at my stomach, as I realized that I'd passed out. I forced my eyes open.

Crushing fear filled my chest when I realized I was alone. The arms that protected me were gone. Frightened, I jerked upright. I desperately tried to focus on the spinning blur of pines and oaks. Every muscle in my body flexed, waiting. I was wounded, half dead, and alone.

Where is Jake?

A hand settled on my shoulder causing a scream to erupt from my throat. I spun, violently throwing what little strength I had remaining into my assailant's knees. He staggered back, but did not fall. He reached for me again.

Frantically, I tried to push my lame body off the ground, but it was impossible to rise without feeling like I would slide off the earth. Arms caught me as I fell.

"Easy, Ivy. It's me," he said. My heart pounded in my ears, distorting a voice I should have known. Twisting my shoulders, I freed myself from his grip.

"*Eric*," I breathed. "What are you doing here?" Nervously, I glanced around for Jake. But we were alone.

Worry creased his brow. "I was nearby. Were you attacked? What happened?" His eyes darted, taking everything in, and then landed back on my face.

With shaking fingers, I pushed a chunk of my hair back. It was a curly mess that framed my face, and constantly fell forward. My skin was damp and cold. "I don't know. I... don't remember." I tried to recall exactly what happened, but I wasn't sure what happened. It sounded insane.

Looking into Eric's face, his expression softened. He stared at me, and whispered, "Oh. Wow." His eyes didn't stray from my face.

My stomach squirmed under his gaze. I had no idea what was going on, but I was frightened, and didn't like the look on his face. Swallowing hard, I tried to remember if we'd spoken at all, outside of class—but we didn't. We were lab partners. I barely knew him.

"We need to get you out of here before they come back."

Assuming he chased off my attacker, I looked at him wondering how that was possible. His frame was slight, and he wasn't made of muscles, although he wasn't scrawny either. He was normal looking. He slid his arms around my back and under my legs, and started to lift me off the ground.

"Eric, you can't… " but I was wrong. He could. And he did carry me. I didn't like it, but I was too weak to walk. The self-consciousness that swept over me didn't help either. I'm not a vain person, but his arms were around me, feeling the curves of my body and it made me uncomfortable. I expected him to slow under my weight, but he didn't. Eric walked quickly in long strides. His scent meshed with the night air. It was familiar—something wholesome from childhood that I couldn't quite remember.

Eric entered the parking lot and slid me down against his old blue truck. After opening the door, he slid his hand under my thighs, as he lifted me in. Then, he slid into his seat, turned the engine over, and peeled out of the parking lot.

Tears flowed down my cheeks, although I forbade it. Crying in front of other people was hideous. I tried to stop, but couldn't. I said nothing and felt nothing, except the deafening pounding of my heart in my ears. I looked at Eric, wondering how he found me.

"Ivy. I need to tell you something. It's important." He glanced at me, then back at the road. "I know you're not alright, but I have to tell you something. It's going to sound weird. Promise you won't freak out on me, okay?"

My voice was flat. It felt like I was speaking from a million miles away. "After tonight, nothing you say can shock me." The old truck's exhaust rumbled, as we left a stop sign behind. Body aching, I slumped in my seat.

"Well, this might," the green tint of the dashboard lights reflected off his face. Clutching the wheel tightly, we turned onto my block. He stopped the truck a few doors down from my house. His golden gaze met mine. "Ivy, I need you to listen. You can't forget. I know you've been through a lot… "

Interrupting, I muttered, "I'm fine." I wasn't, but I didn't want to discuss it. At that point, I just wanted to burry myself under my covers.

Taking a deep breath, he turned toward me with an expressive plea on his face, "Ivy, you have a mark on your head. You're one of us. This is important. If you forget everything else—remember this. *Hide that mark.* Do not tell *anyone* and I mean *anyone*, that you have it. Do you understand?" His hand slid over mine, patting, as his eyes searched my face. I stared at him. He seemed alarmed, like something was wrong.

I reached for the visor. "What are you talking about? Do I have a gash or something?" *Was I scarred?*

Why was he looking at me like that? My fingers pulled the visor down, and flipped open the mirror. A tiny light turned on.

"Don't freak out. Ivy, please?" He said.

I expected to see a bruise or a nasty cut. Not this. At first glance, everything was normal: Pale skin, dark hair, wild curls frizzing from rolling in the dirt. That was all there with one glaring difference. Pressing my fingers to my flesh, I stared at the pale blue mark, glittering above my right brow. It looked like someone took a lightening bug, smeared it on my skin, and then stenciled an elaborate blue swirl on top. Prodding it with my fingers, my jaw hung open. It looked like a tattoo. *Where did this come from?* I removed my fingers from the mark and examined them. There was no blue residue. My fingers slid over the mark. It felt like nothing was there. No paint. No glitter. No bruise. No burn. But it was there—a faint blue shimmering arch with pale snaking vines that formed a sideways S.

"Ivy? Talk to me, Ivy." Eric's voice interrupted my wide-eyed stare into the tiny mirror.

Panic crept up my throat, as I asked, "What is this? This is bad, isn't it?"

Eric spoke to me in the same tone one would when comforting a frightened child, "It's not bad, not at all. It's just *different*. You need to cover it, and don't tell anyone, okay?"

Swallowing hard I asked, "What is it? Did Jake do this?"

"No, he didn't. And it's not bad. But, it's late. And I bet no one knows you snuck out. You gotta stop doing that, by the way." He smiled at me. I stared at him blankly, too shocked to react. His face regained its former seriousness, "I'll tell you everything you need to know. Tomorrow. You'll be safe in your house tonight. We need to get you inside. In the meantime, stay inside, and don't tell anyone. Your life depends on it."

"Eric?" My eyes rested on his face. He was my Biology buddy. He was the other dumb one in a class filled with honor students who made straight A's. We didn't. Other than that, I knew little about him. "How did you know?"

"I'll tell you everything," he lowered his head to catch my gaze, "I promise. Let me know you're safe at home tonight. Go to school tomorrow. Don't mention the park to anyone. And do *not* sneak out again. Promise?"

Numbly, I reached for the lever to open the door, not agreeing to anything. Eric quickly reached across, putting his hand on my shoulder. "They'll kill you, Ivy. Promise me." His voice changed from a command to a plea, "Please." Our gazes locked.

He never said more than two words to me, outside of class. The newness of it was odd, especially after what just happened. I felt my soul leave my body during the attack, but somehow I didn't die. I was alive. Eric saved me.

Breaking the gaze, I said, "I promise." I slid my shoulder out of his grip; my hand lingered on the door for a moment, while I looked back at Eric. "Thank you."

A soft smile spread across his lips, "No problem."

CHAPTER THREE

Sometimes staring at your reflection does *not* help you see what you've become. This was one of those times. I leaned on the tiled counter, hovering close to the glass. Big brown eyes stared back from a face framed with long, dark curls. I looked normal, except for that mark. The pattern grew more intricate and darkened into a violet hue overnight. My fingers slid over it, and felt nothing but smooth skin. I covered it, like Eric told me.

And Jake. God, I was so stupid. Angry with myself, I started tearing through my memories of him, looking for pieces of the guy who attacked me last night. There had to be some scrap of behavior that would have warned me. There had to be.

Three months ago, I saw him for the first time. My friend, Collin Smith and I, were at a community theatre to see *Hamlet.* I loved the theatre. It was a place to get lost in someone else's life, and forget mine for a while.

Swinging red velvet curtains swooshed open, while we sat shrouded in darkness. The stage lights came up spilling softly onto the second row, where we sat. Expecting to snigger at bad acting, I was shocked when I first heard him. Dominating the stage, Jake delivered his lines so beautifully; it felt like he *was* Hamlet. His flowing voice, rich with honey tones, and his sun-kissed body looked like a Greek god. I was mesmerized. Slate blue eyes complimented his complexion, with hair flowing to his shoulders the same color as winter wheat. Smitten, my finger dragged down the playbill, looking for his name.

"Who are you looking for?" Collin whispered in my ear. Raking the playbill, his eyes darted to the stage to see where I was looking.

"That guy," I whispered. Finding his name, JAKE PETERSON, I flipped to the back of the playbill to read about him.

Warm breath slid across on my neck when Collin whispered in my ear, "Oh no. Is the great Ivy going to be someone's groupie? I thought you were above that." Leaning back into his chair, a satisfied grin tugged at the corners of his mouth, and he folded his arms.

Collin Smith was smug and insanely hot. His shiny dark mocha hair fell to a strong jaw, highlighting lips that were usually curled into a playful smile. Combine his startling sapphire blue eyes with his porcelain complexion, and a chiseled chest—well, it was easy to see why he had groupies. His ego issues were the size of the Titanic, and kept us friends - and only friends. At least that's what I told myself. While his groupies found extreme arrogance sexy, I didn't.

Looking smug, Collin knew he said the one thing that would make me feel like a stalker. Closing the paper playbill, I set it on my lap, as Collin stifled a muted snort of triumph.

I pouted through the rest of the performance. After the show, Collin ran off to be fawned over by his groupies. *Yuck.* I cringed. *Lemming hoes.* I was 5'5" of pure groupie repellant. They stayed away from Collin when I was around. Sitting alone, I slouched back into my chair, flipping through the playbill. Collin was my ride home, so I was stuck waiting.

When I felt eyes on me, I glanced up. Jake was smiling, and walking in my direction. The house lights were up, but the room was dim. The lights gave his frame an ethereal glow. Drinking in his beautiful body, I watched him approach. He lowered his gaze with one step, and with the next he looked up into my eyes with a coy smile on his face. My breath caught in my throat. His light brown hair and bright blue eyes made him appealing, but add the shy guy thing into the mix, and I was pathetically love-struck.

His hand extended toward me, and he said, "Hey, my name is Jake. I was one of the actors in the play." Gently, I laid my palm in his grip, staring into his eyes. Excitement flared inside of me, threatening to make me sound like an idiot. He lowered his perfect body into the chair in front of me. Everything about Jake captivated me.

I smiled at him, and slid back into my seat, "I know. I saw you." A super-smile spread across my face. I couldn't help it. Managing to fold my arms, I resumed my normal defensive position, while trying to subdue an adoring grin. "I'm Ivy. Ivy Taylor."

"Ivy, I've got to know - Why didn't you like my performance?" Flipping his hair out of his face, he glanced back up at me, and braced himself to hear my answer.

Confusion made me flinch. *Why does he think that? How did he even see me?* Seeing the audience from the stage was almost impossible. The spotlights were so glaringly bright that the audience disappeared into shadow beyond the first row. We were sitting in the second row. I sat with my arms crossed and scowled at Collin. *He saw me.* My heart climbed into my throat. *Awh, crap.* Jake thought I was scowling at him. Telling this guy that I was frowning at him because he sucked was a total lie, but it would let me walk away without embarrassing myself. Or I could tell the truth and admit that I was drooling. Those were both crappy options, so I opted for denial.

"No Jake. I thought you were… great." Shrugging, I picked up my playbill, trying to hide.

He smiled saying, "Sorry, but it looked like you were in pain. If sitting there and listening to me was that bad—I should quit right now. Seriously," his eyebrows shot up, adding to his plea. "What part sucked that bad? Was it all of it?"

Feeling trapped, I gazed from one end of the room to the other. *Where is Collin?* This was his fault. Jake was taking this the wrong way.

I have to tell him. This is gonna suck. "When you came on stage, my heart stopped. Your voice. Oh. My. God. And the way you were saying your lines. It was breathtaking. I started to skim this," I said holding up the playbill, "for your name and bio. My jerk-friend noticed, and teased me about it. I was, umm, scowling at him, not you." My face felt hot, and my heart was pounding so loudly that I was sure he could hear it. "Well, as much fun as it's been—I gotta go."

Normally, I didn't tell people stuff like that, but breaking an artist's confidence was sacrilegious— especially someone as talented as Jake. I jumped up to make a hasty retreat, but he smoothed his hand over mine, rising with me. Hesitating, I looked at him.

His hair fell into his eyes. Smiling softly, he asked, "Ivy, would you like to grab a cup of coffee?"

We grabbed coffee several times over the next few weeks. I'd wanted him to kiss me after that first date, but he'd insisted on taking things slow. Stupidly, I thought he seemed like a sweet guy, who cared about me. That made the blindsiding attack that bitch-slapped me much worse.

Last night I flew out of my bed, slid out my window, and ran to the park to meet him. Sneaking out was part of my repertoire over the past year. While I ditched most of my juvenile delinquent behavior, I didn't stop all of it. Ducking out my window in the middle of the night was still a norm. I couldn't sleep anyway. My mom had no clue. And no one knew where my dad was. Mom was sweet, but she still thought I was a good girl. She saw the girl I had been, and not the one I'd become. It wasn't unexpected. She had her own trauma to deal with. Hiding my serious crash and burn from her wasn't hard. I hid it from everyone. Only a few people saw me go down in flames after my sister's funeral, even less stayed around to put them out, and help me get on with my life.

Jake encouraged my midnight outings, and was always there to walk and talk. A midnight swing at the park was normal, as my nights became filled with less sleep, and more awake.

Last night played out exactly the way he wanted. He lured me there with the one thing he knew I wanted—a kiss. When I arrived, he'd taken my hand outside the park gate, and we walked for a bit. Leaning against a tree, after we'd walked deeper into the woods than usual, Jake pressed his body into mine. It felt good. His fingers brushed across my face, and gently pushed back a stray curl, causing my pulse to skyrocket.

Moonlight cast a lacey pattern on the ground. His face lingered inches from mine. Warm and welcome, I felt his breath on my chilled skin. Tickling fingers suddenly wiggled against my waist. I retaliated quickly. Falling to the ground, in a tangle of legs and arms, we tickled and laughed. It seemed so sweet, and so normal—until I was glued to the ground. How did he turn into the crimson-eyed monster that attacked me last night? Pain like that was unimaginable. I'd never felt anything like that—ever. And I hoped to God, I never would again.

I clung to the few facts I had, and I sighed. Jake attacked me. Eric saved me. And now I had a mark on my head. Accepting that was all I knew made me nuts, but I knew who had the answers. Eric. My strength returned to me over night, and I was ready to hear whatever it was he had to say.

The clock blinked 7:45am. Grabbing my phone, I threw it in my purse, not bothering to look at the screen, and went to school.

CHAPTER FOUR

I dragged my feet to school. Kids talked, lockers slammed, and the bell rang. The sounds of my normal day droned on like white noise. Continuing to my locker, I grabbed my books.

Although my mark was covered with a thick coating of make-up, I felt exposed. Not knowing what was happening made me twitchy. I grabbed my books and walked to class as the bell rang. My hand pushed the door open, and the teacher shot me a dirty look. I walked quietly to my seat.

Mr. Tanner was a squat man with stern features. Getting excited made his face turn red and his jowls shake. Sweat stains made his once white shirt dingy, and his Dockers clung on for dear life, under his enormous gut. "Tardy. That makes two," he waved a sausage sized finger at me. "One more and you'll be spending the afternoon in detention." Marking his book, he grunted.

If this happened a year ago, I would have been horrified. But now? I didn't care. The sniggers would stop in a second, and they'd all forget I was here. Except for Jenna Marie. She was in every freaking class with me. I think it was some divine joke—putting the pink princess next to the Goth girl. Well, I wasn't really Goth. I just wore solid black a lot. The dark color suited me.

Slouching in class, I watched the clock tick slowly, counting the minutes until the bell. I made the motions as I went through the day, trying not to talk to anyone. I was moderately successful.

Jenna Marie didn't care that I didn't want to talk. She talked enough for two people.

"Pink would be a great color on you, Ivy," her voice was perky. Perky irritated me. Sitting ramrod straight in her seat, she sat across the aisle from my desk.

Starring straight ahead I mumbled, "I like black. Thanks." Talking about my monochromatic wardrobe was a daily ritual for her. This was what I got for getting to class on time. I'd rather sit in detention. My eyes drifted up to the clock, watching the second hand tick one tock at a time. I prayed for the bell to ring.

"But you have such pretty hair. Those beautiful, hazelnut curls would just pop with pink! And you wear black every day." She frowned at me. "I haven't seen you wear another color in over a year. It's time to think pink!" Looking at her, my eyebrows rose in incredulity into my hairline. The bell rang, and snipped off rude words that had formed on my tongue.

When class ended, I sprang from my chair to avoid more pink talk. Shouldering my way out the door, and into the hallway, I paused when Collin came running up behind me.

"Hey Ive!" he called.

"Hey," I answered, looking up at him.

We fell in step and navigated the crowds of kids, open lockers, and the nerds that were always running somewhere. "What's going on?"

Shrugging, he said, "Same old stuff. I just wanted to tell you to wait up for me after school." Arching an eyebrow, a smile spread across his face. Bouncing on his toes, with his hands behind his back, he said, "I have something for you."

"Sure," pausing I added, "You didn't. Did you?" I cocked my hip as my head automatically slanted. I sighed. "Remember? No birthday presents? Geeze Collin."

Celebrating didn't feel right, not this year. My birthday was forever connected to the worst day of my life. And after last night, I just couldn't.

Her voice filled my ears before I saw her face, "Awh, the little virgin said she doesn't want your present Collin. I'll take it." Nicole Scambotti wrapped herself around Collin. He smiled at her. They dated on and off for the past few years. He seemed to like her as much as any of his other groupies. She was part of his flavor of the month club. At the moment it was ginormous boobs on a blonde bombshell frame, with a snarky mouth.

I sneered at her, as I pulled my books tight to my chest. The "little virgin" nickname was my own fault. Collin took me out one night, and I partied a little too hard. Everyone was there, including Nicole. Collin watched me lose control, as I let the glorious numbness flood me. After dancing, I saddled up with some guy I didn't know. We had an embarrassing public make-out session that I barely remembered. The part that I did remember was his hand sliding up my shirt. It thrilled me, and it felt so good to feel something, besides pain. I let his hands linger, but when he went for my skirt, I slapped him away. When he didn't stop, I yelled. Collin pulled him off of me, and Nicole started making virgin jokes every chance she could.

Collin pulled away from her, and spoke softly in my ear, "There are worse nicknames."

I glared at Nicole, speaking loud enough for her to hear me, "Yeah, *skank* is way worse."

The bell drowned out Nicole's pointed response.

Collin pulled her to class, saying over his shoulder, "See ya later. I'll meet you at your locker."

I waved to him, and walked off to class.

Collin liked helping me forget my troubles, and I was always up to my neck in them. Sometimes he would take me to the beach, and we'd sit near the surf. The sea washed the waves in and out, in a hypnotic rhythm that soothed me. Collin would sit next to me, quietly. Something about the sea and the wind made me feel free, like I wasn't trapped in my life. But when things got really bad, I needed more. I started partying, and Collin was always nearby. He didn't stop me, but he kept me out of trouble. My other friends didn't like him for it, but I did. He let me live, and grieve without judgment.

After I while, I noticed that all the things that haunted me melted away around him. And the real Collin, the one no one really saw, was unsure of himself. The uncertainty was alluring. It made me wonder who he really was; the confident guy that walked around like he owned the school, or the shy version that was so deeply hidden that I wasn't sure if it really existed. Collin never made a pass at me; aside from the first day I met him, which was all right because I didn't want to date him. The groupies alone were a health hazard.

That was before my life took an unexpected turn, and fell apart. While the virgin title was still accurate, it wasn't uncommon for me to suck face with some guy I didn't care about. I threw myself at strangers to ease the hole in my chest. I pushed away the guys I actually liked, too afraid of the pain it might cause.

My pace quickened when I saw Eric in front of me, about to walk into the classroom. "Eric," I called. "Wait up." I fell in step with him.

"Hey Ivy. Ready for more biology fun?" he asked as I caught up to him, saying nothing of last night.

"Yup, as always."

Eric had a way of stating the obvious that made me want to smile. He was simple, but in a good way. He was my tether to normal. At least I thought he was. I sat in bio listening to the directions for the next lab. My mind kept tugging me back to last night. My fingers absentmindedly drifted to the mark on my forehead.

I sighed. Eric glanced at me out of the corner of his eye. I ignored him, knowing we couldn't talk about it now. *Waiting sucks.*

I shifted my pencil restlessly, between my thumb and index finger, as a nervous sensation crawled up my throat. I always took notes with a pencil, so I could draw if class got too dull. The yellow stick twirled over each finger with a swift grace - before it flung out of my hand, and pegged the kid sitting in front of me in the back of the head.

The jock shifted in his seat and turned to glare at me. I mouthed, *Sorry.* Eric looked up from his neatly printed notes, and laughed. Two minutes until the bell rang. *Thank God.* I rolled my eyes, and leaned my head on my hand. Staring at the clock, I watched the black hand jerk, and the bell finally rang. The teacher spewed reminders about assignments. I quickly grabbed my books, and looked at Eric, waiting for him to tell me what we were doing.

He closed his book, and stacked his papers neatly. My books had papers sticking out the sides like bunny ears. Organization wasn't really my thing. Eric seemed a little too neat to me, but he was the reason I wasn't failing the class, so I didn't needle him about it.

Eric turned and reached under the lab table in front of us. He held out my pencil, smiling. I took it. "Thanks. I thought Bret was gonna kill me."

"It's only because that was the fifth time you've pegged him with a pencil in the past month." He picked up his books, and I chased him out of the room.

"It has not been five times!" I squeaked, unable to contain my grin. As we rounded the corner, I saw Collin leaning against my locker. I turned to Eric and asked, "When can we talk?" Slowing, I touched his arm, and he stopped.

Eric looked at Collin and then back at me. "I'll walk you home. Let me grab my stuff." It felt a little awkward, but I agreed. Collin and Eric glared at each other. Ignoring them both, I went to my locker.

Collin's arm slid over my shoulder, "Hey Ivy. You ready?" He spoke loud enough for Eric to hear. I watched Eric round the corner, and disappear from sight.

"Uh, sure. I gotta sec. What were you so excited about?" I asked while I fumbled my combination.

His grin was gone, replaced with seriousness that didn't look right on him. Clearing his throat he asked, "So. New boyfriend?"

The lock clicked open in my hand. "No. He's just a friend. Don't go big brother on me and chase him off either."

Collin folded his arms over his chest. "When have I done that?" The corners of his mouth pulled up into a smirk, and I knew he wasn't seriously asking.

I arched a single brow at him, until he shrugged, laughing. "So, what'd you want?" I asked, shifting through my stuff, and grabbing what I needed.

"Just wanted to talk to you. And I've got something for you." He leaned his body into the row of lockers, waiting for me.

I fished out my book, and slammed the locker door shut. I hesitated, looking at him.

"Sure. What is it?" I glanced over Collin's shoulder, seeing Eric walking toward me.

Collin turned to see who I was looking at, and stiffened. I watched the two of them together for a moment. Eric stood a few inches shorter than Collin. Eric was neatly pressed, short hair combed perfectly in place, with his shirt tucked into his jeans, and a pile of books under his arm. Collin had the just-rolled-out-of-bed smoldering look going on. His longer hair went where it wanted, untamed like the rest of him. His dark shirt clung to his body, covered by a black leather jacket, and biker boots. They both looked good, in a different kind of way.

Turning back to Collin, I asked, "Sooo... ?" His blue eyes darted back to my face. Uncertainty flashed across his features, but disappeared so fast that I wasn't sure that I'd really seen it.

He leaned in close, resting his hand on my shoulder, his lips hidden by my hair, as he whispered in my ear, "I'll catch up with you later." He gave Eric a pointed look and walked away. I sighed, watching him leave. He wasn't sulking, but he wasn't happy either. *Crap.*

Eric looked at me, asking, "Are you guys… dating?"

"No," I shook my head. "We most certainly are not. Let's just get out of here." I shoved my book under one arm, pressing through the narrow metal doors that lead out the back of the building, with Eric next to me. Lots of kids walked through an alley behind the school to get to the avenue. It wasn't dark or creepy, and with the company of other kids, it wasn't the kind of alley that gave you the willies. People fanned out as we passed through the metal doors, and I sucked in fresh air. Despite my seemingly dark façade, I enjoyed the sensation of sunlight on my skin. Eric watched me out of the corner of his eye, saying nothing until we were out of the earshot of the others.

"So, tell me." I blurted out when I couldn't wait any longer. "What is this?" I pointed at my head.

As we walked past storefronts, I glanced at him out of the corner of my eye. The conversation was shrouded in the noise of engines and car horns. There was always a lot of traffic at this time of day. Crossing the street, without becoming road kill, was a trick.

Eric shifted his books to his other arm, and his pace slowed. His amber eyes glinted gold in the sunlight. "It's gonna sound weird. You aren't going to believe me."

"Just tell me." *How weird could it be?*

Eric smiled slightly and said, "Last night you asked me if Jake did this to you—if he made that mark. The answer is no. He didn't. The mark on your head makes you his enemy. It shows that you're a Martis. We usually hide it, but when it first appears, life can be kinda rough. In short—you were claimed to fight for the good guys. You were chosen because of your fierce loyalty and courage. That's the reason any Martis is chosen."

"Chosen by who?" I asked.

Eric shrugged. "Angels. They did this to you. When they claim a mortal to fight on their side, that blue mark appears above the right eyebrow—exactly where yours is."

I stared at him with my mouth hanging open, not really believing what he was saying. We'd stopped walking. My eyebrows were receding in disbelief into my hairline. I managed to blurt out, "Then what is Jake? There's no way he's normal."

Eric's expression was somber. "He's a Valefar. They are the only beings that can destroy Martis. You're immortal, unless one of those takes you out.

"There's a war that's been raging forever. The demons were no longer content staying in their realm—the Underworld. They tried to take the angel's realm as well. They fought long horrific battles intent on destroying anyone who opposed them. At some point both sides were at a stalemate. They were equally matched. But the demons wouldn't back down. That's when the demons did something that changed everything—one of them kissed a mortal.

"The demon kiss stripped away the human's soul, and then they infused the victim's body with demon blood. That was the birth of the Valefar. Basically, a Valefar is a human puppet that is kept alive with demon blood. They are like animated corpses, but look exactly like real people. You can't tell the difference unless you catch a glimpse of their mark or their eyes when they are caught in blood lust—they turn blood red. It's the demon blood that made them what they are."

"What do you mean?" I asked. My fingers were pinched tightly into fists. When I tried to relax and unfold them, I noticed how slick they were. His words were scaring me. They sounded totally insane, but my gut was telling me it was real. All of it.

Eric's gaze met mine, "Demons are the only creatures that don't need a soul to survive. And they made the Valefar just like them—soulless. Demon blood is different. Vile. It gives them life in an unnatural way. The rest of us have souls—humans, Martis, even angles.

"When the demons remained in their own realm, the angels left them alone, but when they attacked and started trying to expand their realm; the angels had to do something to stop them. So, they made the Martis. We nearly lost the war because of the Valefar, Ivy. The angels didn't want to engage humans, but they were forced to. And it was for the better—the Martis were able to trap the most powerful demon in a pit in the Underworld—Kreturus. He's still alive down there, waiting for his Valefar to free him. The Martis make sure that doesn't happen."

My throat slid into my stomach. "So, an angel picked me to fight in a battle that I can't see, and my boyfriend was a demon puppet? Is that what you're saying?"

Eric flicked his eyes up at my face, "What do you want to believe? After last night, I can't imagine how you could think what happened was normal."

Shaking my head, I said, "It wasn't normal." I shivered, absently rubbing my hands against my arms.

"He was kissing the soul out of my body—ripping it away from my bones like it was meat."

Eric's hand reached out, and gave my arm a reassuring squeeze. "Ivy, it's their way. That's how they make more Valefar. He was stalking you—hoping to catch you before you knew what you were. He was going to bind you—or kill you."

Eyes wide, I nodded. "He said that. Last night. He said it was the perfect time—because I didn't know what I was yet." Closing my eyes, I blinked hard trying to erase the memory. Looking up at Eric, I asked, "He said I was *new*?"

"Well, you are, right?" Eric answered. "Your mark looked more mature, which threw me off a little bit. But you seem new. When did you first see the mark?"

"Last night. I didn't see it before then. It wasn't there," my fingers absentmindedly touched the make-up covering the mark.

Eric's eyes flicked to the spot, and then returned to my face. "That's what they do—their older Valefar hunt us, trying to find us before we're made. There were hardly any Martis left. When the angels thought we won, when we locked Kreturus in the pit, they allowed the Martis to dwindle. But, when it became clear that the Valefar needed to be addressed, they started adding to our numbers again. It's not unusual to be seventeen or eighteen when you get marked. And the Valefar know that new Martis are clueless."

"What do you mean?" I asked.

"I mean that the Angels don't shoulder-tap their chosen and give them a welcome packet. It's not their way. Martis learn what they are on their own. Anyway, the Valefar befriend humans who they think may get marked, waiting to destroy them as soon as the mark appears. We're easy targets at that point. Maybe that one got lucky?" He glanced at me.

"That was some luck." I heard the disbelief in my voice. That wasn't luck. I was played. Jake knew what I was going to be before I did. How? "Eric, how did he know? I had no clue it was happening. I never even heard of any of this before."

"I don't know entirely, but we suspect they hunt their prey in ways that are unique to Valefar, using abilities we don't have. No one is really sure how it works, but when you're changed to a Martis, it's a process. You don't usually wake up with a mature Martis mark on your head. It's typically a gradual change. First the mark appears like a blue bruise, before it intensifies into a pattern. We assumed the new Martis were being killed because their mark was exposed. But you didn't have that bruise-like mark. I would have seen it. It just appeared, fully formed." He shook his head, "Ivy, I don't know how they hunted you. I didn't even realize you'd get marked." His voice was sincere and somber.

Shaking my head in disbelief, I stood looking straight at him, with my eyes wide. I felt the air fill my lungs as my stomach twisted in knots, not knowing what to believe.

"Ivy," he said, "if you remember anything about the Valefar, remember this. They feel *nothing*, care for *no one*, and are only interested in one thing—*power*. Right now, they are trying to shift the balance of power back in their favor, so they can defeat us."

I swallowed the lump in my throat, "And if they defeat us?"

Eric's gaze broke as he turned away from me, "They can release Kreturus."

A horn blared, making me flinch. Throwing my head back, I looked into the pale blue sky, and wrapped my arms around my waist. I didn't know what to think. Looking over at him, I asked, "So, what do we do?"

"Keep ourselves hidden, and destroy them before they can kill us off." He sounded perfectly reasonable, like killing immortals was an everyday thing.

"Hidden? That's why we hide our mark, right? So the Valefar don't know if we are human or not?" I asked.

"Yes, it makes it harder for them to find us. If you leave the mark uncovered, it's like walking around with a bull's-eye on your forehead—any Valefar can see it, not just their hunters." He paused, "Why, what's wrong?"

I felt myself blanch. "Eric, he knows me. The Valefar that attacked me last night—Jake—he knows who I am. He knows where I live. I was seeing him for a while, before all of this happened."

"Ivy, they can hunt you, once they know who you are. We have to find him, before he finds you, and hope he didn't tell the others. What's his name? Tell me everything you know about him."

I told him what I knew about him, or what I thought I knew.

Eric's hand rose to my cheek, but he hesitated, and then rested his hand on my shoulder. "I'll take care of him. Don't worry about it." His amber eyes were reassuring, but I didn't see how he could defeat Jake.

I shook my head, "You can't go after him. He'll kill you."

"I know what he is. And I've fought the Demon Kissed before, Ivy."

Looking up into his face, I stared at him. "What are you? How do you know all this stuff?"

His amber eyes glittered in the afternoon sun. "I would've thought it was obvious—I'm a Martis."

That's why he saved me. That's how he overpowered Jake. I felt something stirring within me. I didn't like being drawn into this, and not having any say in the matter, but there were much worse people to be allies with than Eric. I owed him my life. I didn't know what to say.

Regret spilled across his face, "Last night—I wish I'd gotten there sooner. I haven't ever met someone who survived an attack. Getting kissed by a Valefar is supposed to be unbearable."

I shivered and said, "It was."

CHAPTER FIVE

Eric deposited me on my doorstep, and went to find Jake. I couldn't pretend the things he said were false. Not after last night. And, not when the fear of Eric fighting Jake was so real. I flopped onto my bed, hoping I didn't send him off to get killed. If something happened to him because of me, I couldn't bear it. *Especially not today.*

It was a year, to the day—October 15th. I stared at my ceiling, trying to not remember. My last birthday was spent finding out what happened to my sister, after the accident. Apryl went on an international vacation with her best friend, Maggie. I was jealous, but I got over it, happy to read her postcards and see what she was doing.

One day the postcards stopped. There was nothing the next day either. Then on my birthday, my life shattered like cheap china. The postcards disappeared because she was gone. A freak accident on a pier and we never saw her again. Mom and I buried an empty casket, and the tombstone had her name, although she was never found. For a long time, I expected to see her walk through the door, laughing. Dreams plagued me like memories, trying to convince me that she was alive. But she wasn't. I had to keep telling myself that. *Apryl is dead.*

Admitting it still made my stomach clench. Every day, I had to relive the same realization—my sister was dead—even though nothing had changed. It was an anchor that didn't become lighter as the year passed. I got stronger, and managed to lug it around without it constantly pulling me under.

My phone chirped with a new text from Shannon. Her message said that we were doing something very un-birthday like. *Pull out your overalls. We r cleaning out d church attic later!*

Jumping off my bed, I crawled into the bottom of my closet looking for old sneakers, wondering if it was stupid to go out. If Jake were looking for me, he would find me, no matter where I was. I couldn't wait here alone. I couldn't. I was going, and that was that.

Shannon's distraction would lighten my mood. While someone else might think cleaning an attic was a crappy birthday present, I loved it. I had an odd fondness for old stuff, and Shannon knew it. She was a year older than me, and my other best friend. It totally sucked that she was in some private school, and I wasn't. My mom was pro-public school despite its harshness, drugs, sex, and normal hoopla. She thought it was better to get toughened up while I was young.

Pulling out a pair of jeans with holes in the knees, I slid them on and laced up my shoes. I threw an old sweatshirt over a tank and tried to tame my frizz. Shannon's one of those girls who never has frizz. She's really clueless about how stunning she is with her perfect skin, and long cinnamon locks. Her frame was slight, and a smidgen taller than mine. She wore her clothes a size too big, which gave her a skater-chick-got-lost-in-J. Crew kind of look. Her green eyes sparkle, and her mouth contorted into a slim smile when she was up to no good.

The floorboards in the hallway creaked, giving away her silent footfalls before my mom pushed open the door to my room. In her hand she held a square box with a bow. I grimaced as she stood there.

"Mom," I whined.

Before I could finish, she waved her hand and cut me off, "I know you said no gifts, but this isn't from me." She approached me slowly. "And it was left for you before you announced your, ah," she paused looking for the right words, "gift aversion." She smiled a sad smile and handed it to me.

It was wrapped in silver paper with a dark blue bow. A to/from tag dangled off the top. My heart dropped in my chest as I recognized the handwriting.

Apryl.

The small box made me feel like I was holding a ghost. If Mom wasn't there, I might have never opened it. Pain and curiosity were mingling, as I wondered what was inside. Pushing back the paper, I uncovered a dark wooden box. It was carved with ivy and flowers. It looked like it was made for me, but that couldn't be possible because it also looked really old. My fingers traced the pattern cut into the smooth wood. Flipping open the lid, a scarlet pillow poofed around a silver comb that sat nestled in the center. It was the most beautiful thing I'd ever seen. The comb had tines that were made of long curved silver with pointed tips. The grip was ornately carved, with stones inset, to reveal a pale purple butterfly sitting on swirls of ivy. It was perfect.

A single sob escaped from my chest, as my fingers shook above the comb, too afraid to touch it. "Where did this come from?"

"Apryl mailed it from Italy last year. Before everything happened." Mom's arm wrapped around my back, "She wanted to give it to you on your birthday. She asked me to hide it. She was sure you'd find it if she brought it home in her luggage."

I laughed, but it had no feeling. That was just like Apryl. She planned everything out, down to the smallest detail. And freakishly far in advance.

"It's beautiful," I said, as my shaky fingers pulled the comb from the velvet. I closed the delicate box and put it on my bed.

"Yes, it is. Your sister was so excited about giving it to you. She knew how much you liked antiques. She was sure this was very old, and it looked like it was made for you." A sad smile crossed her face.

I nodded. Mom took the comb from my hand, and pulled me in front the mirror. In an artful swoop, she twisted up my curly locks and secured them in place with the comb. The silver filigree of the ivy and the gems on the butterfly glimmered against my dark hair.

I stared at my reflection. Remorse washed over me—for all the things I had done, and even more for the things I'd left undone and unsaid between us. Mom kissed me on my forehead. Then, she turned, and left me to gaze at my reflection, alone.

The past and the present crashed together in a deafening silence. I wanted the past to die, so I could distance myself from the pain, and forget—even for a little while. But it didn't happen. Staring at the comb, touching it softly with my fingers, my eyes drifted to my concealed mark. I should have been able to see a slight tinge of purple showing through, ever so slightly. But it was gone. I rubbed the make-up off with the back of my hand. It smeared enough that the purple mark should have showed its full color. The mark was gone.

"Oh, thank God!" I ran to the bathroom and washed my face. The mark was gone. No trace of it remained. I smiled weakly at my reflection, thinking my troubles lessened, as I heard the doorbell announce Shannon's arrival.

CHAPTER SIX

"Ivy, you are so friggin weird," Shannon said, as she crinkled her nose in disgust. "Don't get me wrong. I'm glad I got you the perfect birthday un-present. But we're sitting in a nasty old attic, surrounded by mildewing crap, and your face is lit up like Time Square." She smiled, letting out a little snort, and turned back to the boxes. Shannon didn't get my fascination with old stuff. She could appreciate it, but she didn't revel in it the way I did. Shannon moved a box and peeled the lid back. A spider ran out across her hand. She swallowed a scream before it could escape, and shivered. "That. Was. So. Nasty."

I laughed. It felt odd, but I couldn't contain my excitement. "This is awesome! I can't believe they let us up here. They never let anyone up here."

"Yeah, yeah. I think all the old church ladies were just glad they didn't have to clean out the attic this time." A lazy smile crossed her face. "Enjoy your divine dumpster dive. I'll just start over here. Somewhere. Geeze." I heard her shifting boxes, trying to get to the back of the attic.

Three bare bulbs lit the room. They hung the length of the ceiling, echoing the shape of the nave below. Their bulbs cast a warm yellow light onto the boxes and books that were stacked to the ceiling in neat piles. The stacks divided the room into a maze. While it didn't look like the stacks would topple over, I didn't want to bump into them either.

I picked up a threadbare Bible. Turning the cover open, my finger slowly drifted down a list of names. My eyes soaked them in, one by one. It was filled with families, people who lived and died, with names and dates of the forgotten. The hollow place in my chest burned. Sensations of being robbed flooded me. *I wish I knew what happened to her.* My grip on the old book tightened, as I thought of what I would do if I ever found out how Apryl died. How would I react? Would the pain ease? I got up and walked to another pile, trying to ward off the hollowness that was pulling at me, sucking me into the past. My hands shifted through the pile, touching, but not seeing. Before Apryl died, I'd been such a dreamer. I thought anything was possible. But, I finally came to grips with the reality that my life would go on, without her.

A glimmer caught my attention, and pulled me out of my deteriorating mood. A corner of a golden frame stuck out from under an old sheet. Curiosity clutched me, and I walked toward it wanting to see what was hidden. A dusty pile of books blocked my path. Moving them aside, I wedged myself between the books and the frame.

Shannon's voice called to me, "I'm bringing this box down." She balanced it on her hip at the top of the staircase, "Be right back!"

She was swallowed into the darkness of the stairwell, and I was alone. My fingers wrapped greedily around the frame. I tugged it quickly, freeing it from a lifetime of dust. The frame creaked, as I raised it over a pile of books, and set it down on the floor in front of me. Clutching the sheet, my hand ripped it away, and it slid to the floor. Elaborate carvings of little fat cherubs and ugly looking demons were carved into the wooden frame and gilded in gold. They were all nestled into a scrolling leaf pattern. It was like a *Where's Waldo*, but with creatures of Heaven and Hell. My fingers dragged across the sculpted leaves and cherub curls.

Spiraling colors ranging from pure white, to midnight black, and every color in between funneled through the painting - from top to bottom. The colors were painted in choppy lines that reminded me of cliffs at the shore. It looked like a place where the sea met the mountains, but there was no water, just fierce, jagged rock. At the uppermost portion were angels, both cherubim and seraphim with flaming swords. Slightly above them was pure white light. My eyes followed the swirl to the deepest dark part of the pit. Even the rocks looked evil. There was no light, just soul sucking darkness. I smoothed my hands up and down my forearms, trying to sooth the churning in the pit of my stomach. A little bit above the deepest, black part of the pit, were demons. They were painted as vile things, with dripping black flesh. They resembled short humans with greedy blood-colored eyes, and razor sharp fingers.

As my eyes slid to the middle of the painting, there was a mix of humans and demonic looking beings. They weren't quite demons anymore, but they didn't seem entirely human either. Their eyes were different—hard, cold, and rimmed in red. Above their right brow was a bright, blood red scar. *Valefar.*

My hand absentmindedly rose to my where my purple mark had been. My mark looked like a pixie hit me with a glitter paintball. But these scars looked like oozing, festering mutations of flesh. I felt a pang of revulsion tug at the back of my throat, and closed my mouth to choke it back.

Higher in the painting, there were warmer, brighter colors. This is where the humans were depicted. They were mostly in little groups of young and old. Women were sitting with babies on their laps, and older children surrounded their feet, playing quietly in the grass. The rocks were covered in moss and flowers, and sunshine drenched everything in rich light, vibrant colors, and deep shadows.

As my eyes traveled higher still, there were beings that were human looking, but they seemed more graceful, more compassionate, and more beautiful. Something about their stance said they weren't mortals, although there were no real discernable differences. I leaned in closer to see their faces, tracing them with my finger. I felt guilty doing that to such an old painting, but I did it anyway. I had to.

There were only a handful of these beings, unlike the red-marked-obviously-evil-humanoid-demon folk. The blue ones were scattered amongst the humans with their slight blue mark, glittering like stardust. *Those are Martis.* At the top of the cliff angels were suspended in air, surrounded by a scattering of Martis at the top of the cliff. They were all gathered around two central figures—a young couple.

Dark hair hung in long waves, and wisped quietly around her face for eternity. She was standing on a tiny stone step, above a guy. His feet were dangling. Their fingers were intertwined in the kind of grip that was about to slip away. He'd fall if she let go. He was handsome, with angular features, brown hair fluttering and obscuring his face. His eyes were looking down at the pit below. At first glance it looked like she was pulling him up, away from the pit. But after looking at it for a minute, I couldn't be sure that he wasn't pulling her down. I couldn't tell if she was trying to help him, or drop him. But one thing was clear. The entire painting was poised around these two people.

Her long white gown flowed to her bare feet. Her toes were precariously perched on a single stone. One of her arms was reaching up toward Heaven, and the other was reaching down toward Hell, and her slipping grasp clutched the hand of the guy. Shock flooded me as I recognized the girl in the white gown. *It can't be. That's not possible...*

My heart hammered, as I reached for the painted couple. I felt my skin tingling with the feeling that something bad was about to happen. My thumb wiped across their faces, removing a thin layer of dust. Trembling, I clutched the frame with both hands. Staring. His mark matched the grotesque scarring of the red, evil human-demon things, but it was violet. And the girl... Her mark was a light trail of violet stardust, over her right brow swirled into a sideways S—exactly where mine was this morning.

"Holy crap!" Shannon's voice startled me. The rest of her words were obscured by my shriek. Clutching my chest, I stumbled backwards, tripping over my feet, as my butt hit the floor. The impact felt like I was whacked on my back with a wooden board. I spread my arms out to catch me, before my head hit the floor. Apryl's comb clattered to the floor, skidding to a stop at Shannon's feet. There was dead silence, as her green eyes stared at my face, shocked. After a moment, she whispered, "Ivy, that's *you*."

I blinked hard staring at the painting, wishing it would change. Hoping it would look like someone else, even a little bit. But it didn't. It was me, and *him*. Whoever he was.

Shannon looked down at me, "Why didn't you tell me?"

"Tell you what?" I asked, rubbing my tailbone. I couldn't tell her any of this stuff with Valefar and Martis. I couldn't say I was attacked by demons last night, got plastered with a purple mark today, and saw myself in an ancient painting tonight. *Yeah, sure. That sounds sane.*

She looked at me, and buried her face in her hands. Her fingers clawed at her flesh for half a second, then she let go. She was a moderately patient person, but she couldn't stand it when I hid things from her. "Your mark. Why didn't you tell me you were marked?" She folded her legs, sitting down next to me.

My hand rose to my brow bone, as my eyes widened in alarm. I touched it softly. "How do you know?"

Shannon shook her head. Her elegant fingers reached out and picked up my comb. Her other hand produced a hand-mirror from a dusty pile. After wiping it on her jeans, she held out the mirror. Gazing at my reflection, I saw the violet swirls glittering exactly where they were that morning.

CHAPTER SEVEN

Still in shock, I pressed my fingers to it and rubbed. Shannon leaned back against a stack of boxes, and watched me before saying, "It won't come off. This comb is celestial silver. It hides your mark, so no one else can see it." She gently took the mess of curls covering my shocked face. She pulled them back, revealing all of my violet mark. When she threaded the comb through my hair the color dissipated, like a marker stain that was doused with bleach. Grabbing the mirror, I sat forward, and pulled the comb out. The mark reappeared, bright purple. I put the comb back, and it faded into oblivion again.

My eyes wildly sought hers, asking for answers. "Shannon, how... ?" was all I could manage to say.

"How do I know?" she asked softly. A soft smile covered her ruby red lips. She reached for her necklace, wrapped her fingers around the chain, and pulled. The chain snapped, as the necklace fell to the floor. The patch of skin over her right brow, the skin that had been perfect porcelain, held a glittery blue streak.

Stunned, I felt my jaw drop. "You're a Martis?"

She nodded, "Oddly enough, yes. It was my 17th birthday present, too. I had no idea what was happening. All of a sudden, I couldn't sleep well, and then hardly at all. Then, on my birthday, I woke up with this thing above my eye." She pointed to her blue mark. "So," she asked, "Who told you?"

A smile pulled at my lips. I couldn't believe my good luck. My best friend was going to help me deal with this. "My lab partner," I laughed, breaking the tension. "A Valefar stalked me, and attacked me. Eric saved me and brought me home. He told me what I am."

"Eric," Shannon snorted. "He probably gave you a history lesson. Let me fill in what he left out," Shannon pulled her hair into a loose ponytail while she spoke, "Because I'm sure he left stuff out.

"Ivy, we aren't normal anymore. We aren't even *mortal*. The mark changes us. We aren't human, but we aren't angels—we're somewhere in the middle. The angel's power mixes with our blood and all of a sudden, you have more power than you ever thought possible. We can do things we never thought possible. We don't need to sleep, we're stronger than any human, we can run faster than any animal, and we can see in pitch-blackness without a single shred of light.

"Some Martis are ancient, but many are young like me and you." Her green eyes shifted from mine. "We'll live forever, if a Valefar doesn't destroy us." Her shoulders seemed stiff, like something was making her tense. I assumed it was the shock of finding out that I was marked, too.

"Are there more? More Martis—besides Eric?" I asked excitedly. Maybe this wasn't as bad as I thought. Shannon hesitated. That should have been my cue that something changed between us, but I missed it.

"Yes, there are more. We each have a piece of celestial silver to mask our mark. The Valefar have something that masks theirs, as well. I don't know what it is, but we know that unless they reveal themselves to us, we can't be certain who they are. Hiding our marks is a matter of life or death." Her eyes were unblinking. She stared as she held her hands tensely in her lap.

I wondered if I should tell her. Eric told me not to tell anyone, but she already saw it. Not seeing the harm, I answered, "Eric told me to hide it. Not to tell anyone."

Her eyebrow arched, "He saw it? He saw it was *purple* and said nothing? He didn't do anything?" She stared, looking slightly shocked, and waited for an answer.

Something changed, although I couldn't figure out what. I hesitated, "It was blue that first night. He didn't see it purple. I'd covered it with make-up by then. The mark changed color after I was attacked." *My mark changed color.* Maybe that was what had her upset? Why it would matter?

She hesitated, fumbling the hem of her oversized sweater, staring at me with an odd expression. Her fingers reached for her silver necklace, and picked it up off the floor. The piece of metal disappeared into her fist. "Ya know," she laughed, "I never thought it'd be you. Not in a million years." She rose quickly, pacing the room, not looking at me.

My heart rate kicked up a notch. I jumped up and asked, "What do you mean, *you didn't think it'd be me*? What aren't you telling me?" My stomach twisted. *How much worse can it get?* I was already branded, and enlisted to fight in some battle I wanted no part of, but the look on Shannon's face worried me. Something was wrong. Very wrong.

She stopped abruptly, pressing the silver deeply into her palm. "Ivy. There is a prophecy. It's old." Her eyes shifted to the painting, and then back to me, "It's about you."

Our gazes locked, and I felt the tension claw at my gut. But I had to know. "Tell me Shannon."

"It's supposed to be someone evil. Someone malicious that is so freaking evil that they...But, it's you. How is it *you*?" She shook her head, advancing toward me quickly. Her white fist opened, and she pressed her silver pendant to her mark. A blue sheen glowed over the necklace, and then extinguished, as the silver changed shape. The tiny piece of metal melted in her hand, shifting its shape into a small silver dagger. Unblinking green eyes stared at me, while she held the blade pointing directly at me.

Heart pounding, I jumped away from her— shocked. My back slammed into a stack of books. I felt their balance shift under my weight. "Shannon, what are you doing?" I squealed. The silver dagger gleamed under the bare bulbs. I couldn't take my eyes off its lethal blade.

From that point, everything went wrong. My best friend vanished and I was left with this crazy girl. She looked like Shannon, but she didn't act like her. Something was warring within her, causing erratic jerky movements of the dagger. I could see it in her eyes. My heart was pounding, not believing this was happening. The similarity to last night was unreal. It couldn't be happening. I knew her so much longer than Jake. She wouldn't hurt me. There was no way. My stomach lurched, making me feel sick. My hands shook as I held them up, palms facing her.

She moved quickly. Her face pinched tightly, as the dagger hovered near my throat without touching my skin. I sucked in air, trying to shrink away from the blade. My body pushed into the stack of books. I resisted the urge to push back further, knowing they would collapse.

I screamed, "Shannon. What the hell are you doing?"

She seemed lost, standing there, unable to move. Her lips pressed together in a small line. Her eyes were glassy, but the blade didn't move. Her voice was faint— apologetic in a way. "They commanded us to destroy the Prophecy One. I have to," she shook her head. "I can't save you." Tears streaked down her face.

"Save me from what? Shannon, you're scaring me. Put the knife down." My muscles were so tense; my skin felt like it would explode.

Her unblinking gaze was stoic. The only clue that revealed that she was conflicted was the tears streaming down her face. Her voice was soft, "They told us to kill you, before you learned what you were. Before you could fulfill the prophecy."

"There's got to be some mistake. Shannon, it's me! You know me." My eyes darted around the room, looking for a way out. I pushed back against the books that formed a wall behind me.

Shannon stood there, frozen with her eyes darting between my face and her blade. She spoke so faintly I could barely hear her. "If I could save you, I would. But I can't. No one can save you."

"Shann, you got the wrong girl. I don't know what you're talking about. Why would they kill me? You don't have to save me. I'm still *me*." Holding my body rigid, I tried to stay completely still. Her arm shook, and the cold metal dagger touched my skin. I couldn't stand it anymore. Something snapped inside of me. I wasn't a fighter, but I wasn't going to get killed in a church attic.

Forcing my hands to my sides quickly, I closed my eyes, and shoved. My entire body pressed backwards into the tower of books, precariously stacked behind me. The stack gave. The middle section slid back, forming a hole that engulfed me, before the rest of the wall of books collapsed forward.

Books crashed down from above, knocking over the surrounding stacks. By the time my butt slammed into the floor, books were raining down in every direction. That's when I heard it—the sound of metal scraping across the wooden floor. Her blade fell. Pulse pounding in my ears, I pushed the books off of me, and jumped up. There wasn't a clear spot on the floor, but I saw it. I crawled over a pile, scurrying like a crab, rushing through the haze for her blade.

Shannon was already on her feet, trying to get to her dagger. It was just out of her reach. I had to get there first. I jumped, colliding with the wooden floor, and grabbed her dagger. Not thinking, I ran to the attic window and hurled it into the air. It fell to the ground below, stabbing the lawn.

"No!" Shannon lunged at me, but she missed, and fell to the floor.

"What the hell is wrong with you?" I yelled at her. She sat by my feet with tears streaming down her face. "Why do they want to kill me? Why did you… ?" Exasperation overtook my vocabulary, and I couldn't finish the sentence. I stamped the wooden floor in front of her, yelling, "Tell me what's going on! Tell me now!"

"I can't do it! I can't!" she stammered, rocking, not looking at me. She looked utterly tormented.

This betrayal was more than I could bear. She always had my back, and I had hers. Shaking, I tried to control my rage. My voice left my body in a tight monotone, "If my friendship ever mattered to you, you better stop screwing with me and tell me now." My eyes were burning a hole in her face. My fists clenched tightly at my sides.

"Ivy, you *do* matter to me. What's going to happen to you is unbearable." She wiped her eyes, as her voice took on the tone of someone too grief-stricken to speak. "The prophecy said this: *Purple mark above thine brow, gently conquer the reds as they are now, or to them succumb, devour the lead, and rise as one.*" She sat quietly, wiping her hand across her face. "Everyone thinks it means that the girl with the purple mark is the one who ushers the massive onslaught of evil into the world. You're the girl with the purple mark, Ivy. It's you!" Her emerald eyes stared up at me, unblinking.

Shaking my head, I said, "It's not me. Look at me Shann! I'm not evil. I don't care what the prophecy says. I'm not a Valefar. I'm not bad. You know that. Why can't it be someone else?" With my hands clutching my head, I turned away from her.

Her voice was soft, "There is no one else with a purple mark. There never has been. You might have started blue, but you aren't now. I have no idea how it happened. I just know that painting shows the prophecy of the girl with the purple mark. She's you. You're her. Somehow it happens. Somehow you become evil."

"It won't happen," I bit the words off with contempt, irritated that she didn't believe me.

I looked at her. Her eyes were enormous, and filled with grief. She flicked her head at the canvas, "See the guy in the painting?"

"Yeah," I said looking at him. "What about him?"

"He also has a purple mark, but his is a scar. See, his skin is marred?" I nodded. She continued, "He was demon kissed—he's a Valefar. He's going to pull you down to become one of them. See your hands? You try to pull him up. You'll try to save him. And fail. You'll fail, Ivy. If you fail, you become one of them. And you'll destroy all of us—the Martis, the world, everything and everyone. Ivy, you're the straw. The Trojan horse. The end all. It's you Ivy! Your futures are intertwined. If he wins, you lose."

I swallowed hard, not wanting to believe anything she was saying. "Why would I be involved with one of them? They tried to kill me." Shannon went to speak, but I cut her off, walking toward her, "Shannon, I'm *not* one of them. I'll *never* be one of them." I stopped before her, looking her in the eye. "Believe me. You were my best friend for seventeen years. You have to believe me."

Shannon's voice was strained, "I want to. But it doesn't work like that. A prophecy is a glimpse of the future. This future is bad. And it's because of you." Her eyes revealed the sadness that consumed her soul, "Ivy, who is he?"

Sensing Shannon's conflicting loyalty shifting in my favor, I glanced at the painting again, looking at his face. It felt like I knew him, but I couldn't be sure. I shook my head, "I don't know."

"I can't destroy you. I just can't. But I can't lie. Martis can't lie, so if someone asks me, we have a problem. But they shouldn't because I'm not the Seeker, but still. No, they shouldn't ask me. But, hiding you is going to be hard. I'll make sure you don't have anything to do with that guy. I'll guard you. It won't happen. It can't happen." It sounded like she was talking, trying to convince herself, rather than me.

I latched onto a word, "What's a *Seeker*?"

Her weary green eyes flicked to my face. "The Seeker has been looking for you. Her job is to find out when you are created—the second that purple mark forms on your head—and destroy you."

I hesitated, sure that our friendship was toast. I couldn't trust her anymore, even if she did spare me. My stomach sank. "So... " I said, glaring at her. "You're not gonna kill me? But there is someone looking for me, who will?"

Nodding, her green eyes bore straight into me, "Yes. And Ivy. Eric will kill you, if you tell him."

I answered, "Then, I won't tell him."

"Ivy," she hesitated, "It's not that simple. We're bound to certain acts. Some of us can't resist. Destroying evil is innate—a reflex. I can't kill you, because I know who you are and that you aren't evil now. We've been friends for seventeen years. I know you. But Eric, he won't hesitate. If something goes wrong, and he sees that the mark is purple, it will confirm that you are the one in the prophecy...He won't let you walk. And he won't stop hunting you until you're dead."

With complete certainty I said, "He won't find out." She started to object, but I cut her off. "He *won't find out*. But what about you? Will you hunt me? If I didn't throw your knife out the window, you wouldn't have stopped, would you?"

Shannon looked at me, taking a step forward, and said, "I don't need the dagger to kill you." Tension laced my muscles, as we stood stone still, nose to nose. Finally, she breathed, and continued, "You're not evil. You're not the girl in the prophecy. Not *yet*. Maybe we can prevent it. And I'm not giving up on you until I see reason to." She stepped back, and turned. The veiled threat was there. She would destroy me when she thought there was no hope.

"I'm not her," I said, unfolding my arms, and pointing to the painting.

She walked towards me, arms folded, standing tall and slim. "You will become her. The prophecy says he'll pull you to deepest pits of Hell with him. You'll serve demons and monsters for eternity. The horror flicks that me and you used to watch at the movies - they pale in comparison to that place," her finger pointed to the blackest part of the painting.

"Ivy, if that guy gets to you, you're gonna change. Something inside you will snap, and you are going to *want* to be there. In Hell. To be with him. And I won't be able to do anything to help you. All the Martis will swarm to destroy you, before you destroy everything."

"I'd never betray my friends for a guy. I'd never let the world go to Hell for a guy. You won't have to help me, because it won't happen."

CHAPTER EIGHT

Mental hoopla was slapping into the sides of my skull, giving me a headache, as I stared at the ceiling in my room. I was cast head first into the vat of chicken-fried crap, and I didn't know how to get out. Denying it wasn't really working out. I could say this whole thing didn't happen, but it wouldn't change anything. I'd still be hunted.

The more I thought about it, the angrier I got. I pulled my pillow over my face and screamed. When the air escaped my lungs, my anger fizzled a little. I rested the pillow on my belly, and stared blankly. I had no choice, but to accept everything that was thrust at me, and try to make something of it. The part that bothered me the most wasn't the Seeker stumbling on me in the middle of the night—it was that they thought I was evil.

Having someone call me evil to my face was weird—since I'm not. But it made me wonder if on some level, they were right. Maybe that was where I was headed. I'd done some dumb stuff over the past year, but I wouldn't have said any of it was evil. I partied, drank, and threw myself at random guys. Most teenagers did that anyway. It wasn't good, but I didn't think it gave me a Fastpass to Hell either.

I needed something. This felt too dream-like to be real. If I had something to touch and hold, this wouldn't feel so freaking weird. The plan formed in my mind without much conscious thought. And I waited.

When night fell, I felt a little better. My mom fed me birthday cake and I blew out seventeen candles. Next year there would be one more candle, but I'd still be seventeen. I'd be seventeen when I was seventy. *How was I supposed to hide that?* I'd have to deal with that later.

Staying alive was more pressing at the moment. It was odd, but I had no idea how much I wanted to live, until Jake tried to kill me. I was glad that I was still around to blow out candles. After too much birthday cake, I jumped on my bed forgetting the delicate box was still there. It bounced off the bed and crashed onto the floor.

I rolled over to grab it, but the wood didn't survive the impact. It lay on the floor, cracked. I closed my eyes, blinking back tears. My fingers picked up the box, and I held it delicately in my hands, trying to fix it. It wasn't that messed up. My fingers ran across the crack in the bottom of the box. I pulled out the velvet pillow to see how bad it was, but the inside of the box wasn't cracked. When I flipped it back over, the outside bottom of the box was cracked all the way through. I pressed my nail into the space to confirm what my eyes saw, and instantly regretted it. The box split in my hands.

"Oh no. No." I pushed the pieces back together, but it was too late. They were split clean through. Sighing heavily, I felt the tears well up. I ruined the last gift Apryl gave me.

I dropped half of the broken box on the bed, to wipe a tear from my eye when I saw it. A black chain slid out of the bottom. Looping the chain around my fingers, I pulled it out. It was a necklace with a small pendant, the size of a quarter. It was a solid black stone disc that held two tightly woven ivory peonies. I held it in my palm, looking at it, wondering if Apryl knew it was in the box. I undid the clasp and draped it around my neck. The pendant hung in the hollow of my throat, exactly where I would have worn a choker.

My fingers slid across the rough ivory. Breaking the box didn't seem so bitter now. I found a hidden treasure. And it matched everything. It wasn't too dressy or too plain. I could wear it all the time. I fumbled the cold disc in my fingers wondering why it was hidden in the bottom of the box.

I wasn't tired when I went to bed that night. Sleep was something I no longer needed. I flicked at the frayed edge of my blanket, waiting. Mom had to be asleep. So I waited, twitching my foot restlessly until the sounds of silence echoed through the house. Jerking my body upright, I padded across to my dresser. Looking in the mirror, I ran my slim fingers down my cheeks. I still looked like me, and that purple mark was still there, delicately strewn with lots of swirls. The mark was changing, becoming more elaborate. It changed my life faster and harder than anything I've ever encountered.

I wondered if I'd survive it.

Quickly, I slapped on sweats and swept my hair into a tight ponytail. I stabbed it with my silver comb to hide my mark. Then I launched myself out the window, into the night air. My sneakers struck the pavement in quick blows. I wasn't a runner. I didn't even walk, if I could avoid it. But that night, I ran faster and longer than ever before. I ran until my lungs burned, starved for air.

I stopped. My church sat bathed in blackness in front of me. I walked through the empty parking lot. The trees' canopy creaked, as I walked under their enormous branches. Placing the key in the lock, I turned it once, and pushed the door open. My feet made a beeline through darkened halls, going straight to the attic. I found the frame covered in a sheet, as I'd left it earlier.

I grabbed it and began to tug the metal staples out of the wooden frame. *I'm destroying fine art. Great.* But I had to take it. I had to see what I became and how I became it. The painting had to tell more than it seemed. It was my only link to the person I would become. The person I didn't want to be. The canvas came loose, and I rolled it up silently. Returning the sheet, I placed the empty frame back into the dusty corner. The painting rolled up to the size of a paper towel tube. I shoved it in my jacket, and got out of the building. No one saw me.

Slipping back into the night, my ponytail swished, as I ran. My lungs burned while my feet pounded the pavement not knowing where I was going. I didn't care. The frigid night wind whipped my face until my flesh burned. But I couldn't stop. My worry spilled out of my limbs, and the nervous energy took me further and further from home. As I ran the tall buildings shrunk, and the trees thinned out. Soon only the bare land of sod farms surrounded me.

When I couldn't force my body to run another step, I abruptly came to a stop. I doubled over, and my face turned sideways gasping for air. A massive dark building stood in the distance. I braced my hands on my knees, painting. My sweat-soaked shirt clung to my body. I straightened, recognizing the silhouette of a church spread out in front of me. The dead lawn crunched under my feet, as I walked toward the decrepit building. The magnificent shambles called to me. It spoke to me in the silence, revealing abandoned hopes and promises.

A steeple stretched into the inky sky, and was anchored by a stone building that was falling into ruin. It looked like it was a chapel-sized version of one of the old European cathedrals. The kind with great arches that stretched into space with stones, locked into place, at angles that defied gravity. The doors were made of solid carved wood with decorative ironwork and door pulls. The building sat alone draped in quietness and shadows. Unease gnawed at me. I looked around, not recognizing where I was. And I was alone, unless you count the graveyard.

My hands pushed against the wooden door, expecting to be met with resistance, but it gave way to my touch. I stepped into the building, and out of the moonlight. The interior was black, but I could still see with my Martis vision. However, the comforts of sunlight, like the fact that it chases the creepies away, were missing. I wrung my hands, and walked forward. I passed through a small entryway, and perfectly aligned pews covered in a thick layer of white dust. My feet pressed softly to stone. The sound of my footfalls broke the silence. The stained glass that was intact glimmered in the moonlight. Shattered panes revealed stars, as the coolness of the night air leaked in through the openings. I don't know if I loved it because it was abandoned, or because it had once been beautiful—and now it was broken.

When I reached the front of the church, I stopped. The crucifix was gone. The altar stuff was gone. Everything that wasn't bolted down, like the pews, had walked off. A large rose window hung high above the altar. It had more colors than a kaleidoscope. I sat down, and folded my legs under me, my gaze fixed on the round window. The air was still. I sat alone, in the hallowed space, feeling lost and helpless. Defeat was beckoning me. I slumped forward. The scrolled canvas poked me in the chest.

Reaching into my jacket, I removed the canvas. I unpeeled my jacket from my sweat soaked body, and tossed it to the floor. The chill in the night air made me feel better. Desperately wishing I could control this mess; my fingers unrolled the painting onto the floor. The canvas was small. It was much more manageable stripped from the stretchers. The thought that I'd stolen from a church, well, that hadn't crossed my mind yet. It felt like I had a right to this painting—I needed it. I lived or died by what was in this thing. It was about me, and I had to know how I got to the point in the painting—the point where everything went wrong.

My fingers slid across the oils, as I studied the faces. The humans looked peaceful and happy. No faces jumped out at me. They were all strangers, wearing clothes not recognizable from any era. My eyes slid to the depiction of me. Anguish was washed over my face. The girl in the painting looked the same way that I felt. Confused. Lost. Alone.

Her fingers were woven tightly together with the boy's. He would fall, if she let go. *I wouldn't let go. I wouldn't just let him die.*

Slapping the painting, I spoke to myself, "How does that make me evil?" I didn't understand. I held the canvas closer, shaking my head. At the edge of the painting, there were small markings in gold paint. The frame had covered these before, so I couldn't see them. I looked at them, hoping to make sense of their tiny intricate patterns, but that's all it was—a pattern. Something that would look pretty in place of a frame.

Desperation surged through me, filling my veins. It poured out my mouth in a raw scream. I clutched my face with my hands, not knowing what to do. There was nothing there. There were no clues as to how I would become this sinister monster. When I looked at it again, I had hoped that I would have a revelation or something. But I didn't. Nothing. There was nothing else there. My eyes searched the paint for signs of hope, direction, or anything that would help me. But there was nothing. I'd have to figure it out on my own. Alone.

Brush strokes were painted, cutting into the dark cliffs, forming little paths. All of the paths seemingly led nowhere. *No wonder why all these people were stuck on the cliff. There was no way out.* That summed up my new life. There was no way out. I was the only purple marked freak out there. *Until I messed up, and threw this guy off a cliff.* Maybe that was how I became evil? Maybe it wasn't that I tried to save him, but that I didn't save him. Letting him die, if I could prevent it, wasn't something that I would do. Ever. I lowered my head in my hands. I could barely survive my regular life, and now this was hurled at me. My fingers slid over the smooth paint beneath my skin. This was my future, whether I accepted it or not.

"Fuck," I muttered under my breath. I was slightly shocked at the word, even as it fell out of my mouth.

A voice spoke behind me. "I've never heard you say that before."

CHAPTER NINE

My fingers darted to my face wiping away the tearstains. He didn't approach me. He stayed where he was, behind me, in the deepest shadows.

"Collin," I said quietly, not turning to look at him, knowing he heard me. My sweat-soaked shirt clung to my body. I wanted to throw on my jacket, but the painting was hidden underneath, and I didn't want to admit that I stole it. From a church. *Oh, God. What was I doing?*

Before I gave it much thought the hairs on my neck prickled. My stomach churned in response, feeling like I ate a glass sandwich. Something felt *off.* Turning, my eyes cut through the darkness, looking to see what was unsettling me. It was Collin. The shadows couldn't hide the anxiety in his body. His stance was rigid, his tension echoing my own. His arms were folded over his chest, as his muscles flexed, pulling his arms tightly into his body. His hair swept across his eyes, and appeared to be damp, like mine. *Did he run here?* I watched his chest rise and fall slowly, as he drew in long breaths. It was only Collin.

I dismissed the feeling, thinking my brain was fried, and too paranoid to distinguish danger from craziness. I wasn't going to throw all my friends away because of Jake. The betrayal stung, but I wouldn't let it make me afraid of everyone. And this was typical, mysterious Collin. Showing up when I was a wreck, like he always did.

Breaking our gaze, I turned my face down, and stared at the floor. And just in time, too. The tears welled up in my eyes and overflowed. I hated crying in front of people, but after everything I'd been through, my brain finally caught up with my heart. Betrayal, fear, lust, love, and anger all swirled bitterly together.

I didn't hear him approach. Collin sat down beside me, not saying a word until the tears slowed. Eventually, he reached into his pocket and held out his hand over my lap. As I looked up at him, he opened his palm. A silver-colored ring with a blood-red stone gleamed at me. He pressed it into my hand.

"What's this?" I sniffled.

"Your present." Before I could protest he said, "I'm not taking it back. I got it for you. I thought you could use it today. It's a ruby in white gold. I heard that it's supposed to purge the sorrow from your soul. Maybe it's an old wives tale, but all the same, I thought you could use it today." He smiled weakly at me, knowing he was treading in dangerous territory.

I slid the ring onto my index finger and looked at it wondering if he just made that up. "I don't feel any different."

He smiled, "Maybe it takes longer than two seconds." He scooted closer. Aware of his proximity and my sweat-coated body, I felt awkward. It should have made me feel better that his skin was dewy too, but he smelled good, and I reeked. I stood up, and held out the ring in the moonlight. *Could rubies really absorb sorrow?* My hand touched Apryl's pendant without thinking. If it could, even a little bit, I'd wear it.

I turned expecting to find Collin on the floor, but he stood behind me. Misjudging the distance between us, I aligned my body too close to his. I sucked in a deep breath, startled. When I looked up, we were nose to nose, almost touching, but neither of us moved. We stayed there, gazes locked. Something stirred inside of me. The sensation made my arms feel light, like they could float up to drape around Collin's neck on their own. Wrapping my fingers in his soft hair would be so easy, but my arms remained at my sides.

A dull image washed through my mind. It felt like an old memory, dull and hazy with age. It echoed of fingers touching flesh, sliding slowly across a soft cheek. The sensation scraped my stomach softly, causing my heart to beat faster. His warm breath caressed my skin, as we stood surrounded by shattered glass. My pain melted away, flowing out of me, taking my anger and sorrow with it. There was nothing left, except me. And him.

Warmth shot through me, forcing me to breathe deeply at the unexpected response. Collin's fingers neared my face. Hope filled me, wishing he would do what I just saw in my mind. I stood still, looking up into his eyes, too afraid to breathe. My lips parted, as I took a shallow breath, closing my eyes and slowly opening them again. The realization that I wanted the premonition to happen consumed me. I've never felt like that before.

There was so much emotion connected to a thought, and his presence. His hand slowed, nearing my face. It froze in the air, almost touching me. Butterflies plagued my stomach, as anticipation got the better of me. Yet when he moved again, his fingers touched only a curl, avoiding my flesh. I waited for him to slide his hand across my cheek. I waited for the sensation on my skin. Instead, he placed the stray curl behind my ear, and withdrew his hand. Disappointment surged through me, as our gaze broke. The magic of the moment shattered, and he stepped away.

What was that? My body shivered, as I turned away from him, taking a few paces. I wrapped my arms around my torso, looking over my shoulder at him. His gaze looked anywhere, and everywhere—except at me. We rarely locked eyes. We never touched. And it was because this kind of thing happened. It felt like mind games, but I didn't want to admit it was more than that.

My voice came out gravelly, "Why'd you come here, Collin?" I didn't look at him.

"You called to me," he said softly. "I had to come." He turned, not knowing what to do. I bristled at his unexpected response. Something was bothering me, but I couldn't really put my finger on it. I liked that he showed up when I needed someone, but I never knew how he did it. Or how he found me. Or why he wouldn't touch me when he found me shattered. Most friends would at least offer a hug. But he didn't. It felt intentional, like he avoided touching me at all cost. Suddenly the idea was intolerable.

Irritation surged through me. Not knowing how to answer I simply said, "I did not *call you.*"

Collin was silent for a few minutes. He seemed unsure of himself, which was strange for him. I could hear his breathing, slow and deliberate. He made a few false starts and then said, "You should go home, Ivy. Don't come out here alone. It's not safe." Slowly, he turned away from me to leave.

I didn't move. Staring blankly, tears ran down my cheeks, and a whisper fell out of my mouth, "Nothing is safe. Not anymore."

Collin stopped and turned, looking at me. His lips parted, like he wanted to say something, but he didn't.

I felt broken, standing before him, completely exposed. The rawness of it surged through me, making my stomach twist. My gaze avoided his eyes. The air felt thick, and the two of us stood around like we'd done something wrong, though we'd done nothing.

I couldn't stand it. I wanted to ask, *Why won't you touch me?* But I heard my voice ask, "How did you find me?"

His blue eyes held my gaze intently. His lips parted, as I waited for words. But, the only thing that I could hear was his breath escaping from his body. He broke my gaze and ran his fingers though his hair, pushing it away from his face. His skin was smooth and perfect. No scar. But, the Valefar hid it, like my mark was hidden now. Shock flooded me as I realized what I was thinking. *Did I really not trust him? Is that what I think of him?* No, I was paranoid. *I could trust Collin.*

He took a step toward me, but not as close this time. He folded his arms, holding them loosely to his chest. His voice was soft, "Ivy, you called me. You call out to me. I don't know exactly how I know where you are, but I do. It's like your spirit calls to me and I can't ignore it." My gaze fixated on his mouth as he spoke, "It doesn't matter where I am, or what I'm doing, or who I'm with... When I hear you," he paused, "when I hear your distress... I can't ignore it. It's like a siren song. I can't resist it, Ivy. I have to come to you."

His words penetrated my mind, slinking back into the dark spots that were becoming larger, and untrusting. My skin prickled, as my heart raced. I could feel his eyes on me, waiting for me to look at him again.

But I didn't know what to do. The desperate feeling of wanting to know, without a doubt, that he was normal drowned me. I didn't know what insanity prompted me to do it, but I did. Taking a step towards him, I closed the gap between us.

Looking up into his face, I said, "Kiss me, Collin." Vulnerability and doubt lined my thoughts. There was one way to prove it—a kiss. If he kissed me, I would know he was normal. Just Collin. If he didn't, then he was something else. Fear and distrust were warring with the loyalty I felt toward him. I had to know. This was the easiest way to find out.

Collin's face faltered. His certain stance melted, as he physically pulled back from me, hands rising, so I could see his palms. "Ivy. That's not … a good idea."

Fixated, I took a step toward him, watching his confident façade fade away. I could feel the lub-dub of my heart deep within me. This would tell me he was normal. I needed him to be Collin. *Nothing more. Dear God, nothing more.* "You wanted me once. I know you did."

Collin slid his foot backwards, increasing the distance between us, but his eyes didn't leave mine. "Ivy now isn't the best time. I couldn't take advantage of you when you're like this." His foot slid back another step.

My gaze was locked on his unblinking blue eyes. My voice whispered, "Just one kiss." I took another step toward him, closing the space between us.

He put his hands up in the universal symbol for stop. We didn't touch. He broke my gaze and looked away. "I can't. Ivy. I don't feel like that. I'm sorry." The answer to my question was staring me in the face. He wasn't normal. I just didn't want to admit it. Not yet.

"Collin," I asked softly, "What *are* you?"

His blue gaze was wide, as he ran his fingers through his hair. "What does *that* mean?" He sounded offended and started to shift away.

I shook my head, "You know what I mean. You don't touch me. Ever. Why not? I know you like me, but you won't kiss me. I thought it was me, that I wouldn't let you. All this time, I thought you were respecting my distance. But that's not it, is it?" My heart raced in my chest. I couldn't handle another betrayal, and not from him. *Just tell me, Collin.*

Smiling his boyish grin, Collin started to say, "Ivy, that's crazy. We're just..."

But I didn't let him finish. Reaching up to his neck, I threaded my fingers through his hair, pulling him to me. Collin's body went slack in my hands, as I felt him press against me. It felt heavenly, until my hands slid, and touched his skin. An icy hot surge burst into me, traveling through my hand, and into my body like a gigantic static shock. We both jerked, breaking the contact.

Shock was painted across my face, as I looked at my shaking hand, then back at Collin.

His voice was strained, "What the hell was that?" Shaking his head, eyes wide, he continued to move away from me, "That was too much. I can't be what you need. Ivy, I'm not that guy. I'm not." He turned away from me, walking in long strides, disappearing beyond the doors at the back of the church and into the night.

Dread filled me as I grabbed my jacket, stuffing the painting under my other arm, and sprinted in the opposite direction. I ran toward the back of the church, and up a dim stairwell. Crashing through the first door I found, I slid into the room, and pushed the door shut behind me. Collin didn't follow. Not this time. He was gone. And it was my fault. I hadn't meant to run him off. I just wanted to know why he wouldn't touch me.

What the hell is wrong with me? Emotions bubbled into a frothy mix of humiliation and regret. Anger seared through all of it. Collin was one of the only friends I had left, and I screwed it up. Growling in frustration, I turned and hurled the painting at a pile of books. It rolled behind them and out of sight. Sliding my back down the wall, I lowered my butt to the floor, banging my head softly into the wooden shelves behind me. He didn't want to touch me. The reality crashed into me with a deafening blow.

CHAPTER TEN

School dragged on. My life as a poser Martis proved to be under-whelming during the school day. No one hunted me there. At least, I didn't think they did. I still wondered who the Seeker was, and how close she was to finding me, but no one stood out as an angelic stalker. My new life was weird, and I was having trouble with it. Learning how to survive, without exposing my secret, made me want to hurl. Putting aside all thoughts of the Martis and Valefar who wanted to kill me, I made it through the day. Somehow, I also managed to avoid the biggest mistake I'd made in years. Collin was conspicuously absent, which meant he cut, or he was avoiding me. Or both. *Suck.* I didn't know how to fix it.

He *ran.* Like I scared him—like he couldn't stand the thought of touching me. It was just too messed up. Not having any idea what I would say to him, I was glad he was avoiding me. And it wasn't like I could tell him the truth, which would sound insane.

Hey Collin, I'm acting like a nut-job because a demon slave tried to rip out my soul the other night, then my best friend attacked me. I felt utterly alone, and you were there, and... well. It didn't matter anyway. I couldn't tell him.

The last bell rang at 2:26pm. Not wanting to go home yet, I slowed my exit, walking with Eric, lost in thought. We pressed through crowds of kids, heading toward my locker. Something told me that I should be cautious of Eric, but right now he was one of the only people I could talk to. It forced a friendship that was based on lies, which made my skin crawl. I hated lying, but I had no choice.

Our conversations got progressively more normal, as my life got stranger. I smiled at him, "I don't know how you can stand having me as your lab partner. I'm gonna tank our grades."

We shouldered our way down the hall, through crowds of scattering kids. A light box flickered overhead. Eric had a soft smile on his lips. "Nah, Ivy. It'll be fine." Shannon's warning echoed in my mind, as *He'll kill you.* I couldn't see it. That made me either reckless—or retarded. Probably both.

"You always think everything will be fine," I said half laughingly. "Seriously, I mutilated our worm and the frog. If the pig wasn't already dead, I'd feel sorry for him. As it is, I can tell it's just a train wreck waiting to happen. I'm gonna feel like its Wilbur… or it'll make me think of ham." I cringed. "Well, either way, it's got a C written all over it."

Eric's soft steps fell in perfect pace to mine. They matched his sweet, quiet demeanor. "I *am* serious. It'll be fine." He looked at me out of the corner of his eye, still smiling, amused.

"The only reason you're the other dumb one," God help me, I used air quotes for *dumb one*, "is because I suck your lab grades down. I don't think that's fair either," I said looking him square in the face. "You know all this stuff. And I keep messing it up." Our paces slowed in sync, as I neared my locker. Eric stopped, and touched my arm. Still emotionally raw from my encounter with Collin last night, I flinched. His hand withdrew. Not meaning to shake him off, I reached out for him. My fingers wrapped around his forearm gently, and he paused, looking at me. "Eric,

I'm jumpy. That's all. It's not you. I swear. What were you going to say?"

I wasn't interested in Eric. Not like that, but I didn't want him to think he was gross or something. I wasn't a touchy feely friend, but I didn't shirk at my friends' touch either. I guess I was somewhere in between.

He smiled, nodding, "Nothing, it's just. Well, I'm going to the diner in a sec. You want to come?"

"Sure, just let me grab my stuff." I didn't want to go home yet. I'd be okay, and if Jake showed up, Eric was a good person to be with.

Eric started to say something, but his mouth faltered and snapped shut. His smile faded just as quickly. I looked up to see what caused his abrupt change. My eyes wandered across the groups of kids and landed on my locker. Collin was leaning against it, surrounded by a gaggle of girls. I groaned out loud. Eric sniggered.

Turning to Eric, I asked, "I'll meet you over there?"

He gave me a look of condolences, and said, "Sure. See ya there." His pace quickened. Eric and Collin glared at each other as he passed. I turned my attention back to my locker. Embarrassment related to last night crept over my skin, making me feel hot. I didn't want to talk about it. I didn't want to see him, mostly, because I had made an idiot out of myself.

I said nothing, and opened my locker. Collin watched me. I tossed my bio book into the bottom, and then stood on my toes to sift through the crap at the top. My math book was up there. Somewhere. Not finding it, I lowered my heels to the floor. *Ugh. It must be down bottom.* The bottom of my locker looked like a ski hill made of paper, books, and the occasional Spork.

I crouched down to sift through the pile, squatting, wishing I could leave without it.

Collin crouched next to me, "Ivy. Dear. This may be obvious, but you are a slob." A playful smile flashed across his face, as he looked at me. He was going to act like last night never happened. *Oh God.* Then it would be hanging there, perpetually stuck, like a scratched CD, skipping back to the blunder for eternity.

But, like him, I didn't want to talk about it now either. "Go away Collin," I said, not putting much feeling into it, digging through papers, slowly unearthing textbooks. He continued to crouch next to me, laughing lightly. He bumped into me, and knocked me off balance. If I'd been paying attention, it wouldn't have happened. But I wasn't. Unable to shift my weight fast enough, I fell backward, and landed on my butt. When I looked at him, a coy smile tugged at one corner of his mouth.

I grumbled half-heartedly, "Grow up!" I rolled to my knees, reaching into my locker, and grabbed my bio book. Turning, I held the book with two hands, and whapped him in the chest. He toppled over from his crouched perch. But before he fell, he stuck his foot out and took me back down with him. My laughter broke free, as the rest of my bad mood fizzled. Our jean clad legs tangled together, and I fell onto his chest with the bio book separating us. For a second, my life felt normal. I had one of my best friends back, but the feeling faded quickly. The close proximity conjured the memories from last night. Quickly, I pushed myself off of him. I sat down on the floor in front of my locker, pushing my hair out of my eyes. Collin rolled himself upright, still laughing.

"Get a room!" some guy yelled, as he sprinted past. Most of the students had either left the building, or were headed to their after-school activities.

We looked at each other and laughed lightly, but the laughter ended too soon to be real. *Crap.* This was what I'd done to our friendship. The halls were empty.

Desperately, I wished last night hadn't happened. I wanted my friend back. Collin leaned his head back against the locker, and we looked at each other. The silence continued. Comfortable silence was normal for us, but this wasn't it. I felt weird. I just wanted his friendship, to be secure in knowing that I still had it. Fear clutched at me, realizing the thought I was dreading. *I've lost him.*

"No you haven't. You'll always have me," he said relaxed.

The smile faded from my face. I lifted my back off the locker slowly, heart hammering, "What? What did you say?" *Holy crap. Did he hear me?* Panic shot through my entire body. My stomach twisted in knots. His eyebrows shot up, as he squirmed, looking away from me. He ran both hands through his hair at the same time, avoiding my gaze.

"Collin... ," I paused, feeling stupid. Almost too stupid to ask the question, but I had to know, "Did you... *hear me?*" My pulse raced. Our eyes locked, and I couldn't look away.

The corner of his mouth tugged his face into a lopsided smile. Nervously he asked, "So, you're finally gonna admit it?" I started to protest, but he cut me off, "No. No, you can't deny it now. And yes, I can hear *you.* And I know you can hear *me.*" I jerked away, feeling panic rising into my throat. Leaning his head against the locker, he ignored my panic. "Don't act all shocked. You've known for as long as I have. Since that night your friend went psycho on me. I know you noticed." He paused, looking around to make sure we were really alone. "We were at that party, and your friend was telling me off. You came over to drag her back to her hag cave, and it happened. Our eyes locked, and you brushed my arm as you passed. It was eye to eye, flesh to flesh. *I felt you. I heard you.* And I know you heard me. You just never wanted to admit it." He shrugged, "Neither did I. But there it is."

My eyes were wide, as he retold a memory that haunted me. It made me think I was totally insane. Things like that don't happen. I thought about it a million times, wondering what occurred. When I passed him that night, I meant to tease him, and get him off balance, so that he would leave Shannon alone. I locked eyes with him, brushing my arm against him as I passed. But I made a mistake. I didn't account for what happened. When we touched, it felt like I licked an outlet. When the static jolt passed, warm fuzziness flooded my brain, melting me, while the rest of my body felt like I was naked in the snow. It was bizarrely uncomfortable. But that wasn't the most uncomfortable part—feeling *him* was. His soul, his being, or whatever you want to call it, spoke to mine. I *heard* him. I *felt* him. I knew exactly what he was talking about.

Swallowing hard, uncertainty grabbed me. I knew he was right, but I still couldn't accept it. "No," my voice was soft, barely audible, "It's only intuition. Or a hunch. There is no way you're reading my mind." My curls fell over my shoulder, forming a wall to hide behind. I refused to look at him.

"Then look me in the eye. Prove me wrong." He waited, but I wouldn't look up. I couldn't. Fear clawed through my stomach in waves. I didn't know what was happening. "Ivy," his voice softened from arrogant I-told-you-so, to kind, "It's all right. You avoid it for the same reason I do—it makes you feel vulnerable. And it tingles a little bit." Looking out of the corner of my eye, I saw him smiling. "I know you avoid it—on purpose—because you want to ignore our bond."

A single brow shot up, as I stammered for words. Looking him square in the eye, I asked, "*Our bond?* Oh please. There is no bond. What's wrong with you?" I laughed nervously. "And whatever you're doing is *not* mind-reading." I folded my arms, slamming my back into the locker.

"What *I'm* doing?" he laughed. "This isn't *my* doing. It's *you*, Ivy. I can't read people's minds. You're doing it!" His blue eyes were wide, as he turned toward me.

"I am not!" I protested. "I don't know how you do that to me."

"Yes you do. If we lock eyes, I can hear you. If you touch me, all your senses flood me. It's overwhelming at times. It scared the hell outa me at first, then I realized it was something that just happened when you were around. Since you seemed content to ignore it, I did the same."

"There is no way that *I'm* the one causing that!" I desperately wanted him to be wrong. It couldn't be me. There was no way. Jumping to my feet, the desire to run away flooded me. Heart racing, I started to walk away quickly down the hall, but Collin was right behind me.

"Ivy, wait," he said following me. But I couldn't stop. I felt my body shaking, terrified of his words—of him. His steps hastened behind me, and then he whirled in front of me so fast that I jerked back. Suddenly, Collin stood in front of me ready to pin me to the locker if I moved. I turned my face away from him, refusing to look him in the eye, hoping that he wouldn't touch me. My heart hammered against my ribs, making it impossible to ignore my fear. "Ivy," he breathed the words inches from my turned face, "I didn't think you were such a coward."

I bristled. My face snapped up, and I looked up at him. "What?"

His expression was full of pity. "I would have never said anything, if I knew you'd run. Out of the two of us, I thought you'd handle this better." He stepped back, breaking our gaze, and gestured for me to leave. Stunned, I stood there, unable to move. Cowardly wasn't something I wanted to be. His opinion bruised my ego, and made it impossible to flee. I said nothing, not knowing what to do.

Collin said, "I know this is weird. But it's there. And I don't want to lose you over it. Last night... " he paused, turning from me. My eyes lifted, looking at his back. His hands desperately clung to his head. He wasn't handling this well either. Somehow, that gave me courage when I had none.

Taking a step, I walked up behind him, reaching for his shoulder. Before I touched him, he spun around, almost knocking into me. His vivid blue eyes locked with mine. Uncertainty grabbed me, choking my throat. Swallowing hard, I asked, "That's why you ran? Last night. You were afraid? Of me?" My heart pounded as I watched my words melt into him.

Collin looked away, unsure. His arms folded, as he looked at the floor. His dark hair swept across his eyes. After a moment he nodded, saying, "See for yourself."

"I did. I was there. Remember? I saw, but I don't know what happened. Why did you run?" My body trembled, and I fought to stop shaking. The idea of *this* terrified me, and acting like it was real, made it worse.

Stepping toward me, he said, "No, you can *see* for yourself." He reached for my hands, taking them in his own. His body tensed with contact, sharply taking in air. He lifted my hands to his face, and released his grip. Standing in front of me, his sapphire eyes were intense, watching. My hands rested gently on his face, as I slid my fingers down to his cheeks, adjusting my reach to his height. His warm skin was smooth, but that feeling was sucked away before I had time to think about it. An icy hot jolt shot through me, and then faded into the bizarre naked-in-the-snow sensation that made me squirm. My heart raced inside my chest. I was losing my nerve.

His voice was soft, "Look at me Ivy. Look into my eyes, and don't look away. Let it happen this time. I'll show you why I ran. You can see it." My hands shook, as they touched his skin. I gazed up into his eyes— terrified. It wasn't the same terror as being attacked, knowing my life was at stake. It was something more carnal, more intimate than I'd ever shared with anyone. It was total exposure of soul and self, with nowhere to hide. I hated it.

My heart raced wildly, until the onslaught of sensations subsided. Drawing in a long breath, the bond shifted. It made me feel like I *was* Collin. I could hear and feel his thoughts. His whims. His dreams. All of it. It was floating around me, inside me, brushing against my consciousness. His defenses of charm and wit flew by, as I fell deeper into his mind. Secret thoughts flew past, as I saw the things he guised from the rest of world. Then I found myself settling into his memory from a few moments ago. I felt the pure joy he felt when he had knocked me on my butt. Collin's chest rose and fell, as he breathed slowly—his blue gaze intense. He stood stone still, watching me, allowing the invasion into his mind. I looked at him, eyes unseeing, sensing his memories through my touch. They had his voice, and his perception of reality.

Then, I saw last night, but from his eyes. He heard my voice in his mind, as he sat laughing with friends. Then my crushing sadness washed over him. He was flooded with raw emotion that was too painful to ignore. He battled it, but it was consuming him. The wave of remorse, anger, and fear that washed over me as I sat crying on the stone floor of the old church, consumed him. My anguish became his anguish. Unable to ignore it another second, he was suddenly running toward me. I felt his feet pounding the ground, as his heart heaved. He ran, not knowing where I was. Everything happened so quickly. The version of the memory I saw wasn't in real time. It flew by like a TiVoed commercial that no one wanted to watch.

Suddenly, he found me alone in the dust. The old church surrounded him, dropping into his memory like a blanket, coming slowly into focus. The change of pace jarred me, as the sensation of my brokenness surged through him in full force. It was more intense than before. He loomed in a dark corner, watching me, unable to move. Remaining hidden by shadows, he thought he was safe. Unseen. He watched my back, as I breathed deeply with my damp shirt clinging to my skin. My ponytail flopped over my shoulder, as I slumped forward. The emotions he felt flooding from me were filling him in unrelenting waves, and caused his body to tense. His sentiments were too tangled to read, but as he watched me I knew that he was torn.

Suddenly, the memory scattered like tiny grains of sand blown away by the wind. My contact with his skin broke, as my fingertips touched his collar. I rested my hands on his shoulders for a second, breathing heavily, before dropping my arms and stepped back. A cold wash of panic rinsed over me, as I accepted the truth.

It was real. *Oh God.* I could feel everything he felt, see what he saw, and it was more vivid than being there, watching it myself. It was like I was inside of him, experiencing it with him. I nervously chewed my lip. Thoughts flew like drunken bats, crashing incoherently through my mind.

Heart pounding, eyes wide, I asked, "Did you read my mind, too?"

He shook his head, with his eyes downcast. "No. Not really. It seems to go one way, for the most part."

I released the breath that I didn't realize I was holding, looking at his face. Sapphire eyes watched me, before Collin broke the gaze. He possessed a melancholy nature that I was too shaken to notice. I'd seen it in his mind. No I *felt* it in his mind. It weighed on him, baiting him, making him reckless. Collin's arms folded over his chest, as his hair slid into his face. He pushed it back, eyes darting between me, and the floor.

Swallowing hard, I thought about him doing the mind speed-read to me. The idea made it feel like someone poured ice down my back. I closed my eyes slowly, not knowing what to think, too afraid to move.

His voice broke the silence, "That's why I couldn't kiss you."

Shock washed over me, overriding my fear. I looked straight at him. That was the last thing I expected him to say. "What?"

His eyes were so blue, and his expression was tormented as he spoke. "Ivy, your emotions flood through me when we aren't even touching. A slight caress from you, something I would barely notice from other girls, is so intense that... ," his words trailed off. "I don't know what'll happen—with a kiss." He shook his head, almost ashamed of what he'd said.

An odd sensation snaked through my body. I wanted to consider what it was, and tell him it was okay. But it wasn't. I had a deadly secret. He'd see it, Hell, he'd feel it if we kissed. He'd learn what I was, and about the Martis. If he stuck around after seeing that, there was no way he'd stay knowing about the prophecy. I was damned, destined to destroy everyone.

Looking down, I heard myself agreeing with him. "You don't have to explain. You're right."

Silence filled the air until I couldn't take it anymore. Emotions swirled relentlessly inside my chest, filling me with regret. My voice was weak, "I'll see you around, I guess." Careful not to look him in the eye, I turned and started walking away. No voice called after me. No footfalls came running up behind me. My stomach sank in the deafening silence, realizing that my fear came true. *I lost him.*

CHAPTER ELEVEN

Cold air blasted me in the face, as I pushed open the metal door, and headed across the parking lot. My steps smacked into the pavement fast and hard. It was such a stupid mistake. Why couldn't I leave things alone? I cut through the empty alley, as my feet carried me past the blaring horns and noise on the street. My brain sorted through jumbled emotions. I could think about it later. Eric was waiting for me at the diner. I sucked in cold air, and let the chill flood my body. A crisp burst of wind tore through my hair, peeling my jacket open. Clutching my coat tighter, I leaned into the biting gust.

When the breeze died, I looked up. My dark hair was tangled across my eyes—and I saw him. Pulse racing; I stopped dead in my tracks. Jake was staring at me through the blur of traffic across the busy street. He leaned against a storefront—watching me. My heart jumped into my throat. Startled by a car horn, I glanced away, and that was all it took. Jake disappeared.

Frantically, my eyes raked the street looking for him, but he was gone. That was it. Knowing I couldn't risk staying still for another second, I ran until I reached the end of the block. The silver beacon stood on the corner. Big neon letters said DINER. It was circa 1950 on the outside, complete with shiny silver siding. The interior was more modern, but still had a counter with bright red stools and gleaming chrome legs.

I jumped through the door, looking for Eric. He sat at a table in the back corner. I slid into the booth opposite him, utterly freaked. An overhead lamp just missed crashing into my skull. Eyes wide, I said, "I saw him."

A waiter slapped down two glasses of water. Condensation beaded on the clear glass, and ran down the sides.

"Where?" Eric asked.

"When I came out of the school. He was across the street. I saw him between the cars, but he disappeared." I felt my face falter. "I didn't see where he went." Panic was rising in my throat.

Eric's amber eyes narrowed. "So, he's still alive. I tracked him, and found where he lived, but he was gone. There was no way to tell if he survived the night he attacked you."

I shook my head, rubbing my hands up and down my arms. "What do we do?"

"Hey, it's okay. There are a few places where Valefar can't attack. One is a church—holy ground. The other, as weird as it sounds, is your home." Eric leaned back.

"My house? Why? Is that like, some weird vampire thing? Do I have to invite him in or something?" I wanted to lay my head on the table. Instead I slumped forward, holding my head between my hands.

Eric smiled slightly, "No, it's a magic thing. You have a parent—someone who loves you. It's a natural ward against demon magic. They can't enter your house, because your mom lives there, too. That's why I kept telling you to stay home. It sounds weird, but it's true." He sipped some water, and then said, "Now, the best way to catch him is to wait for him to take another shot at you."

His words choked the air out of my lungs. How did my life spun out of control so quickly? I summed it up in one word, "Suck."

"Yeah." Eric watched me as he spoke. He leaned forward, with his arms outstretched across the table. He spoke softly, "He won't hurt you again. I promise, Ivy. I won't let him. I won't let anything bad happen to you." His fingers clutched the edge of the table.

I desperately wanted to believe him, but my twisting gut was telling me otherwise. "How?" I asked. "I know you mean well, Eric, but can't protect me from him. You don't even know where he is. I'm a walking target. It's only a matter of time."

"Ivy, look at me," Eric's hand gripped mine, and my gaze slowly lifted to his face, "He won't hurt you again. I swear. I won't let anything hurt you." His eyes were earnest, but he was promising something that I knew he couldn't deliver. Even if he could protect me from Jake, I couldn't expect him to keep his promise if he found out what I really was. Pulling my hand back, I leaned back into the booth.

"Eric," I sighed, not knowing how to say what I felt. "You can't protect me. You just can't. Things are... *bigger* than they seem."

Leaning forward, he asked, "What do you mean?" A large Greek woman cut off our conversation. She stood at our table, and cocked her hip, waiting. She wrote our order onto her pad, then left, leaving us alone again. Lowering his voice, he repeated, "What do you mean, *things are bigger than they seem?*"

Swallowing hard, I answered, "Just that... Things aren't simple. Not anymore. It's complicated, Eric." The desperation that clung to the sides of my stomach all day slid up my throat, choking me. I knew I was saying too much, but I needed to confide in someone. I might have said more if Shannon hadn't planted the seeds of distrust in my mind. But she did.

The expression on his face was soft, and concerned. "Is it Collin?" he asked.

"Not really," I paused, reconsidered then said, "A little bit." I wanted to tell Eric that my mark was tainted, but I couldn't risk it. I didn't know enough about him or the Martis to decide yet. Besides, boy problems would be overlooked as normal teenage drama.

Eric leaned back into his side of the booth. Looking down at the white table top, he said, "You know, I wasn't sure if you were still gonna come before."

"Why's that?" I asked.

Eric shrugged, "Well, you spend a lot of time with that guy. And he doesn't really like me, so I thought he'd talk you out of it. What'd he think about you hanging out with me anyway?" His chin tilted up enough to catch my eye.

"Actually… He doesn't like it." I felt the smile pull my lips.

Eric picked up his glass and took a sip. "Why's that? Do you think?"

I shrugged, "He's just protective. That's all. 'Til now, he's been the big brother I never had. You know, always poking his nose where it shouldn't go." I smiled, thinking about it.

Nothing escaped Eric's notice. Tilting his head, he asked, "*'Til now?* So something changed?" Leaning forward in the booth, he added, "You didn't tell him that you're a Martis, did you?"

I scoffed. Shaking my head, I answered, "No. I'm not stupid. He doesn't know. I didn't tell anyone. Except... " The approaching waitress silenced my words. Eric looked appalled that I told someone, but I knew he wouldn't care once he knew who I told. The waitress slapped down white plates with fried food. The scent of grease filled the air, reminding me that I was hungry.

After she left, Eric leaned forward, asking, "Who? Who did you tell! I told you not to tell anyone."

"I found a Martis last night. I told her. Shannon McClure."

Eric visibly relaxed, and I could see the tension flow out of him. "That's okay. She's okay. How'd you know she was Martis?"

"It was an accident," I replied. "She saw my mark, and then revealed herself as a Martis." I told him the rest of what happened—well, most of what happened. I left out the part about my mark turning violet, Shannon attacking me, and my involvement in the prophecy. I peered over my plate, considering Eric. If I could tell him everything it would make life so much easier. Maybe he could help me un-defile my mark, and wiggle out of the prophecy. But, if I was truly damned, there was nothing he could do about it. And he'd turn on me. "Can I ask you something?"

A smile tugged the corner of his mouth, "Sure, what do you want to know?" He leaned back into the booth, arms spread wide. He was as confident as Collin, but carried it differently.

"It's kind of personal. Can I ask anything?" I grabbed a couple of pink sugar packets to occupy my hands while I spoke, flipping them around between my fingers.

He pressed his lips together, "Personal? Sure, I'll answer. And, Martis can't lie, ya know. I'll answer anything you ask." A playful look crossed his face.

"Tell me about you. I don't really know you. What you like. What movies you watch. What stuff you like to do. When you think about it, it's really weird. I don't even know how old you are."

The expression on his face shifted from confidently amused to surprise. "What do you mean? I'm seventeen, like you. You know me, Ivy."

Smiling, I leaned forward, saying, "Huh. Apparently Martis can't lie, but they can dodge questions." I waited for him to speak, but he just smiled at me. "You are *not* seventeen, Eric!" I laughed. "You just look like you are. Martis are immortal, right? So, what year were you born, seventeen-year-old?" His smile grew. The right corners pulled tighter, revealing dimples that were normally hidden. I shifted uncomfortably in my seat. "Stop looking at me like that. Answer the question, Mr. Question Evader."

Eric let loose a loud laugh. It was a wonderful deep rich sound. "So you figured that out fast. We can't lie, but we don't have to answer."

I made a mental note that the lack of lying was supposed to include me, but obviously didn't since I'd been lying like crazy since the attack. "But you said you would." I leaned back, watching him. He was enjoying this.

Nodding he said, "I did. I'll tell you anything you want to know, if you're sure you can handle it? And remember, I can ask the same of you. We're both bound by the same magic to speak the truth." Taking the ketchup bottle, Eric whacked on the 57 mark until his chicken looked like it was shot on the plate.

The corners of my mouth twitched, "I can handle anything. So, whatever I ask, you'll answer?" I picked up a fry. He nodded, popping a piece of chicken into his mouth. Questions buzzed in my head, "You mentioned magic. And I saw how strong Jake was," I shuddered. I couldn't help it. "He pinned me to the ground. That was magic, right?" Eric nodded. "So, what can we do? Do we have magic like that?"

He dabbed his mouth with a napkin. "Yes, we have our own abilities, unique to the Martis. We have immortality, strength, speed, but we have different manifestations of power. We can conjure the physical form of light—that's pretty cool. Some of us can heal, see the future, and others are great warriors who survived millennia of horrific wars." He spoke like he was remembering something.

That was the first time I had any inkling of the power Eric wielded. The powers intrigued me, but I wanted the basics first. "How old are you, Eric? When were you born?"

"I was born near Greece," his amber eyes watched me intently. "Ancient Greece. I was chosen to be a Martis a long time ago." He paused, looking at me. "It was at the end of 39AD." He sat back into the booth waiting for my reaction. My fingers dropped the fry I was holding. It bounced off the plate, and rolled under the table.

Shaking my head, I said, "I knew it. I knew you weren't dumb."

He leaned forward laughing and said, "What!"

"In class," I said leaning back into the booth, twirling a fry. "You act like you have no idea what's going on, but whenever I was graced with some of your meager verbiage, you sounded too intelligent to be getting 70's." I raised my eyebrow and leaned forward pointing a fry at his chest. "You're a faker. A really *old* faker."

In honor of my ridiculous statement, I received another wholehearted laugh. His caramel eyes sparkled and his face lit up. "Yeah, now you know. I'm really an underachiever—a really old underachiever." He laughed as he bit a fry. "You're gonna be fun. I can tell."

"So, you've been seventeen for almost 2,000 years? That's got to be—weird."

Nodding he said, "Sometimes it is. Sometimes it's not."

"How'd it happen?" I asked.

His eyes shifted toward the table, as his mood shifted to serious. "I was betrothed. The wedding was supposed to be a few days after I was marked." His face darkened, "I barely survived." He continued, "But I did survive, and after I found the rest of the Martis, I did better. They helped me, and gave me this," he said lifting a silver X on a chain out from under his shirt. It was an old cross.

My eyes lifted to his right brow. It looked perfect, no stardust. No pixie trail. "A cross?" I felt my eyebrow arch.

Nodding, he replied, "It's celestial silver. It hides us, so no one can see our mark. It's, also, our most powerful weapon. Only celestial silver can kill a Valefar. You need it so you can defend yourself." He looked at my hair, gesturing, "How'd you get yours? I was trying to get you a piece, but I couldn't get it that fast. It's very rare, and held under lock and key."

My heart sank, as his words washed over me. "My sister sent it to me. I got it the same day you found me in the park."

"Your sister?" his eyebrows bunched together.

"Yeah, she sent it back to my Mom, when she was in Italy last year, before she died. I don't know where Apryl got it." My fingers touched it gently. "Is it really celestial silver? That's kind of weird, right?"

Eric nodded. "Yes. To both questions. It *is* celestial silver; otherwise it wouldn't hide your mark. And it is weird, since it's so rare." He zoned out, staring at the comb. After a pause he said, "So your mom hid it for a year?"

"Yeah. It was a birthday present. She was supposed to hide it. Apryl always did stuff like that." Looking at him, I saw his expression change, "What's the matter? It's just a coincidence." I shrugged, popping a piece of chicken into my mouth.

His amber eyes focused on my face, "There are no coincidences. Not when Valefar are around."

I bristled, "What are you saying? That Apryl was… what? Valefar?"

He shook his head, "Oh, God no. I didn't mean that." He looked at his plate, shoving more fries into his mouth.

It felt like he was hiding something from me. "Then, what did you mean?" My arms folded, defensively.

"Ivy, I mean I personally don't believe in coincidences. That's all. I've learned to look at things from all angles. It's kinda required to stay alive." His amber eyes flicked to mine, "Listen. Your sister's present was a blessing. It came right when you needed it most. While you may accept that's all there is to it, and that may be all it was, I have to consider what else might have happened."

I said nothing. I couldn't compare him to Jake, because Eric wasn't Valefar, but my brains kept trying to draw the same conclusion, warning me not trust him. The problem was that I *did* trust him. He saved me. Of course I trusted him. I felt my arms loosen, as my offense faded. "Did you know her?" I asked softly.

Looking up, he said, "Apryl? No, not really." He patted the napkin across his lips, and then placed it on his plate. "Ivy, I'm glad you have a piece of silver. There are two things every new Martis needs. One is silver."

"What's the other one?" I asked.

"Not what, but *who*. There's some*one* you need to meet—an old Martis. Older than me. Come on. It's not far. I'll take you since Jake is lurking." He slid out of the booth and asked, "Where are your books?"

I glanced down at the table, "I left them at the school." Shrugging, I added, "I didn't need anything anyway." I'd left Collin in such a hurry that I didn't grab them.

He laughed, "We have a test tomorrow. If you used your textbook for more than a doorstop, you'd get straight A's. You know that, right?" He leaned against the side of my booth wearing jeans, sneakers, and a crisp white tee shirt. The scent of dryer sheets and Ivory soap lingered. Eric smelled wholesome.

Laughing lightly, I scooted out of the booth, saying, "Yeah, yeah. You sound like my mom."

CHAPTER TWELVE

Eric drove without saying much, lost in his own thoughts. As we passed the Cape Cod style houses that lined the streets, we entered a neighborhood filled with life. Pumpkins lined front porches; while the more decorated houses had haystacks perfectly piled, and cornstalks tied to the porch post. I loved autumn on Long Island. It was my favorite time of year.

We pulled up to St. Bart's parking lot a few minutes later. It was a nondescript looking church. That meant no one noticed it, because it had nothing striking about it—at all. The façade was brown, the grass was fading with the upcoming frost, and there were a few evergreens on the lawn. In other words, it was ugly, but not eyesore ugly.

Eric pushed the doors open, and I followed him inside. The hallways were silent and dark. We wound through a maze of halls, and passed a few nuns. We entered a sitting room with a haggard old nun sitting in a rocking chair. It was hard to tell, since she was wearing nun clothes, but I was sure she was built like a brick. Her body had a rectangular frame, bent with age. Her face had angular features, which must have been pretty in her youth. Sun damaged skin freckled her cheeks, and wiry hair that was devoid of color framed her aged face. Her gaze was intensely focused on the book in her hands.

Eric cleared his throat.

The nun looked up and smiled, "Ah, Eric. My favorite. Come on over here and help an old lady up." Sister Al put her book down on the table. She raised her hand to Eric. He took it, and placed his other palm on her elbow to steady her.

This was the woman who was going to teach me how to stay alive?

"Ivy Taylor, wipe that smug look off your face." Al's voice was noticeably less sweet than it was a moment ago. Her black habit swished around her ankles, as she spoke. My eyes darted to the floor. "That's better," she said. "Things are not always what they appear."

I nodded, at a loss for what to say. "Yes ma'am."

The nun laughed at that. "I'm Sister Althea. You may call me Sister Al." She extended her speckled hand toward me. I placed my grip in hers. Her ancient shake had the vigor of a twenty-year-old.

"Pleased to meet you," I said. My gaze darted to Eric, who had sat in one of the padded chairs. "My name is Ivy Taylor."

"I know who you are child. I know that there are great things planned for you. I know you *survived* already," she winked when she said *survived*, "and I know that you feel cast adrift and afraid."

I felt silly for admitting it to a stranger, but she was right. "That sums it up pretty well."

"Uh huh. I know so." She pointed toward a chair on the other side of Eric, and returned to her rocker. "I'm older than dirt, honey. I know lots. Just ask Eric." She paused for a moment, watching me. "There's something different about you," she said. I tried to hide my panic, but I had a feeling that I couldn't hide anything from this woman. There was something about her. The nun continued, "Yes, something's different. You carry a burden larger than most. But it's not beyond you." Her feet rocked her slowly as she spoke, "Many people wander through this life, unsure of who they are. It doesn't matter much to them. But it matters to you. The problem is that you see yourself, without really seeing yourself. You have no idea who you are yet. That's a little unusual, but manageable."

"So, what do I do?" I asked unsure. She was speaking in riddles. I felt like I should take out a note pad, so I could figure it out later. I hated riddles, mainly because I sucked at them.

Her aged eyes locked with mine, "You need to get rid of that anger seeping into your soul before it pollutes you." She watched me. Closely. I didn't move. I neither denied, nor affirmed it. I knew I had issues. But Eric didn't seem to like her answer. Her arthritic hands grasped the rocker as she leaned forward toward Eric. "You show her how to handle that anger. Teach her to defend herself. And then we'll train her up right, showing her how to use all her powers—as a Martis." Her ancient eyes bore into mine, making me flinch.

Eric faltered, reaching for the right words, "Sister, I don't know what you mean."

Her head snapped toward him, "You do so, boy. And I expect you to teach her. Without losing that anger festering inside her, she'll never become who she's meant to be."

I snorted, "*Meant to be?* You think this is all *destiny?*" I couldn't help it. "This isn't destiny! This isn't fair!" This wasn't my destiny! It was a death sentence.

Sister Al's eyes swept across my concealed mark before she smiled gently, and said, "No, it's not fair that you were turned so young, while I was turned so old. It's not fair that you had no choice. But you have a choice now. You can choose which side you want to fight for. You can choose whom you align yourself with. And you can choose how you live. Life isn't fair, child. But you wouldn't have been chosen if there wasn't something special about you." Her skin was weathered like old leather, but her eyes still sparkled like they were young. "Come here Ivy."

I looked at Eric and he nodded, encouraging me to go. To trust her. I looked at the woman. She was a nun. If I couldn't trust a nun, I was severely damaged. Feeling silly, I padded across the carpet. It muffled my clumsy steps. I stopped in front of her rocker.

Sister Al leaned forward and said, "May I?" I nodded, not knowing what she was doing. Sister Al pressed her gnarled fingers into my palm. They scratched against my smooth skin like sandpaper. I felt my body tense, unsure of what she was doing. Her gaze remained on my hand, as she blinked slowly. When she released me, she turned her face up to mine. For a moment she said nothing, no sparkle in her eyes—no smile on her face. It was an expression I recognized in the eyes of my mother when she was notified that Apryl died. It was like time froze, and she was too stunned to blink or breathe. Sister Al held the same anguished expression.

When she spoke, her voice was low. "Dear girl." She closed her eyes, shaking her head slowly. "You have a unique set of circumstances, don't you?" I didn't say anything. I just stood there, wide eyed waiting for her to out me. "Your vice is also your savior. That is a very sticky situation."

"What is it?" I asked. My stomach folded over, squashing itself into nausea.

She smiled softly at me, releasing my hand. "Passion. You have the strength to follow through the things that you care about, but you also have the ability to be influenced by the things that haunt you. It's going to be problematic at some point.

"Your passion will keep you alive Ivy Taylor, but it will also risk your soul. It dictates what you do, how you live, and with whom you lay your loyalties. Oh child. You have so much good in you, and so much darkness too." Her voice trailed off.

Uncomfortably, I stood there and felt like a big fortune cookie. Sliding my hands in my pockets, I noticed Eric's eyes on me. His expression wasn't good. I tried to repress a shiver, but it raked my body, causing my shoulders to twitch. Wanting to kill the horrific silence, I asked, "You read palms?"

Surprise melted the serious look off her face. "Ha!" she snorted, "No, child. But I suppose you can call it something like that. It's part of the power of the Martis. I'm a Seyer, rare as we are."

I nodded, not knowing what to say, or what she meant. An uncomfortable silence dragged on, while the two of them stared at me. My fingers nervously clawed my leg through my jean pockets. Finally, I turned my back on them, unable to stand their stares any longer. I paced the room, slowly. Waiting. Eric's eyes were on me, watching me. He missed nothing. Maybe he was dangerous.

"Eric," she said. "I want her training to start immediately. Teach her how to fight. We need her to survive, especially after what happened the other night. That Valefar will be gunning for her. And I want *you* to train her. Not one of the others. You and only you. If you need help with something, you may ask the other Martis, introduce her, but do not allow her to train with them. Got it?" Her gaze landed on him with an intensity that backed the importance of her words.

Eric's eyes darted between me, and then Al. "Sure, but why me?"

A smile pulled back the corner of her mouth. Aged teeth were revealed behind her thin lips. "You're the best warrior we have. She needs to learn from the best. That's all. It won't interfere with your other duties. You teach her to fight and I'll teach her the rest. Me and you'll get her trained in no time." She folded her gnarled knuckles in her lap, smiling up at me. It was a knowing smile, one that said bad things were coming.

I looked back at her aged face, wondering how I was supposed to survive this. I couldn't fight. When someone messed with me, I didn't fight back. I wasn't that girl. But after Jake attacked me, I wished to God I were that girl. Lying there helpless, well, I was done with that. I never wanted to be trapped like that again. And if it came time to have my soul ripped from my body, or kill—I'd kill. The thought shocked me, but logic intervened. Of course I'd kill. I never wanted to live through that pain again, and I didn't want anyone else to, either. Not if I could stop it. Determination shot through my veins, flooding my body with resolution. I would learn this. I could do this. I had to.

I nodded at Eric. "Just say when and where. I'll be there."

"She's kinda creepy, Eric." I didn't know where to start, but that summed it up. I buckled myself into Eric's truck.

He snorted a laugh and said, "She's one of the eldest amongst us. She has some very unusual gifts, and she must think you do too."

I squirmed, "What makes you say that?"

"She's treating you differently. And I've never heard of one of us having your vice before," he sounded concerned. "Apparently that's your strength too."

"That pretty much sums it up. I'm a passionate nut-job." I watched the world fly by out the window. The sun had been swallowed by the night sky, and the streetlights glowed a dull yellow.

"Passions are good," he looked at me, quickly adding, "when they're kept in check. We need to check yours and keep them there." He pulled over to the curb a few houses down from my home. "Anger is never good. Do you know what she was talking about? Do you know why you're angry?"

I kept my eyes staring through the glass at the world outside. Houses lined the street with people inside their happy homes, living normal lives. A life I wanted so desperately that it made me ache. I nodded, "Yeah, I know." My voice was faint, drained.

Eric said, "I can't pretend to understand how you feel, so I won't. I was thrilled I was chosen for this. I can't imagine being mad about it." He picked at the seal on his window and glanced at me over his shoulder. I shrugged.

Something told me being marked as a Martis wasn't what pissed me off. For some reason, Eric assumed that was the source of my anger. In a small way, perhaps it was. I wasn't happy about being thrust into this—that was for sure. No, the anger that burned within me so fiercely, so passionately, was not from being claimed. It was from being tainted into the beast Shannon described. It was tied to the fear and pain of the memory of my best friend turning on me. And wondering who else would prove disloyal when they saw my mark was the color of the Damned One.

"You're different… " I faltered, not knowing what to say.

"Why? Because I was glad this life was thrust on me? On some level, you're right, Ivy. I won't deny it. I was thrilled when this happened to me because it meant that I could really help people, and make a difference— even if it cost me my life. I share your passion and zeal." He paused, glancing at me out of the corner of his eye. "We're more alike than you realize. Don't worry. It'll work out."

"I'm not worried," I lied.

His eyes studied my face. Eric never judged me, he just took in what he saw—a broken mess—and acted like Eric. "Ivy, you were dumped on your head into a life you couldn't even imagine a week ago. You're going to go home, eat dinner, and stare at the ceiling until dawn. I know. I did that too. But it gets better."

I nodded unenthused. "Yup. Sure."

"Don't act like that. You've been offered a life that most people dream about. And you out of all people should understand that," he scolded.

"What does that mean?" I asked.

"It means that you get to live a life that makes a difference. It's a change that you can *see* over your lifetime, whether it's for seventeen years or seventeen hundred years. If you destroy one Valefar, you made a difference. You save people. You spread goodness into the world and strike out evil. You get to see your life is not lived in vein. Ivy, hardly anyone is ever granted that gift—ever." His voice became higher as he finished, "And for some reason it was granted to you, and you're mad about it."

His words soaked through my shocked shell. That was part of me—the Martis part. I could feel it swaying to his words, like they were music to my soul. "You're right."

"What?" he said surprised.

"I can admit when I'm wrong. I'm wrong to feel mad about all this, but you don't totally understand."

"Well, help me then. Tell me." Eric's face pleaded. He leaned closer to me, his features illuminated by the dashboard lights.

Should I tell him? The words wanted to roll off the tip of my tongue, *Something's wrong with me Eric. Help me.* I wanted to trust him so badly, but I couldn't. I couldn't tell him. I bit my lip. "I can't."

Looking up at the upholstered ceiling, he let out a whoosh of air, "I can't figure you out. Ya know that? You sit in class and are smart and pretty. You don't test well. Anyone can see that it's the test, not you. Anyone, *but* you. It makes you think you're dumb. That same creativity that skews your test scores also lightens your soul. That joy pours into the people around you. I see *you* Ivy. You're a good friend to Shannon. And you're a good friend to that idiot Collin, even though he doesn't deserve it." He shook his head and said, "I don't get it."

I looked at him. I'd known him for so long, but I never heard him say so much. I asked, "What don't you get?"

Eric's face was scrunched tight, "How can you be willing to share that with him? But not me?"

"I don't understand what you mean," I squirmed in my seat.

"You trust him. He treats you horribly, throwing you into situations that you shouldn't be in, and yet, you trust him. I treat you so much better. But before today, you never gave me a second look." His eyes locked with mine for every heartfelt word. I didn't know what to say. Collin didn't treat me horribly, but a lot of people thought my trysts were a result of his influence. They weren't. They were my own doing, but I wasn't ready to tell Eric that.

So I said, "I'm sorry." I paused, trying to tell him. To explain. I took a deep breath. "It's just… I have a lot of trouble trusting people," Eric went to interrupt, but I held up my hand to mute him. "Please let me finish. It's something that I've wanted to change, but I can't. I keep trying, and I keep getting it wrong."

"What do you mean?" he asked. He shifted in his seat, leaning a little more toward me.

I was slow to answer, not wanting to say it. I wanted to be wrong about Eric. I couldn't get stabbed in the back again. "Jake. I trusted him, and… " I didn't have to say anything else. He put the pieces together. It's beyond sucking when someone you trusted betrays you. Jake betrayed me, in the worst way possible.

Eric's arm reached out and brushed my hand. I looked up. He said, "I'll make sure your faith in me is well placed. You can trust me Ivy. I promise." His hand was on the seat, next to mine; his eyes were searching my face to see if I believed him. I wanted to, but trust didn't work like that anymore. Wanting it wasn't enough.

"I hope so."

"No, you *know* so. Listen," he was confident, "You need friends now more than ever before. You have to trust someone. You can't do this alone. Loners end up dead. I've got your back, Ivy. I'll train you. I'll protect you. I won't ever give you a reason to not trust me. I promise." His amber eyes were sincere. Guilt racked me, but he kept pushing. I was sitting there lying to his face. He thought I was a pure Martis, his ally. And I knew I wasn't. I was some messed up hybrid demon angel thing that had to rely on him, or I'd die.

I said, "I hope so."

"Trust me, Ivy. It's all I ask. Trust me." His eyes bore into me.

I knew when my anger started. Although I didn't like to talk about it, I didn't see what harm it could do now. I shook my head, "The source of my anger isn't totally from being marked. It isn't from now. Jake wasn't all of it... It's from before. From Apryl. I lost part of me when she died. It did something to me, and I couldn't get rid the anger that burned in my chest. It's still there. Hollow. Tainting things. I can feel it."

Eric's hand slid over mine briefly. "Ah, I do know about that. Al knows more than she says."

Leaning my head back against the seat, I asked, "What do you mean?"

He sighed, mirroring me, "It was a long time ago. I tried to hide it. I didn't think anyone knew. Lydia, my... Well, I was angry. I lost her, kind of the same way you lost your sister. That's why Al wanted me to help you. She knew I went through something similar." An odd sensation flooded me. I'd never talked about Apryl with anyone, outside my family. None of my friends had to deal with death. I was stuck learning how to cope, alone. It took me a minute to identify the sensation bubbling up inside of me—hope.

"You were angry?" I asked. He nodded. "The blackness, Eric. How did you keep it away? How did you keep it from swallowing you whole?" I felt my brow pinched together, and the moisture in my eyes. Verbalizing my battle made it seem like it would end soon.

His caramel eyes looked sad. "It did swallow me. I let the darkness flood me, until I didn't want to take another breath. I know what you're talking about. It takes time... and trust. So, what do you say?"

What am I supposed to say? I shook my head, "It'll take me time. I want to trust you, Eric, I do. It's just that... "

Leaning forward he said, "What? Tell me."

I shook my head, "I'm a mess." Was it possible? If I hinted enough, would he get it? If Shannon knew of the prophecy, he had to know too. "I'm not what you think." I reached for the door, and opened it, as I slid off the seat.

Before my feet hit the ground, I felt Eric's hand on my wrist. "Wait. I'm not gonna push you. You tell me when you're ready. In the meantime, know I'm here, and I'm your friend. And Ivy," he smiled at me, "I already know you're a mess. It's part of your charm."

CHAPTER THIRTEEN

The week passed without incident. While other aspects of my life leveled out, one part didn't—Collin. We were avoiding each other. I saw him in passing, walking down the hall or on stage after school. Eric was always nearby, so I didn't try to talk to him. Even if we were alone—what would I say? I wondered if we could go back to being friends, but I doubted that was possible.

At night, after Eric brought me home, I'd sit alone—staring at my ceiling until dawn—hiding in the safety of my parentally warded home. I'd hear Collin's words echo inside my mind. The recollection of his silky voice and intense sapphire eyes washed over me. The memory left me breathless, like I was falling in a dark dream, with no way to wake up. Collin's absence made me realize how much he meant to me, no matter how much I wanted to deny it. Damn. What was wrong with me? A kiss with him would reveal everything. It would leave me completely exposed, and endanger Collin. The best way to deal with this problem was to ride it out. The lust would burn off, and I'd have my friend back—I hoped.

Attempting to shift my thoughts to something more productive, I tried to discover how I got tainted in the first place. It didn't seem like something very common, since the prophecy was around for a while and no one else had this problem before. I invited Shannon over one night, and we tried to figure out how it happened. She sat on my bed, acting like we were just *us* again. It made me sad, because I knew things we would never be just us again. There would always be an element of mistrust between us.

She said, "I researched some stuff for you. There wasn't tons of info. I think I got it, but it's weird. " She looked up at me, pulling her feet in tighter. Shannon liked to curl up into a ball when she was stressed. Apparently, she was beyond stressed because she couldn't scrunch her body smaller.

"I can handle weird. Tell me." My heart raced slightly. Hope flowed through me. I'd learn what caused it, and then I could change it, right? I tried to stop pacing.

"It comes down to blood. Demon blood is powerful, and it works differently than angel blood. Angel blood builds up and makes you more—you. Just better. Demon blood is more like acid, snaking its way into your body, slowly corrupting, slowly empowering." She paused, looking at me. "When a Valefar binds—enslaves—a Martis, they have to remove the soul and then add their blood. They gouge the victim's forehead, and cover the scar in demon blood. It enters the bloodstream through the mark and binds the victim to the Valefar at the same time. But you have no scar. He didn't get that far. But… there had to be blood. Did he bleed? Any chance, during the demon kiss, you accidentally… swallowed his blood?" Shannon asked the question like it was the most bizarre, unlikely thing in the world. And it was… or would have been, if I didn't fight back. But, I did.

My stomach sank, "I bit his lip. I couldn't break the kiss. He was too strong… so I bit him. Hard."

She looked disturbed, "You drank it?" Her lips pulled into an expression of disgust.

"No," I said, "I didn't *drink it*. I spat it all out. His blood ran down my face, and got all over me. But, I don't think I swallowed any." Clutching my arms, I pulled them tightly into my chest, and began to pace again. I clearly remembered having the blood in my mouth, but I couldn't remember swallowing it. And part of the night was a blur. I didn't know what happened. One moment I was conscious, and the next I was in Eric's arms. I still didn't know what he did to revive me. I thought I died. "What *if* I swallowed it?"

She leaned back against the wall, dangling her legs off the side of the bed. "I don't know. No one ever *drinks* it. Those who do, usually die—or turn Valefar. No one has been stuck in the middle before." She smoothed her long hair over her shoulder. "It's possible that you swallowed a tiny amount, and that was what caused your mark to change color—tainting you—like the prophecy said."

I looked at her, horrified. "So, that's what did it? Demon blood… " The only thing I could do to free myself, was also the thing that damned me. *Shit. How did this stuff happen to me?* Feeling ill, I wrapped my arms around my middle, and stared out my window into the inky sky. The chill from the glass seeped through, and I shivered. "What about my soul? He took a huge chunk, but I don't know how much. I thought he'd taken all of it. I thought I died, Shan."

Her expression was grieved. "You still have soul, otherwise that mark on your head would be bright red. And you'd be dead. Martis are amongst the living and must have a soul to survive. Valefar don't. That's why they drain us first, and add blood later. As long as you have enough of your soul, you can't become one of them. Not completely."

I closed my eyes, pressing my hand against my forehead. *I damned myself. I did this to myself.* After a panic attack that lasted a day or two, the anger slowly turned into something else—something dark. If Jake hadn't attacked me, it wouldn't have happened. I wouldn't have been tainted. I wouldn't be the girl in the prophecy. But, I was the one who did it. I was the one who made him bleed. In the end, it was my fault. I had to keep this a secret. No one could know that I swallowed demon blood, because everyone else who did so died or turned Valefar. Everyone—except me.

The days passed and I said nothing. The darkness, the cold fingers that felt like death had robbed me again, were suffocating me. I didn't tell anyone, although I knew Al and Eric could tell that I was suffering. We continued training, but I made little progress.

One day the training changed from the normal physical stuff, to something better. I was glad for the change and walked with Eric into the gym. We passed a gaggle of nuns, and some Martis who came to the church to train with Eric. The place was becoming overrun with Martis. It was no accident that they were all swarming around me. But no one noticed I was different. No one saw. And I hid it as best I could.

Apparently Eric was a kick ass warrior. It was clear he was one of the best in the world. Martis came from all over the place to learn from him. They whispered of his abilities, and were in awe. I'd seen some of them training with him. They fought gracefully, nothing like my pathetic sparring. No doubt, I was his worst student.

After he pushed through the doors, he stopped in front of me. He wore blue jeans and a white tee shirt, same as always. His amber eyes were playful. "I want to show you something. One second." When we walked in there were three other Martis in the room. Eric walked over to them. They all chatted like they had known each other forever. He turned toward me, while he spoke too softly to hear. The Martis laughed, and threw their bags over their shoulders, and cleared out.

The last one to leave was a woman with jet-black hair named Elena. I'd seen her training with Eric over the past few weeks. She called over her shoulder, "Good luck newbie!"

My eyes went wide as I looked at Eric, not liking how this training session was turning out. "Why are they looking at me like that, Eric?"

He smiled, walking over to me in long strides. "Are you nervous? I thought Ivy Taylor could handle anything?"

"Yeah," I said, "that was before things got all freaky. What are we doing? Why all the secrecy?"

"It's not so much a secret, as a safety precaution. And Al wanted you in here alone when we trained. So I threw everyone else out. Awesome, right?"

"Yup. Awesome." My mouth flattened into a thin line. I didn't like being treated different. People would notice me. They already had. Eric spent more time training me than anyone else. I just laughed, shrugging it off that I was impossible to train. He sat down on one of the mats and folded his legs. I mirrored him.

"Ivy, I am going to show you one of the coolest things that Martis can do. Al wants to make sure you learn how to do it. And it takes time to learn." He smiled at me, and leaned back on his arms. "Martis have the ability to turn light into physical matter."

My eyebrow arched. That was unexpected. "What are you talking about?"

"It's part of the power of the angel blood. Martis can call meld light into a physical form. We can use it for lots of things. It's typically used by Polomotis when they battle and Dyconisi when they heal. I haven't seen enough Seyers to know exactly how they use it, but Al said you would use it and that I should teach you."

I nodded, not sure what I thought. He sat up, holding his palm in front of him. His fingers twitched as he smiled, his gaze on my face, while my eyes were watching his palm. A point the size of a pinhole faded into existence, glowing a dim blue. As his fingers twitched, the orb grew larger and larger. Soon it was a floating sphere with a bright blue center, encircled by another sphere of translucent white light.

It was beautiful. I reached out for it, extending my fingers to touch it, wondering what it would feel like. I looked to Eric for permission, and he nodded saying, "You can touch it." I reached out, extending my fingers toward the orb. Its soft light radiated calming warmth. Its surface was smooth with an underlying softness, like a pearl. Mesmerized, I ran my finger over the slick surface, finally pressing my palm into it. The light enveloped my hand. The inside of the sphere wasn't liquid, but it wasn't solid either. It felt like warm pudding, congealed into a smooth liquid. I wiggled my fingers through the goo and pulled my hand out, expecting it to be wet, but it wasn't.

"Eric, what is that? What do you use it for?" I asked, looking at him. He watched me intently as I examined the orb, smiling.

"It's light. Well, a piece of light. The healers use it to heal wounds. It can heal just about anything in the right healer's hands. Good healers can use vast quantities of light and do amazing things. Warriors use it in battle. We can use it for anything from illumination to using it as a weapon. But, the only way to make sure a Valefar actually dies is with celestial silver. The light can stop them, and save us, but the Valefar won't be completely destroyed and can resurface later, if we only use light."

"Can I hold it?" I asked.

He shook his head. I watched as the orb's light dimmed, as it disappeared from his palm. "You are going to learn to call it. That way Al can teach you how to use it."

A smile tugged the corner of my mouth. Anticipation flooded me with giddy excitement. I wanted to be able to call the sphere of light, because it was cool. So, maybe my reasons were shallow at that point, but the sphere had a mesmerizing factor like watching the bubbles inside of a lava lamp. He told me the basics, and held his palm under mine, after scooting closer. "Since it's light, it's warm. You can reach out for it, and it'll come to you because you are Martis." Eric's hand cradled mine. He called the light and the orb formed on top of my palm. I could feel the warmth form on my flesh before the blue pinhole appeared. But, the light didn't grow. It disappeared. I breathed in deeply, and looked at him. I wasn't wholly Martis. I wondered if the light would listen to me, or if the darkness that was within me would chase it away.

Eric could tell I was tense, but he had no clue why. "You can do this Ivy. This is basic stuff. Whatever Al has you do with it is way harder. You totally don't need to worry." He smiled at me, and then repositioned his hand under mine. "You try now."

Although he explained it to me several times, actually doing it was difficult. I concentrated on the warm air swirling around my fingers, tracing the heat source to the light that illuminated my hand. I called to it, willing it to pool in my palm the way Eric did. I watched, as I felt my hand remain at a constant temperature. There was no pin prick of heat, no blue pinpoint of light. After a few moments Eric's voice broke the silence. He dropped his hand and slid in front of me.

"Huh. You did exactly what I told you? Felt the warmth in the air, and then backtracked to the light? Calling it to you?"

I nodded. "Maybe I need more practice?" What else could I say? That my demon blood kept the light from coming to me?

Eric's brows scrunched together. "No. This doesn't usually take practice. It's more of an understanding and execution. Let's go over everything again. Maybe we skipped something." Eric started from the beginning, and repeated everything he already told me. When he was done, he told me to spread my fingers wide and fixate on the sensation of the air flowing over my skin. Then we resumed our positions with his hand cradling mine. "Now, focus on the air. Feel it touching your palm; it's pressing lightly against your flesh."

I focused. I had to make this work. By sheer will power, it had to work. I knew failing once would be a fluke, but failing twice—on something so basic—well, there was no way to hide that. Concentrating harder, I focused on the air surrounding my palm. I felt its subtle movements as it moved slowly over my still palm. I felt the air trapped between the back of my hand and Eric's growing warmer. The warm air traveled the entire length of his fingers, filling the small chasm between our hands. Breathing deeply, I focused on the warmth—feeling it radiate around me. I pictured the blue sphere, calling to it with my mind, commanding it to come to me. Eric had told me that when I found the light it would flow to me like honey, slowly surging towards me in golden beams. To my horror, I felt the honey rays around me refusing to answer my call. They moved toward me initially, but as they were about to form into the blue mini sphere, they were repulsed by me. My hand was empty, for a second time.

Eric was baffled. His forehead wrinkled as he spun around in front of me. "What happened? Did you feel it?"

I nodded, not wanting to look at him. The light didn't want anything to do with me. I was tainted, and it knew. Soon he would know it. "Yes, I felt it."

"Okay, let's try one more time. This time I'm going to sit in front of you and watch you. But I'll call the light. You are just going to hold it. If you were able to feel it, you should be able to hold it. This is easy Ivy. I'm sure it's your teacher, and not you. Smile, okay?"

I smiled weakly at him, already knowing what would happen. Humoring him, I did it anyway. Eric called the light, and soon had the beautiful double sphere swirling in his palm. He sat directly in front of me. With his free hand, he lifted my palm. I spread my fingers to receive the orb, and then cradled the back of my hand to hold it in place. He inched the sphere toward me slowly. My heart slid into my stomach. I couldn't stand to watch this. He put the hand that held the orb of light directly over my palm and slowly started to shift the orb to my palm. The sphere took an odd shape, and began to pour towards my open hand. Hope flittered through me as I saw the light flowing toward me. I called to it, begging it to stay this time. But it didn't happen. Right before the light touched my flesh, I felt its repulsion. As the orb shifted from Eric's palm to mine, the light disappeared.

Eric stared at my empty palm. His fingers pressed my flesh as he spoke, "I don't understand. Anyone can call light. But it won't go to you."

I pulled my palm away from him, tucking my arms tightly around me. "It doesn't seem to like me."

"It doesn't work like that. Light doesn't like one Martis more than another. It doesn't care. It calls like to like—like two drops of water melding into one." He looked up at me. His expression was confused. He sat waiting for an explanation to come to him—one that made sense. But nothing came. We sat there staring at each other.

I was the only one who knew why the light wouldn't come to me, that it could never come to me. While my angel blood allowed me to call it, my demon blood repelled it. I swallowed hard, wondering if it was so obvious to Eric. Eventually he suggested we go to Al with this problem. I didn't protest. When he told the old woman, she thanked Eric and asked him if he had any ideas. He blamed the failure on his teaching skills. Al kindly thanked him, and asked to speak to me alone.

My heart was going to explode. How long could I hide this? She had to know. Al sat in her usual spot, her old eyes looking at me. "So, the light won't obey you?"

I swallowed hard, "Guess not."

"That's an oddity, for a Martis." There was a long silence, like Al was waiting for me to confess. But I wouldn't. She finally said, "We all use the light differently, according to our abilities. Eric uses it as a warrior, and others use it to heal. For my kind, the Seyers, we call it into our visions. We can see things that haven't happened yet. Being able to call light is a safety precaution. It ensures that I don't get trapped in a vision. The light shields us, and protects us. While I'm uncertain of your abilities at this point, I know that you must be able to do this. If the light won't come to you—you won't have that protection, Ivy. That will be dangerous."

Trying not to squirm, I said, "I'll practice. I know I can do it."

"Do you?" she asked. "You really think that the problem was that you didn't try?"

I backed to the door, ready to leave. "That had to be it. I'll practice until I get it." She nodded at me, and I left. I had to perfect something that I couldn't do. And lying this time wouldn't fix it.

At the end of the week, Eric told me that Al wanted to talk to me alone. That worked well, because Eric had a meeting. So we agreed to meet up after school. We parted ways, as he took the shorter path to his locker. It was weird, but I felt safe around Eric. I knew it wasn't real though. As soon as he found out what I was, he'd turn on me.

As I turned the corner, my eyes were fixated on the smooth floor, until I was a few feet from my locker. I shuddered and looked up. Collin's arms were folded tightly against his chest, accentuating the firm curve of his arms. A dark blue shirt clung to his torso, and he had on his black leather jacket. The leather was well worn. It was his favorite coat.

I stopped, unable to move in the middle of the busy hallway. It was like dropping a rock in the middle of an anthill. Everyone moved around me in swarms. Mixed emotions flooded me. I wanted to see him, but I couldn't bear the thought of talking to him. I desperately needed a friend. Someone I could trust with everything, but no matter how much I wanted to tell him, I couldn't. I'd have to do this alone. Swallowing hard, I stepped into the stream of kids, and crossed to my locker. The entire time, Collin's eyes were intensely focused on me. He ignored those who called him, never shifting his gaze. Shifting his body, he leaned against the next locker, and then gestured for me to come and open mine. I faltered, as my pulse quickened. Reaching for my locker door, I averted my eyes, trying to hurry. I said nothing.

"So, you're going out with him?" His jaw was clenched, as he asked what everyone naturally assumed. Somewhat confused, I paused, looking at his feet. My head leaned on my locker, as I pressed my eyes closed.

This is what bothered him so much that he broke the silence? It was nothing, but Collin didn't know that. Eric and I were together every day, during class, after class, at rehearsal, and after. This was the first day I was alone after school. Eric and I talked about it, and though it was best to let others assume we were dating, even though we weren't. It made life easier, and I needed easier. Collin wasn't easier. I longed to tell him, and feel the burden of the past few weeks melt away. But I couldn't. I had to lie. Again.

"Maybe I am," I lied, looking into my locker. I stood there, seeing nothing, barely moving. The hairs on my neck prickled, as I felt his gaze on my face.

He didn't respond right away. His eyes lingered on the side of my face, with his lips pressed tight. Finally he said, "Or, maybe you're not." There was no shift to his stance, and his arms remained tightly locked at his chest. More people walked by, calling out to him, but Collin ignored them completely.

A nervous laugh escaped from me. This was my chance. I could tell him the truth, or part of it anyway. I could say we aren't dating—that I didn't like Eric that way. I pushed a curl behind my ear, and turned to him. I was careful to look at his cheek and not his eyes. But, instead of the truth, I uttered the words that would protect me, "Of course we are. Don't tell me you're jealous, Collin." I smirked at him.

He expression was intense, unblinking. "You never touch. He doesn't hold your hand. I haven't seen you touch him—at all. That's a bit odd Ivy." His eyes were fixated on my chin. He could have taken the information out of my mind, if I looked up. But he didn't. He waited for me to answer.

I rummaged through my locker, acting like I didn't care. "Maybe for you it's odd, but not me. I'm not like that anymore." Memories of kissing nameless boys surfaced along with the pain I'd tried to contain last year. I pushed the thoughts back down. Shaking my head, I glanced up at him. "I'm not like that anymore."

His voice was so quiet it was almost inaudible, "Just tell me." His chest rose and fell in deep, controlled breaths. His fingers were gripping his arms so hard that they were turning white. It didn't matter what he asked or what I wanted. I couldn't tell him. Regret pooled in my stomach, making my lips twist. I bit them gently, to remove the scowl from my face.

I heard myself say, "There's nothing to tell. I'm not like you. I don't screw everything on two legs, okay?"

He smiled slightly. It was a cocky boyish grin that I rarely saw on his face. It was the look that said I was right, and that he didn't mind so much. He earned his reputation before I knew him, and it was general knowledge that he wasn't a one-girl kind of guy. I thought that was why he let me be last year, when I lost it. The pain of losing someone I loved was unbearable. Drowning it in lust was the only escape I found. His hair slid over his eyes, as he looked at the floor. "No. Not everyone." His blue eyes cut into me. A shiver spilled down my spine. "Not you."

"No, not me." I whispered, heart pounding. I looked down at the books that I had pulled tightly to my chest. Realizing my words sounded a little too remorseful, I smiled softly, "I think that was the first time someone shot you down."

The corners of his mouth pulled up, and the death grip he had on his arms lessened. "Pretty much. You wouldn't even look at me. You remember that?" His arms loosened, and slid into his pockets. A smirk crossed my lips. I remembered. The theater kids I hung around with after school had thrust a script into my hands. They made me cover for someone, and banished me to prompt in one of the wings backstage. I sat in the darkened alcove alone, messing up cues, and losing my place in the script. It was mortifying.

Collin exited after his lines, and saw me alone in the darkness. He moved confidently toward me. The pick-up line he used rolled right off of me. I was so flustered about looking like an idiot that I thought he was teasing me. Shock had silenced him when I walked away. At some point I realized it was real—he liked me. But too much time passed, and I wasn't willing to admit that I'd mistaken his advances as anything but teasing. So, it became a game—a game where he'd say incredible things to convince me to go out with him, and I'd always laugh and say no. The things he said were slightly absurd, which made me laugh. My playful rejections became equally amusing. But that was the past. Why was he bringing this up now? Nodding, I leaned into my locker, looking at his chest. Looking at his eyes was safe, he still wouldn't hear my thoughts, but if I forgot and touched him he could.

"Enough other girls looked at you. One more didn't matter." I shrugged, "Some people are meant to be friends. That's all."

He shifted his feet, leaning his back onto the locker, his blue gaze intense and unblinking. "You don't kiss him."

The smile slid off my face. *Why is he pressing this?* I straightened, ready to leave, but before I walked away, I found myself toying with telling him a secret. I never told anyone about this hidden part of me. Telling him this little bit of truth felt dangerous, like parading a mouse in front of a sleeping lion. And it gave me a sense of control that I was utterly lacking. Squirming slightly against the locker, I looked up to his jaw line. I felt the secret burning on my lips, as I uttered the words, "I don't kiss guys who I really like. I never have. Okay?"

A single brow floated up on Collin's face. His lips gave me a disbelieving smile, and I instantly regretted telling him. My defenses shot up as I scoffed, "Oh, stop it. It's not that weird." I pulled my books tighter to my body like they were a security blanket. My heart pummeled in my chest. I accidentally told him a much more personal secret than I'd intended. I could feel the burn rising in my cheeks as my embarrassment became visible.

"Ivy," he said with a smirk on his lips, "of course it's weird. You've kissed half the school, and there wasn't one guy in that lot that you liked even a little bit?"

"That's a grossly inflated number. And no. There wasn't." A coy smile came over me before I could wash it away. I could see how it would be weird for the girl who kiss almost anyone for over a year, to never kissed someone she truly liked. No one knew.

Collin's features were totally serious. His voice was rich, asking softly, "Why? Why won't you kiss him?" He was completely focused now, watching me, waiting for me to look up. I shouldn't have said anything. My throat felt dry. I swallowed hard, not wanting to answer. How do I tell him this part? I wasn't sure if I wanted to tell him. I knew if I didn't answer, he would press until I did. It would make it a much bigger deal than if I spit it out now. And as long as I didn't touch him, he wouldn't know the whole truth.

Acting like it wasn't a big deal, even though it was a defining keystone to my ideal relationship, I spit out some words. "Because, I like him. And it doesn't work both ways. Friends aren't dates. There's a relationship there that's too precious to mess up with hormones. Maybe it's stupid, but I don't think it's possible to have both."

He leaned a little closer, intrigued. "Both what?" Our eyes were getting dangerously close to meeting.

"A friend who's also a boyfriend. That stuff's for fairytales, Collin. It doesn't happen in real life." The words were distant thoughts, lodged at the back of my mind for years, but their truth resonated with me as I said them. It wasn't possible to have everything. That was a dream—an unattainable dream that silly people spent a lifetime to find out.

His response surprised me. "I can't believe you said that." Forgetting to avoid his eyes, I looked straight into the rich blue pools. I couldn't look away. *Don't touch him, and you'll be fine.* Waves of emotions washed over me, but they were so jumbled that I couldn't tell what it meant. "Ivy, that's the ultimate goal when you're playing the field—finding the person who gets you— someone who knows you, your faults, and likes you *anyway*. Why wouldn't you want that? Why separate them?"

Things felt familiar, like they had gone back to the way it was before. Before everything got weird. Before my life was ripped out of my hands. I was content to revel in it for the moment, but his directness made my eyes sweep downward. I didn't know if it was to avoid judgment, or to push him away. This was one of my precious secrets. He didn't understand, but I wasn't sure if I wanted him to. I finally answered, "Because they can't co-exist. They just don't. It's not a matter of separating them. They don't go together. There's no such thing as true love."

"Really?" he asked. I nodded. His voice sounded breathless, "Ivy, how did you get so cynical?" He tilted his head, sincerely asking, "So, tell me; why can't you have both? Why can't you have the guy who is your best friend, and your lover? Why can't he be the same person?" His sapphire eyes searched my face, unafraid, waiting for me to answer.

I looked into his eyes, and suddenly it didn't feel like we were talking about Eric anymore. My heart slid into my stomach. These were things I never told anyone. I wondered if I was making a mistake. I said, "I couldn't risk it. It's too reckless. Relationships are destroyed when a couple breaks up—even if they were friends. Sometimes it's better to hold onto what you have, rather than risk what might be." I felt so exposed, and normally that would terrify me, but with Collin, right then—it didn't. It felt normal, and I didn't want it to stop. He made me feel *found*, and I'd felt lost for so long.

A sad smile formed on his face. "But, Ivy, you risk losing everything you could gain if it worked out. It has to work out for someone, sometime. Why not you?" His eyes were so blue.

Shaking my head, my eyes remained locked with his. Courage and recklessness mingled together. What he was suggesting was not possible. "When has anything ever worked out like that for me?" I didn't feel as bitter as it sounded, "It's not in the cards for me, Collin. I'm content with things the way they are. I don't get the fairytale. I'm the emotionally scarred girl with the cynical view of life, and I'm okay with that. I know who I am. I know what I get."

He leaned on the locker facing me, moving even closer. He closed the gap so that our bodies were almost touching. His warm breath slid across my skin when he spoke, "Out of all people, I would have thought you'd be the one to hunt it down, and then hold onto it."

My head jerked back a little bit, surprised at his words, "Why would you think that?" There was no way I would risk that. Not after losing my sister, and dealing with the agonizing pain that followed. I had no desire to love anyone, especially if I had a choice about it. Love only brought pain.

His hand ran across my cheek. An icy hot shock flowered under his hand before he pulled it away mumbling, "Sorry, I forgot."

The touch made me jump, but it felt different—desirable almost. No thoughts leaked through then. A few emotions, but they were the obvious ones displayed on Collin's face. He paused, looking at me, but avoiding my gaze. He shrugged, "It's just—you're not someone who does stuff half way. At some point, I thought you'd give up the dating half way thing and shoot for the stars. I just thought... you'd want it." His eyes flicked back up to see how I took his words.

I was stunned we were having this conversation. The grip on my books had loosened at some point, as I looked up at his downturned face. "Collin?" I asked. He looked at me. "Is this what you came to ask me about?"

Shaking his head, he said, "No, it wasn't." He took in a deep breath, and ran his fingers through his dark hair.

"Then, what was it?"

His sapphire gaze was soft, as it met mine. "The bond—it's changing."

"What do you mean? I didn't notice anything."

Collin smiled sadly at me. "I wasn't sure. I had to talk to you to find out." He swallowed hard, "Ivy, it's growing." His words weren't meshing with reality. Growing? I hadn't noticed anything. What was he talking about?

Shaking my head, I said, "No, it's not. Collin, we just stood here and talked, and it wasn't weird. I kinda liked it. It felt like us, again. The way things used to be." But as soon as the words were free, I regretted them. The creases in his forehead didn't fade, and his eyes remained locked with mine.

His voice brushed gently against my mind, *It doesn't require touch anymore, does it?*

I sucked in air and took a step back, dropping my books to the floor. They tumbled out of my hands, and made a loud slapping sound as they fell. The hallways were empty now, and no other sounds diminished the noise. Shaking my head, I said, "No. It can't do that."

Collin took a step toward me, his hands outstretched for me, but he quickly jammed them in his pockets. "It does. It already has."

Eyes wide with panic, my heart raced wildly in my chest. I trusted Collin, he was one of the few people I did trust, but I didn't want this. It would ruin everything. Shaking my head, I still couldn't accept what he was telling me, what I knew to be true. "No.

No, it can't—we *have* to touch. It can't just work without that. It can't." Hysteria was creeping into my voice. I hated that it was there, but I was in a constant state of emotional overload for too long. I couldn't force it away.

"I know you liked my touch before. I know the sensation didn't freak you out, and that you didn't take a mind-dive." He took a step closer to me, carefully. Slowly, like I might run. "Ask me something. Something you didn't say out loud during this conversation. Something towards the end. Something that you thought, but didn't say."

A chill settled on my flesh that had nothing to do with the temperature. Vulnerability washed over me. He couldn't know. I didn't think it. I barely thought it. I finally spoke, asking the question that terrified me, "Why do I really think I can't have both?"

Collin inched closer to me, and wound a long curl around his fingers, careful not to touch me. He kept his fingers there while he spoke, "Because you don't want to fall in love. Not if you can prevent it, because the pain of losing him would be unbearable. You've decided it's better to not love. Losing your sister almost destroyed you." His eyes met mine and didn't falter when he said, "It's not that you can't have both—it's that you don't want both. You just want to survive."

Trembling, my heartbeat roared in my ears. He articulated the reason I couldn't bring myself to say. The excuses I made for pushing people away. It was fear—cold, raw fear that propelled me into survival mode. And I stayed there, too afraid to come back.

CHAPTER FOURTEEN

Eric was smart enough not to ask what happened. We drove in silence. I watched him navigate the mid-day traffic. His perfectly combed hair framed his face. There was a faint smile on his lips. It was always there. He didn't flip people off, he didn't curse, and he didn't lie. Me—on the other hand—I wasn't so good. I lied. A lot. Still watching him, I slumped back into the seat.

Eric caught me looking at him out of the corner of his eye. "What?"

I shook my head, looking away, "Nothing. I just never noticed before—you're a good guy. Like *good good*. You're just… you. I never noticed, but then, I didn't notice a lot of things." My mind started to drift, as I watched the world blur by out the window. The last year of my life was pretty much a haze. I missed a lot of stuff.

"You noticed enough. And don't worry about today. I have to meet with Julia, you talk with Al, and then we can go to the gym and practice some more." The church had an old gym, complete with circa 1945 gym equipment. It was a relic, but it provided a safe place for me to learn. Valefar couldn't enter churches. Since the gym was attached to the church, we were safe.

"Thanks Eric," I pulled my curls over my shoulder, and away from my face. "So, what do you think Sister Al wants with me?"

Eric looked in my direction briefly, before turning his gaze back to the traffic. "Maybe she figured out what your gift is?" All the Martis were sorted into one of three groups based on their natural abilities or giftedness. This gift was supposed to help me fight Valefar. It was supposed to make my life easier, but it was taking Al longer to determine my gift than usual. She wanted to speak to me about it today.

"Maybe," I replied. I was waiting for the other shoe to drop when Al pegged me with a gift. It was going to be a big fat Valefar shoe that clunked with a resounding GONG. Lowering my head, worry pinched my face. I hoped she found a gift that was normal for a Martis. I couldn't afford to blow my secret—not yet.

We pulled up to the back of the church building, and piled out of the truck. Eric walked next to me. It felt like we had both called in to the principal's office. Eric said nothing, as he pulled the door open. Stepping over the threshold, I immediately smacked into someone. The tall brunette was irritated with my clumsiness. She acted like no one had ever stepped on her before. She looked like an Italian supermodel, so maybe no one had. Her waist was tiny, and her hips curved just so, and met up with some killer legs. Most girls couldn't get legs like that, even if they stayed on a stair climber all day. Her dark hair was smooth, and pulled back neatly into a clip at the nape of her neck. She was dressed like a librarian, wearing a gray pencil skirt and a sweater vest. And she was glaring at me.

Eric's hand was on the small of my back, as he pushed me back towards her, and into the room. "Ivy, this is Julia. Julia, Ivy Taylor." He looked at Julia, adding, "She's new."

A single perfectly plucked brow arched on her angular face, as her brown eyes evaluated me. She spoke in heavily accented words, "Pleased to meet you," though I could tell that she wasn't. "I am the

Regent Martis of the Dyconisi." Her thick Italian accent continued, "Are you going to be a warrior or a healer?" My mouth opened, but I didn't know what to say. I looked at Eric.

Eric answered for me. "She doesn't know what she'll be yet. Al's been working with her to figure it out."

Julia *hmmed* me.

Feeling a trickle of panic, I realized that her gaze scared the crap out of me. I stepped a tad closer to Eric, and asked, "What are you talking about?"

"Sister Al will tell you. You need to go talk to her," Eric said sweetly.

Julia's arms were folded. "Yes, it is *her* job. Go and speak with her. Report back when she is through." And she waved me off. Julia's words carried authority, and I doubted there was anyone who didn't listen to her.

I opened my mouth to say something, but Eric cut off my retort, "Let me point which way to Al. Come on." He pulled on my arm, leading me out of the room. When we were in the hall he said, "That person's important. She's my boss—sort of. And someone you don't want to piss off. Be nice." Releasing my arm, he left me in the hall, alone, and walked back to her. I frowned, and padded away slowly.

The tightness in my chest increased, as I came to Al's door. I closed my eyes for a second, and took a deep breath. I wasn't afraid of the old woman— actually, I liked her. However, wondering if she knew, or suspected that I was anything but a Martis made me dread talking to her. Talking to her alone made that feeling worse. It was only a matter of time until I blew my cover. Either Al would discover what I really was, or I'd do it to myself.

"Are you gonna stay outside forever?" Sister Al's voice spilled into the hallway. "Get in here girl. Don't make me wait all night."

I stepped over the threshold and into the sitting room. The nun was in the rocker she favored. "It's, like, 4 o'clock," I jibed. We'd developed a little rapport. She was actually very funny, which shocked me at first. I'd thought nuns would be serious, and demure. Al wasn't.

"Stop being a smart mouth and get in here, girl. Close the door behind you." I pushed the wooden door shut, and walked to the empty seat next to her. Before I sat down, she said something that made me freeze. "Ivy Taylor. You are *not* what you appear," she said.

My eyes shifted, avoiding her gaze, as my heart lurched. "I don't know what you mean," I smiled. Smiling made liars seem more truthful. I hated lying to her, but I couldn't tell anyone.

Her gnarled finger pointed at the floor in front of her. "Sit. Let's talk." I folded my legs under me and sat like a six-year-old on the carpet; then I tilted my chin up to look at her.

Weathered skin hung loosely on her face, covered in tiny creases. She looked at me, missing nothing.

I liked to rip the band-aide off in one fast, painful, pull. I blurted out, "What are we talking about?" *Time to get this over with.*

"As you know, each of us has a different purpose. It's time you get yours. I'm a *Seyer*. I mentioned it to you before, but I never told you what it actually means. A Seyer literally sees the future. We see visions, and then it's our job to bring them to the Dyconisi. They make laws, rules, and ideas about what we see." She paused, folding her old fingers into her lap. "There are very few Seyers left. I'm one of the last. That's why you come to me. I can see what you will be." My stomach felt like I ate a lead pancake, as dread filled my veins. Assuming she wasn't nuts, seeing what I was, was a major health hazard.

"So you know? You know that I'm... what I am?" I felt the purple mark burn on my head. I wanted to dig my nails into my flesh and scratch it. But, I kept my fingers laced in my lap.

"Yes. And you don't have to be afraid of me. I see what you are." She paused, "But you don't. I'll tell you the basics. I'm sure you want to know what gifts Eric and Shannon have.

"Eric is a *Polomotis*—a warrior. His job is to protect the Martis and the innocent. He is ranked highest amongst Polomotis in this area of the world. He can formulate military strategy with our limited resources. It's servants like Eric, who protect us, all of us, from the Valefar. Without them we would be vulnerable... and most likely very dead." She cleared her throat.

"And, Shannon, she's a *Dyconisis*. A healer. She can heal wounds. Only physical ones. Not spiritual wounds." She paused and looked up at me. "There's a difference."

I nodded. "Yes, there is." I knew the difference very well. "So, she can heal a wound—a physical one. But she can't heal a broken heart? Right?"

She nodded, "Yes, exactly. Our Dyconisis heal and study our laws. Which do you think you are, girl? A Polomotis, Seyer, or Dyconisis?" Her old eyes studied me. The rocker creaked as she pushed gently, swaying the chair.

"I have no clue. I don't feel like any of those things." I looked at her. I couldn't tell what I was, or what traits I had. I didn't have visions. I couldn't heal, and Eric already showed me that I couldn't fight.

"True," she agreed. "And while you don't see yourself as a warrior—you will be. You will be the greatest warrior we have seen for quite some time."

My eyebrow shot up, as I stifled a laugh when I realized she was serious. "But I can't fight. You saw me with Eric. How can I be a warrior?"

Her aged face considered me before she spoke again. "Eric is going to have his hands full with you. And while you rebel against laws, you can't help but find comfort in them. And while you cannot heal yourself, you seek to heal others." She paused, "But out of the three, the biggest portion of your soul is a Seyer's. You are a Seyer, Ivy Taylor. Like me."

"But, I don't see anything. I don't have visions," I answered.

Nodding, a soft smile spread across her face, "But you will. The time will come. And you will see. It'll lead you in the right direction. When it touches you, grab onto it. It will be soon, girl. And I'll teach you, don't worry."

Millions of questions flooded my mind, but it kept spinning back to one. One she already alluded to, but didn't say for certain. "Can you see my future?"

She nodded. "Yes, I've seen it."

My heart was hammering in my ears. She had to know. *Why didn't she just say it?* I asked, "Then you know?" I was half hoping she would say it was okay that I was tainted. Then there would be hope for me. Staying stuck in the middle, hiding my festering soul, was tedious.

"I know all I need to know," she said, evading my question in a typical Martis fashion. Her ancient eyes were sharp. She leaned forward in her rocker, "Ivy, your position is Seyer. We'll help you be what it is you're supposed to become. Seyers are rare. Very rare." An ancient finger pointed at my chest, "Especially your kind."

Instinctively, I flinched. She knew. She had to know. I wanted her to say it. But she didn't. That was the end of our discussion, and she shooed me away. I slowly made my way toward Eric, slightly fazed. If Al knew I was the prophecy girl, why didn't she rat me out? Slowing as I neared the room Eric occupied, I could hear their voices carry into the hall.

Julia's rich accent spoke, "...not acceptable. We cannot allow something like this to occur. Have you found nothing since you've been here? We can't have the same thing happen again, Eric. You know your duty—and how important it is for us. Who is she?"

Eric's voice followed. "I don't have her exact name, but I know that she's formed. There are too many Valefar here, and it's not like last time. There are more Valefar on Long Island than on the entire east coast. They're searching for her as well. No, this is the right place. It's her this time. It's the right spot, Julia. And, I know how important this is. If the prophecy comes true, everything we've worked for will be lost. I won't let that happen."

"Good," she replied, "Destroy her. And I want you keeping me updated. When you find her, bind her the way we discussed. She will have new traits, and we believe that will hold her. Then the Tribunal can meet and dispatch of her properly. Creatures of Hell need to be destroyed, so they don't resurface at a later time. We cannot have her return." It took every ounce of strength I had not to run screaming from the building. They were talking about me. I leaned in toward the room, trying to be totally silent.

Eric said, "When I find her, you will be the first to know. We're close. Very close."

"Thank God," the strain in her voice lessened, "You and I have looked for this creature for over a millennia. This is one of the only times we have had any indication that the time and place are correct. And last time was a nightmare. You are sure the Valefar are here for her?"

Eric cleared his throat. His voice sounded amused. "Yes. There are too many here for it to be a coincidence. The Martis are gravitating here as well. That is only supposed to happen when the girl in the prophecy forms." He paused, "Unless you believe there is something else going on?"

"No. I think you are correct." Julia said. "And, the prophecy is still hidden, so they cannot take it. They must be looking for her. You have more guard here than usual?" Her voice was tense.

"Yes," Eric answered. "And we have been working closely with the Seyer to make certain we know when the girl is within reach." The words began to sink in as the shock melted through my skull. Eric *and* Al were looking for me. My heart raced as my eyes bugged.

"Ah," Julia scoffed, "Seyers are a dead breed. You do not need to rely on her kind. Logic and discernment, that you did not possess last time, will lead you to this girl. The prophecy must not come true. Protect your kind."

"I will." His voice steeled, "She will be captured. And I will kill her myself, permanently—if required."

Eric turned his head, and saw me in the doorway.

CHAPTER FIFTEEN

"Hey Ivy," Eric reached for me, pulling me into the room. I wiped the expression off my face before they could see the full-blown panic in my eyes. I couldn't believe it. Eric was the Seeker. He was looking for *me*. "We're done here. So what'd she say you are?" They waited for me to answer. Terror pushed my pulse to an ungodly rate, as I fought to suppress my panic.

"Yes. Tell. What she say? I need to document your vocation before I leave." Julia's face held a bemused expression.

The one they were hunting was staring at them, but they had no clue. I held my voice steady, shoving my shaking hands in my pockets, "She said I'm a Seyer." Eric's mouth opened slightly.

Julia scoffed, "Heh. A Seyer!"

Eric's eyes darted between Julia's face and my nervous stance. He rubbed my forearm in a comforting gesture, "That's great. And rare. Wow." I smiled weakly, trying not to flinch away from his touch. They were reading my nervousness wrong—thank God. They thought it was because I was a Seyer.

I asked, "Really? Al made it sound like it was no big deal."

"And it ain't," the old woman's voice rang out behind me. "Each of us got a different part in the bigger picture of things. Ain't that right Julia?" Silver hair framed her face.

Julia sighed, waving her hands as she spoke, "Si, si. We know how you feel Althea." She looked away, rolling her eyes. It seemed like they had this discussion before.

Al took a step toward Julia, gesturing to me, "Ivy will help us with the prophecy."

My heart dropped into my toes. *What did she say?* "Excuse me?" I squeaked.

"Really?" Eric questioned, looking excited.

Julia humphed and folded her arms. "We know the prophecy. Our warriors will eradicate the problem—not this little girl."

"That's not what I've seen. It's this *little girl* who will be the one to *eradicate* the problem." Her old eyes looked at me. Panic was gripping me from my throat to my toes. Its tendrils laced into my stomach, and squeezed.

Al knows what I am. She's going to turn me over. I fought every urge of self-preservation that was franticly flowing within me, and kept my feet glued to the spot.

"Psh. You do your way. We do ours. I'll report your new *Seyer*," she said it with disdain, "and your prediction." Julia picked up her patent leather purse. Sister Al walked her out, leaving Eric and I alone.

"So," Eric turned towards me with a proud smile on his face, "A Seyer. Wow." Heart pounding, I nodded, avoiding the urge to run screaming from Eric.

Why did it have to be Eric? What was I supposed to tell him? That I was the one he was trying to kill. Faking what I was, was going to get much harder. Looking into his face, I saw peaceful amber eyes, not the warrior hunting me. I only saw Eric—sweet, thoughtful Eric. How could I be so incredibly wrong about people? Was my perception that bad? My stomach was in knots, as I held my fists tightly in my jean pockets. "I'm gonna meet up with Shannon, if that's okay?" It was difficult to look him in the eye, but I managed a weak nod.

Eric smiled, "Sure. You all right?"

"Yup. I'm good." I pulled my hands out of my pockets, and folded them over my chest. Slowly, I turned to walk away from him, and out the front doors. Shannon's little red car was waiting, just like we planned. Silently, I slid into the seat, and closed the door.

"What's wrong with you?" she asked. The sunlight gave her hair a golden glow. She put the car into drive, and pulled into traffic.

I sat there for a second, unsure of what to do. The tension in my forehead wouldn't ease up. I pressed it with my fingertips, as we drove in silence. The truth slammed together in the back of my mind. I desperately wanted to deny it. Eric's words mixed with the things Shannon had told me earlier, and it made me feel sick. But, I knew it was true.

The tightness of my throat choked my voice, making my words barely audible. "Eric's the Seeker."

Shannon gasped, swerving the car slightly when she looked at me. "How did you find out?" Her voice was several octaves higher than usual. "Ivy, what happened?"

"I heard him talking to someone named Julia. They think I'm a *creature*...and they know I'm nearby. They just have no idea how close." My voice faded into shocked silence.

Shannon's foot turned to lead. We arrived at my house much faster than normal. She turned and asked me, "What are you going to do?"

Unbuckling, I shrugged. "They don't know it's me."

"Julia's trouble," she said. "Eric *has* to listen to her."

Still shocked, I stared out the windshield, looking at nothing. "Eric was told to help me—and kill me." Shaking my head, I exited the car.

Shannon called behind me, "Ivy, do you want me to come in? You don't look good."

Turning to her, I said, "No. I just want to be alone." My hand pushed the door shut, and I walked up the sidewalk, shocked into silence.

As night fell, the feelings that I suppressed were flowing to the surface. I had severe control freak tendencies, and when I had no control—I freaked out. The urge to repeat my past behavior was consuming my thoughts. I had to do something to lift the chaos. Staring at my reflection, I assessed my outfit. Black chiffon shirt with a fitted bodice and flowing sleeves paired with a little black skirt. I grabbed my black boots and shoved my feet in. These were made so that I could run, if necessary, but they looked awesome too. Stabbing Apryl's comb in my hair, I arranged a half up and half down style. Porcelain skin absorbed the purple pigment as my mark disappeared.

The crumpled invite was on my dresser. I'd gotten it via a guy at school over a week ago. I had no intention of going, until now. The party was in Babylon. That wasn't too far from here. There would be kids from other schools, and lots of boys I didn't know. Resigned to easing up some of the chaos, I turned and launched myself out my window and into the night.

When I arrived at the house, the party was well underway. It was one of the huge homes that lined the waterfront, with an equally huge lawn. It had a brick circle drive that was full of cars, with a huge three tier fountain in the center. Kids were milling about, unaffected by the crisp night air. Most had a drink in their hand, talking loudly over the throbbing music emitting a BOOM BOOM BOOM from the house.

I ducked through the door and navigated the crowds of kids, until I found the dance floor. The large room was filled with the smell of sweat, and lingering smoke. Windows opened to the back of the house, showcasing the waterfront. There were way too many kids in the space. It connected to another room that had an equal abundance of people. Hoping to get lost in the crowd, I shimmied my way through the maze.

Nicole and her drones stared at me as I passed. "Come to get laid, Virgin?" Nicole yelled, laughing at me. Her gaggle of friends sniggered. Her words caught the attention of a few guys standing nearby.

I walked up to her, looking into her perfect face, and answered loud enough for others to hear, "Yes." Nicole was at a momentary loss for words. As I stepped away from her, a boy with brown hair and brown eyes smiled at me. His hair was hanging in his eyes. I walked over to him, and whispered in his ear. He put his hand on the small of my back, and grinned at Nicole, as we walked away. I smiled at her over my shoulder, waving, and said, "Thanks!" Her face pinched into a scowl.

We walked toward the back of the house, toward the darker corners of the room. Brown-haired boy leaned in, speaking loudly in my ear, "Hey. I'm..."

Turning toward him, I put my fingers over his lips to silence him. "I don't want to know who you are." Sliding my body up against his, I pushed him back into the wall, lacing my arms around his neck.

A smile spread across his face, as he realized what I was offering. His hands slid down my back, cupping my butt, as he pulled me to him. "Perfect."

"Stop talking," I commanded, pressing my body into him. My hands slid up to his face, and I pulled his mouth down on mine. I didn't know who he was, and I didn't care. It was perfect that way. Only a stranger could offer the escape I needed, and help me feel like I still had some control over my life. We stayed intertwined in the dark corner of the room, with hands sliding, touching, and tasting. The couples around us were moving at a slower pace, but I didn't care. His lips moved down my neck. I started to melt, my knees buckling at the sensation. The rush of emotions was flooding me, and numbing my pain. It wouldn't last long, but I might be able to make it last longer if I didn't hold back this time. Thoughts ran through my mind, and I realized I'd decided what I came here to do before I arrived.

Did this really hurt me? I couldn't remember from last time. It damaged my reputation, but I couldn't remember anything else. Other sensations were slowing my thoughts. One strong hand was sliding under my low neckline, as his teeth grazed my neck in sharp kisses. A sigh escaped me, and I leaned into him. I threaded my fingers through his hair, and pulled firmly. His face came up from my neck with a boyish grin. He was breathing hard, and glistening. The room was warm before, but now it felt incredibly hot. Closing my eyes, I inhaled his scent. He smelled like spicy aftershave.

"Take me upstairs," I said breathlessly. Smiling wide, we turned to walk up the stairs. His hands moved roughly over my body, as we stumbled up the stairs, and into a dark hallway. The guy was cut like a skater, with strong forearms, and an athlete's tight body. I slid my hands under his shirt, as he pushed me into a wall at the top of the landing.

His lips moved across my neck, making me feel wonderfully warm. A hand slid under my shirt, and over my bra. The intoxicating bliss surged through me, and I moaned. He responded by sliding his other hand up my thigh, well under the hem of my skirt. Leaning into his hard body, I felt *found* for a moment. The overwhelming sense of being *lost* faded. It felt like everything would be fine. Strong arms held me, and nothing else could touch me. At least, I didn't plan on it.

The icy hot sensation snapped me back to reality before I heard his chiding voice. "Ivy! What the hell are you doing! Look at me." He pulled me away from skater boy. Collin's blue eyes came into focus, as my buzz faded, leaving nothing but my drowning fear.

"Hey dude," brown-haired boy said, "back off. She's mine." The guy tried to get Collin to let go of me, but he wouldn't.

Too dazed to realize what was happening, I felt Collin in my mind. By the time he saw how screwed up I was, it was too late. I couldn't hide my sinful intentions. His grip didn't loosen. Instead, he shoved back my make-out buddy. "Fuck off. She's mine." I tried to twist my wrist out of Collin's grip, but stuff got weird fast. His sadness and concern started to leak into my emotions and swirled together. But instead of mixing, they were remaining separate like swirled ice cream.

Heart racing, I tried to pull away from Collin. "Leave me alone, Collin. You don't know…"

His grip tightened, as he stood between us. His face lowered and came down into mine, our noses almost touching. "I'm not leaving you to ruin your life. You said you were done with this shit, Ivy. What are you doing?"

"Hey man. She said back off. Back off." Skater dude tried to be valiant, but failed.

Collin turned slowly, with rage in his eyes. He looked slightly insane. "If you want her, you're gonna have to take her from me." Collin yanked my other arm before I knew what happened. Moving quickly, he slung me over his shoulder, and ran.

"LET ME GO!" I screamed. I shrilled a terrified yell, as he bounded down the steps, and out the front door. My body bounced like a rag doll, and I half hung on for my life. Collin ran through the house, and burst through the front doors. He slowed in front of the illuminated fountain. I screeched, "Noooo!" before he dropped me, but I was already airborne. My body twisted, as I tried to stop myself from hitting the waist-deep water. The cold liquid sucked me under, crushing the breath out of my chest. My butt bumped into the cement bottom, and I staggered to my knees. The wind sent a chill through me, and my body shook as I glared at Collin. Water drained from the hair that was plastered to my face. Apryl's comb was barely hanging on. Water filled my boots, and lots of other places that cold water shouldn't go.

Anger flowed through me, white hot. At first, I just breathed, watching him. A crowd followed to see what would happen. Some kids said something about not wanting to be on the receiving end of that. Eventually, I threw my leg over the side of the fountain, and ran at him. My body slammed into his. My fists smacked into his chest, as I yelled up into his face. "You had no right! Who the hell do you think you are?"

Collin didn't move. He let me vent, watching me with irritating calmness. His eyes had turned back to their normal hue, and not the impossibly deep blue that looked insane a few moments ago. Now I looked insane. The crowd was laughing. Some shouted stuff at us, but I was too pissed off to understand. I ignored all of them, except Collin. "How could you! What makes you think you could do this to me!" The shrill in my voice was dying, as the coldness seeped in. My anger was burning out, and the cold was taking over. My black chiffon outfit clung to my body; making me feel colder than I thought was possible. I stepped away from Collin, tears streaming down my face. Between sobs I said, "You should have left me alone."

"I can't leave you alone," he stood, arms distance from me, looking hopelessly lost. "Nicole baited you. You didn't really want to be with that guy."

"Nicole did *not* bait me. I came here looking for him." I couldn't look at Collin. He didn't understand. And I couldn't tell him. His hands reached for me without hesitation, and he firmly gripped my upper arms. There were no icy hot tingles, just a blast of remorse that flooded through the bond.

"Ivy," he breathed. "Just tell me. What's got you so scared that you'd do this?" His voice was softer, "You used to tell me anything. And everything. We had no secrets. Just tell me." His breath washed over my skin, startlingly warm.

Twisting my shoulders, I cleared my mind as I broke contact with him. "Things changed. It's not like that anymore. I'm not the same girl anymore. If you don't like it—too bad." I folded my arms tightly, trying not to shiver. He straightened, looking as if I'd kicked him in the stomach. He took a step toward me. His eyes were trying to lock with mine. Determination was exuding from him.

"I know something happened to you—and it has you scared to death. The fear is rolling off of you, thick and heavy. It's drowning you. You're reaching out for random guys, so you can feel something besides the horrifying terror that's consuming you." I kept my face downturned, toward the ground, saying nothing. My entire body was numb. I couldn't tell him he was right. He already knew it, anyway. His warm hand touched my face. He pulled it up to look him in the eye. "You're still the same girl, whether you see it or not."

Swallowing hard, I shook my face out of his grip. I answered, "You've never been so wrong."

CHAPTER SIXTEEN

Shannon emerged from the crowd with a surprised look on her face. She inserted herself between Collin and I, and then pulled me away from the staring eyes of the crowd we'd attracted. Nothing was said. Nothing had to be. I could see the look on her face, and I saw the thanks she nodded at Collin before she drove me home.

Soaked to the bone, I sat in her car, and blasted the heater in my face. Every attempt was made not to take out my anger on Shannon. I did something incredibly stupid, and got caught.

After a long silence she said, "Dumping you in cold water was the best thing he coulda did for you." Turning my wet head, I stared at her. My eyebrow shot up, as my mouth fell open. She was siding with him? "No," she said. "I'm serious. For Martis, cold water is like a reset button. It has the same shocking effect that cold water has on humans, but without any of the risk of hypothermia. The cold is supposed to purge ailments from immortals. Did it help?"

"Help?" I chattered. "Help! No, it didn't help. He threw me in cold water, in front of everyone. Now, I'll be the wet virgin. Awh, suck. That's so much worse!" My head slumped forward, as I clutched my face.

"Ivy, you're an idiot," her sharp words shot through my pride in a way uniquely Shannon. "I'm not talking about your social standing. There's no way that little display helped your social life. Although the skaters may avoid you now." She smiled, suppressing a laugh. "Did it help you purge whatever was bugging you? I'm assuming the idea of being around Eric, and knowing who he is, had you freaked. Are you better now?"

"Maybe." She glared at me while I sulked. "Okay, yes. It helped. That's gone for now. But won't it just come back?"

She glanced at me out of the corner of her eye, "Only if you let it." Her face took on a star struck expression. "I wish I had enough guts to throw you in a fountain." She laughed, "It's almost like he knew that would snap you out of it. Too bad he's not a Martis." She wagged her eyebrows at me.

I stared at her in disbelief. "Awh crap, Shan. Now you like him? You can't like him. You hate his guts. He hates you. You can't like each other. My head will implode."

The car came to a stop, a few doors down from my house. She smiled at me. "Maybe he's not so bad. I mean, he kept you from indulging your inner-Valefar. Ivy, Martis don't sleep around. That could have damaged the ratio of your inner good to bad. We don't know what hurls you into the prophecy. Collin may have kept you from making a huge mistake." She shrugged, "So, maybe he's not so bad."

"Come inside. I need to tell you something—about him—and me." Seeing an odd look cross her face, I quickly added, "And it's not what you think."

After I changed into dry clothes, I felt better. Oddly, the dunk didn't leave me chilled all night. It felt more like jumping into a cool pool on an insanely hot day. I felt refreshed, and the crushing fear was gone. Shannon sat at the foot of my bed. I plopped down on the pillows by the headboard.

"Shannon," I said, "I think I've done something to Collin. I didn't tell anyone else about it, because I thought it might be Valefar induced."

Shannon nodded, green eyes widening. "Ivy, what'd you do?"

Taking a deep breath, I continued, "I don't know. He can hear me. And I can hear him. It's like mind reading, but more vivid. This sounds weird, but it feels like our spirits are intertwined—like we're bonded or something. Tell me you've heard of this?" I gripped my fingers tightly.

She leaned back against the wall, looking very intrigued. "It's only with Collin? Not anyone else?"

I nodded, "Only him."

"Hmmm. Seyers have unique powers the rest of us don't, but I'm not aware of anything like this. But, it doesn't mean it's not there. It means I'm not a Seyer." She pulled her hair over her shoulder, twirling the ends.

"Who told you I'm a Seyer?" I asked. "I skipped that part earlier today."

She shrugged, "Eric called me. I thought that probably added to your freak out, so I tried to track you down. By the time I found you, Collin had you in the fountain."

"The Seyer thing didn't help," I acknowledged. "Al made it clear she knows I'm different, although she didn't say she knows what I am. She seems to think I'll do stuff. I have no idea if she knows that I'm tainted. But this? Shannon..." I sighed, running my fingers through my hair. "I'm afraid it'll hurt him. I don't know what it is, and whatever this is, this bond, it's changing. It feels different. In the past I could only hear his thoughts by looking him in the eye and touching him.

But tonight there was no need for either of those things. He heard me anyway."

Shannon was quiet before she asked, "Did anything else change?"

Thinking about it, I wasn't sure. The anger earlier had clouded everything else. Nodding, I said, "I can *feel* the bond. It felt like an old rubber band, tugging me toward him. When we separated, it didn't like it. It felt stretched beyond comfort, and then it snapped. I was so mad, I didn't notice."

"You need to talk to Al. She's your mentor. She'd know if bonding like that is Martis or not." She sat up, looking at me.

"It's the *or not* part that concerns me," I said.

School the next day sucked. I managed to ruin my reputation, and flamed Eric's in one glorious streak. There were hushed whispers of stopped conversations when I walked by. From what I heard, I cheated on Eric with skater-boy, which was horrible, because everyone thought Eric was a sweet guy. How could anyone do something like that to him? Then I was accused of having a fling with Collin, which is why he tossed me in the fountain in a jealous rage. Basically, I was crowned class slut. Nicole, of course, was thrilled with Collin's humiliating actions. She made sure to tease me, as I walked into my first period class.

Mr. Turner paired everyone up for class work, and I had the joy of working with one of Nicole's drones. Lily had an oval face, platinum blond hair, and bright red fingernails. She also had the trademark big boobs that made Nicole's clique noticeable. She sneered at me when I scooted my desk over. "That was trampy—even for you." Her lips pulled back into a disgusted expression, as she glared at me.

"Whatever, Barbie. Let's just do the work." I couldn't look at her. Normally the clones didn't bother me, and their chatter rolled off my back, but I felt raw. Her words stung.

She sneered, hissing as she leaned closer to me. "What's it gonna take for you to notice him? It's cruel—what you do—leading him on. Dating any other guy. Sucking face with some skater freak, when he's right in front of you."

I dropped my pen, and glared at her. "I am not leading Collin on. Listen, I..."

She cut me off before I could finish the rest of my thought. "No, you listen, you little slut," she sneered poking her pen into my arm. "Nicole didn't want me to say anything, but I can't stand watching you torture Collin anymore. Since you're too stupid to notice, I'm telling you—he loves you. Get it through your thick skull." My mouth fell open in disbelief, but I couldn't get a word in. She hissed, "A guy doesn't act like that for a fling. He doesn't scoop up a girl and carry her away from another guy if he's just a friend. The rest of us hang on him, but he doesn't notice us, we're like air—invisible. But not with you. Never with you. He runs after you, checks on you, does stuff for you, gave you that ring you're wearing. He loves you. Stop treating him like crap."

Shaking my head, I said, "He doesn't love me. It's just lust. Or something."

Her perfect eyebrow shot up. "Tell yourself whatever you want, but you better stop hurting Collin. Nicole's gonna kill you. And I can't stand you either."

Her words hung in the air. The horrible certainty that her clones thought he loved me, made me feel sick. If he did love me, the way I acted was horrifying. No. They couldn't be right. It wasn't possible. This was payback for messing with Nicole last night. Collin couldn't love me. He couldn't.

The rest of the day passed, and I dreading seeing Eric. People were talking about him and it was entirely my fault. I didn't know how he'd respond. When I turned the hallway to the bio room, I saw Eric leaning on the wall. His arms were folded, as he watched me approach. My pace slowed. The burn of humiliation rose to my cheeks. When I reached him I said, "Eric, let me explain."

His amber eyes were cold. He lowered his face to mine, and said, "Explain. Explain how you could do something like that. You didn't even know him." Straightening, he stepped back.

"Eric..." the bell rang. His disappointment deflated my desire to fight back. My entire defense, the need to conceal the demon blood coursing through my veins melted. I couldn't hide this anymore. It was eating me alive and destroying every friendship I had. Horrified, I heard the words slipping out of my mouth before I could stop them. "Eric, I'm not like you. I'm different. There's darkness inside me that I can't control. Yesterday, I heard you talking about killing someone, permanently. I was overloaded. I can't stand the thought. Oh God, Eric." The confession spilled over my lips before I could choke it back, "It's me. I'm the one you're looking for."

His lips cracked into a smile, as he laughed. He put his hand on my shoulder acting utterly amused. "That's what freaked you out? You think you're the one we're looking for?" He laughed some more, shaking his head. "I suppose that warranted your reaction, but I assure you," he smiled, "I'm not hunting *you*."

He didn't believe me! Unbelievable. I told the Seeker the one he was hunting was standing right in front of him, and he blew me off! I felt irritated, but it also assured that I was well hidden. He didn't suspect me at all. From the look on his face, he thought I was foolish for thinking such a thing. Eric forgave me easily. It was part of his charm, but it also made it harder. There would be a time when he realized who I was. The betrayal was going to be horrifying, and there was nothing I could do to stop it.

My mood was crap by the time I got to the nun. Sister Al was telling me about the premonition type of Seyer-ing that happened before a vision, when I blurted out the question that I was dying to ask, "Is it normal for a Seyer to have a heightened sense of another person?"

Her wrinkled face seemed surprised by my question. "No. That ain't normal, but none of us is the same. And you were cut from a different mold, child. Any fool can see that. Why you askin'?" Her old eyes held mine.

I couldn't look away. I wanted to tell her. I wanted to trust her. But my mouth wouldn't spill the truth. I shrugged. "I thought maybe we just had heightened senses in general."

She replied, "Ask your question, if you got one."

"I have a connection with another person. It's like we can hear each other's thoughts. It feels very - weird." I paused. She didn't look at me like I was insane, so I began again slowly forming the words that described our bond. "And the connection, this bond we have, it's growing. When I try to pull away from this person, it's starting to physically hurt. Something inside me is being stretched. And it snaps when I leave." I stopped there, expecting her to tell me I was nuts.

"Hmm. It's not with everyone—only one person?" Her ancient fingers made a tee pee on her chin.

"Only one," I breathed.

Her old eyes considered me. "And it's changing?"

I nodded, "Yeah. It's getting stronger. In the beginning, it was only a sensation. Then it required eye contact or touch. I'm afraid I won't be able to keep my secrets to myself. Like the Martis. What do I do?"

Her face was serious, as she tapped her upper lip. I expected this sage to have all the answers that I would need for the rest of my life. I hung on her words, waiting for them to enlighten me, and get me out of this mess. Her answer was shocking. "No idea, but that's an interesting situation. You'll have to let me know how it turns out."

"What!" I squealed. "You have to tell me. I don't know what to do. He's not Martis! He's a mortal!"

She leaned forward, "It's a *him*?"

"Yes. Can you tell me now? What do I do? The only way to keep him out of my head is to push him away. But the bond is pulling me toward him. I don't think I can stay away, especially if it's doing the same thing to him." And I didn't want to stay away from him. He was my best friend, no matter what recent events transpired.

A smile spread over her lips as she leaned back laughing, "Oh child!"

"This isn't funny! I need to know. I can't stand it." I was out of breath. Panic was rising within me.

Al finally answered, "You can't stand it, because you try to control everything. But you ain't gonna control this. And you can't bend it to your will, neither. The two of you were made to do something together. At some point. It doesn't matter what you do—it will happen. Fighting it is pointless, even if you don't like it. And at some point, he will find out what you are." She leaned forward, "We all will. When you're ready."

My heart caught in my throat. Her old face watched mine. Great. She was going to play with me until I told her. Well, that I could control, and I wasn't telling her that I was the only Martis walking around with demon blood right then. That was the end of the discussion. I'd have to deal with Collin myself.

CHAPTER SEVENTEEN

A week passed since the fountain incident. Collin kept his distance. We had trouble patching things up after the fountain incident, and we weren't talking. My anger faded, but I couldn't talk to him yet. The words Lily had said really messed with me, although I found it impossible to believe her. There was no way he loved me. And besides, I knew there was another reason why Collin kept away from me. I could feel it. The bond was changing again. It seemed to have a life of its own. I didn't discuss it with Collin, but I knew he was also aware of the shift. Apprehension laced his thoughts. When we passed each other in the halls, I felt the bond pull, urging me toward him. Often, it made us pause. We would stop—unable to speak. Our eyes met and we would stare at each other, as wordless thoughts past between us.

Kids noticed. They were saying that some new dramatic thing happened between us, though nothing had. The staring was an attempt at locking down my mind before thoughts could slip out and into Collin's mind. When he was nearby, I forced everything out of my mind. He did the same, but the bond grew more uncomfortable. Each time we finally moved enough to snap the bond my heart would sink, and the pulling in my chest snapped, in a short painful pop.

I straddled my stool in bio, and slumped down on my desk. The tabletop felt cold against my cheek. Staring at the wall, I thought about it, waiting for the bell to ring. Things were getting really weird. When Collin crossed my path, I was solely focused on breaking proximity, and subduing the bond before information leaked out. *Stupid-ass bond.* It was getting hard. Very hard. Being a hallway apart wasn't helping anymore. We could hear each other at a longer distance, and through walls. It was particularly bad in math, when he was in the room next to mine. His muted thoughts came through the cinder block walls. The worst part was the pulling sensation. There was a wall in the way. It's not like I could move it and go to him! But the bond didn't care.

The chair next to me scraped the floor. I heard Eric ask, "You okay?"

Leaning back, I raised my head, and smiled faintly. "Yup. I'm fine. Just a little strung out." He nodded. Class went on as usual. When the bell rang, we walked back to my locker together. There was no circle of blonde girls. No Collin. Eric left me, and we planned to meet around front. I was disappointed that Collin wasn't there. I almost wished he'd say something, so we could move past the other night. But, he didn't. Neither would I. It's not like I should apologize. But still. If I was given the opportunity to allow things to blow over, I would jump at it.

The kids still regarded me as the school slut, but I was no longer the topic of choice. Thank God. That was horrifying and lasted long enough. Eric made up some story about taking me back, despite my wild ways—which was true, since he couldn't lie. And we were a fake couple again. Eric drove to the church, saying little. When he finally spoke, it wasn't something that I wanted to talk about. "Why'd you do it?"

Turning my head, I looked at him quizzically. "Do what?"

His face saddened, and he wouldn't look at me. "The skater. At the party. I heard lots of stories. I didn't hear yours."

"I don't really want to talk about it, okay?" I stared out the window, leaning my head against the glass.

He cleared his throat, clearly uncomfortable. "Ivy, Shannon told me that Collin threw you in the fountain. You were fighting with your best friend? The whole thing sounds weird."

I shrugged, "It was weird."

Eric looked at me, gripping the wheel tighter. "Things tend to fester and putrefy, if you don't deal with them. You tend to shove your problems in a box, and then they blow up in your face."

I bristled, "They do not... Well, maybe they do—a little bit. What would you have me do?" I looked at him out of the corner of my eye, straightening in my seat.

"I'd have you deal with it. Whatever it is. However you can. Sealing it inside of you doesn't work out very well." He shrugged. "I know, because I did it. I was really angry when I was first changed. Not because of the mark, but because of what I lost. The Valefar killed her..." his voice grew quieter, as he turned the wheel, pulling into the parking lot. The gravel crunched under the truck as he slowed to a stop. "Lydia meant everything to me. I lost her because I was a fool. Whether you want to admit it or not—Collin means something to you. Don't be a fool and throw it away."

"Maybe I am a fool. What kind of girl would I be, if I did like him? You said it yourself, he treats me like crap." I didn't want to talk about this anymore.

Eric pushed my hair out of my face, turning my chin toward him. His caramel eyes were compassionate.

"Ivy, I envy you. You have no idea how much I envy you. I know what he did for you. What he's done for you. Love doesn't come along too often. Believe me, I know. When it does, only the foolish let it fade. Even if it is him." Eric slid out of the truck.

Stunned, I sat there unable to move. Love? Wouldn't I know if Collin loved me? I heard his thoughts and emotions through the bond. Admiration leaked through before, and even lust, but not love— never love. No, they were wrong. I don't know what they were seeing, but I knew—without a doubt—Collin did not love me. We were friends. That's all.

When I finally went inside, Al was waiting for me. Today she was going to prep me for my visions. Since I hadn't had one yet, she thought they would crash into me like a freight train. The gift was on or off for me, with nothing in the middle. Since that was the way my life usually went, I didn't doubt her. I was excited about learning this part. There was the remote possibility that I would see something about my future—about the prophecy. Then, maybe, I could fix things.

Al rocked as she spoke. "Seyers get glimpses of the future. They can't see everything—just parts and pieces. If you get enough details, you can try to figure out what might happen. When you have your first vision, it will feel like a dream. But, since we don't sleep, you won't be sleeping. But you'll be vulnerable. The first thing you do when you feel a vision coming is to remove yourself from danger. Then when you are in the vision, collect as much detail as you can. You're gonna need it to figure out what you saw. Then come tell me about it."

"Okay," I didn't know what to say. I figured visions were like dreams, so I thought I would just have to wait and find out. And it didn't seem she could really teach me anything else until I'd experienced one. I'd have to wait and see how it went on my own.

"Is there anything you want to tell me?" she asked.

I stiffened slightly. "Like what?"

"Oh, I don't know," she smiled. "You just seem like you have choices to make, and you haven't made them. If ya leave the pie in the oven too long, it burns."

What the hell was she talking about? Pie? I blinked. "I don't have pies, Sister."

"Yes, ya do. Everybody's got pies. Pies about what to wear, what to eat, who to date, who to fight, who to tell… " she paused. Her weathered skin wrinkled around glittery eyes. "And if we don't decide, everything just burns. If we don't choose when, someone else will choose for us, like the fire department tells you when those pies burn your house down. You get what I'm saying to ya?"

No. "Yes," I smiled. I had no words to retort to the pies, but I did feel a little hungry. "Well, thanks."

Eric hung his head in the room. "You ready?" Sister Al looked at me, waiting for my reply.

I nodded at Eric and said, "I think so." Turning to Al, I asked, "Are we done?"

"We are." She looked slightly offended. But I couldn't say anything. I nearly peed myself when she brought it up. I knew she'd seen my future, but I didn't know how much. It was possible she didn't know that I was tainted. And I didn't want to be the one to tell her. Then I thought of her metaphor. Burnt pie. That's what happens when you wait too long. The decision gets taken away. It clicked slowly, but it clicked. I said the only thing I could think to say, "Thank you." I placed a hand on her shoulder, as I passed.

She covered it with her gnarled fingers and said, "I'll help you. I promised. Nuns don't lie, girl."

Eric was an awesome teacher. He didn't mention my failures. I kind of sucked at everything. Patience was a requirement when working with me, and he had it in abundance. I'd mastered a few moves, but was shocked when he said, "Let's just have fun today." The look on his face let me know right away that I wasn't going to think this was fun.

"Fun? What are you talking about?" I asked. Practice was never fun. I usually got my butt kicked. Dread ran through my veins.

He grinned, "We're done when one of us is immobilized. Use the things I taught you. Don't leave the gym. And no weapons."

"Eric, I don't have any weapons," I laughed. Like I shoved something down my pants. What was he talking about? The Martis that had trained with Eric slowed, grinning, watching us. Their feet stopped as they watched the exchange.

Flicking my comb, he said, "No silver. Keep it clean." Grinning like crazy, he bent at the waist, gesturing for me to come toward him. "Come get me."

The dark haired Martis laughed, as she sat down with the two men, ready to watch us spar. My eyes flicked between them and us. I folded my arms, feeling more than silly. "Eric. Seriously? And what about them?"

"They can watch. We just did the same exercise. It'll be good for them—and you." He grinned at me, saying,

"You better start, or I will." Slightly shocked, I stood there with my arms folded, refusing to move. Disbelief spread across my face. Seriously? He wanted me to trap him? Apparently, I waited too long because he lunged at me at full speed.

I shrieked, and ran, narrowly escaping his grasp. "This is so unfair!" I yelled over my shoulder. "You're gonna trap me in five seconds!"

The other Martis laughed. Elena, the Martis woman with black hair yelled, with a smile on her face, "Fight, girl! Stop running. He'll catch you! Use your offensive moves."

His hand swiped at my waist, as I twisted to see who spoke. I turned, ducking and ran under his arms. "I can't beat you! You're 2,000 years older than me!" His foot went out when I was half way through, and I tumbled to the ground. Instead of taking him with me, I twisted into a ball, and rolled away. Jumping to my feet, I expected him to grab at me, so I stayed low. His hand swiped—and missed. I laughed, jumping over a mat, and then climbed up the rope.

Eric stood at the bottom. "That was dumb. Now how do you plan to get away from me?"

I yelled down. "You said you had to immobilize me. I can still move." I waved my arms at him to demonstrate. "You don't win. Stalemate." My heart was pounding and I used the moment to catch my breath, knowing Eric wouldn't allow a stalemate.

His hands tugged the rope and I felt it move below me. He shot up, climbing quickly. He moved much faster than before, and was halfway up before I caught my breath. My fingers released the rope, as I felt the air swirl around me in a WOOSH. As I dropped, Eric screamed, reaching for me but missing. My feet landed on the floor with a deafening thud, followed by some nasty shin splints. Eric was stunned into silence, and remained motionless on the rope. My gaze shot to the Martis—their mouths were open.

Crap. What did I do? I sprinted from the place that I'd landed, and across the room. A sickening sensation formed in my stomach. No one had moved or said anything. Knowing I screwed up, I kept running, and crashed through the gym doors. I had to get away. The looks on their faces told me something was wrong. I did something wrong, but I had no idea what. I was done with this. Done pretending to be Martis. Surrounded by the four of them, if they knew what I really was, I'd be dead.

I ran down the dim halls, away from all of them. Eric's footfalls came crashing down the hall behind me, increasingly faster. I pushed through the exterior door, running full out across the back lawn of the church. His fingers rustled the back of my shirt, before I turned sharply, narrowly evading his grasp.

"Ivy! Stop!" he called after me. But I wouldn't stop. I had to run. I couldn't stand it anymore. I didn't want to see the betrayal on his face when he pieced everything together. Panting hard, I hurled my body out of his reach. I ran faster, lunging for the woods, knowing that it would be easier to lose him between the trees. Eric's fingers wrapped around my arm, and he jerked me backwards. I felt my balance go off kilter, and couldn't recover. My body came crashing down on the lawn at the edge of the forest. Eric pinned me. Squirming to roll over and twist out of his grip was pointless. His grip was iron clad.

Breathing heavily, he said, "Why'd you run? And by the way, I win." He lowered himself and sat on my legs. I let out an exasperated noise, flexing every muscle in my body. Panic flooded me, and I tried to kick him off. My chest couldn't suck in enough air fast enough. My arms flared, throwing punches wildly at him.

"Whoa, Ivy," he said, pinning my arms to the ground. He hovered over me as I thrashed.

"Get off of me! Let me go!" I screamed. My heart raced so violently that I thought I'd die. Eric was breathing heavily, above me. He released my arms, but didn't get up. I was still pinned to the ground. I closed my eyes, rubbing my hands across my face. He said nothing, and sat there, staring at me. I finally dropped my hands, noticing how stupid it would have been to run into the woods now. It was dark, and clouds obstructed the moonlight. Jake could be in there. Eric lifted himself off my legs, and sat next to me. He didn't say anything. He just stared at me.

When I couldn't take it anymore, my voice rasped, "What? Go ahead. Say whatever you're thinking." My hand wiped beads of sweat off my forehead. I clenched my fists to hide how shaken I was.

Eric replied, somewhat stunned, "Okay. How'd you jump like that? I've never seen a Martis jump from that high before. It didn't even look like a jump. It looked like you flew to the ground." His amber eyes were burning holes in my face. I couldn't look at him. The thought of lying to him made me sick—I hated it. But there was nothing else to do. The lies protected me, but the reality that I was different was surfacing. He'd know soon.

I continued picking the grass out of my hair, and cautiously looked at him out of the corner of my eye. *Just say it, Ivy. He suspects something anyway.* But I didn't. I steeled my voice for another lie. "Jeeze, Eric. I don't know. So, I can jump far. So what? I got lucky or something."

Eric's expression was unreadable. "I don't know what that was, but it wasn't luck."

CHAPTER EIGHTEEN

It was after six o'clock when Eric and I arrived back at the school for stage crew. I chattered, as usual, and he was quieter than usual. That worried me. Eric parted ways with me when we got to the stage. He went into the cage to do technical stuff, while I went to paint something. Something always needed to be painted, and I loved to paint. I grabbed a brush, looking forward to burying my bad mood in latex. Jenna Marie came up behind me. She had on a pink apron with bows on it. Her hair was slicked back into a ponytail.

She blurted out, "Ivy, are you dating Collin *and* Eric?" Shocked at her question, I choked on my spit. A few other perky girls I didn't know loomed behind her. None of them ever needed coffee. They were naturally chipper.

I returned my gaze to Jenna Marie trying to regain my normal placidity. "No, Collin and I—we're just friends. I'm dating Eric." She was so insane. Changing the conversation, I asked, "So, what are we painting?"

Smiling she said, "Just finishing up some odds and ends. I was retouching the flats, but I need to do some tables. Will you finish for me?" She handed me her brush, and another pink apron.

"Yeah, sure." I grabbed the brush, ignoring the offered apron. I walked to the flats that were laid out backstage.

Her voice called to me, "Not those ones. We got those already. I was retouching those flats." Her delicate fingers pointed to the stage where seven out of nine flats where already erected. "Touch up the seams," she said and walked off.

I saw the problem before I walked up there, but it was too late now. I'd volunteered to be within a stone's throw of Collin. After avoiding each other for over a week, I ended up being right next to him. It was too late now. A few eyes were on me, so I walked up the wooden steps to the spot where Jenna Marie had indicated. With the brush in my hand, I wiggled behind the actors, careful not to get paint on them. I set myself down in front of the bucket of paint, and dipped the brush in.

I have no idea what happened after that. Collin was too close. It was like my brain melted and the only thing I was aware of was Collin Smith. His thoughts brushed against me softly, making my body lean toward him. I forced my spine straight and sat on my feet. I brushed strokes of black, and tried to tune him out. The more I tried, the worse it got. I finally moved a step away from him, over to the next flat. Then I moved to the next. When I was at the edge of the stage, I tried to snap the bond, but it wouldn't give. I couldn't leave. My heart bounced in my chest. Feeling his eyes on me, I wondered if he felt the same thing.

Yes. His voice brushed the inside my mind. It felt like a soft caress. I immediately wanted another. I had to get away from him. I needed to break the bond. If I could move my legs off the stage, and down the stairs, then it'd break it. *Move!* I commanded my legs, but they were aching to walk towards Collin.

I saw Eric watching me from across the stage. Something else was going on. His attention was on the actors. Suddenly the teacher's voice cut through my mental haze. "Don't come back until you're serious! You're messing up everyone else. Damn it! We're two weeks away from opening night, Collin. You always pull it off at the last minute, but not this time. Get outta here and don't come back until you're ready." A script was hurled at him. Collin caught it, and stormed off the stage.

I heard the metal door to the basement scrape open. They kept all the props and old sets down there in the school basement. The room was dark and musty, and directly under the stage. Collin's voice whispered in my mind, *Follow me.*

Like I had a choice? The bond tugged sharply, propelling me toward him. My feet slowly walked down the stairs, not knowing what was happening. The lights were off. Proceeding into the blackness, I could feel Collin's stormy mood, but I didn't see him until I was on the lower landing.

He turned on me. "What the hell was that? What are you doing to me Ivy?" His eyes were wide, and I could sense his fear.

Trying to stay calm, I answered, "I'm not doing it, Collin. That's why you've been avoiding me? It's getting worse. Isn't it?"

His eyes were fierce as he looked at me. "Yes," he snapped. After a moment, his expression softened. "I stayed away because of this and because of the other night with the fountain. I didn't think you'd talk to me anytime soon." He took a step away, and ran his fingers through his hair. "It is much worse, Ivy. I can't even be near you without wanting to… damn it!" A surge of anger flowed into me through the bond. Collin, who was always so controlled, was losing it.

"Without wanting to what?" I stood in front of him, and looked up at his face. Everything was flowing through the bond. Nothing was hidden. I felt his heart racing and the tightness in his chest. He knew I was scared, too. I couldn't hide it.

His eyes were the same vivid blue that I'd only seen once before. His words were spoken so softly—like he was ashamed. "Ivy, I want to touch you. To taste you. Kiss you." His fingers lingered, as he reached for my face, but he promptly folded his arms again.

Butterflies swirled in my stomach, as he spoke. I looked up into his eyes, unable to speak. His muscles were flexed tightly, and his breathing was short and hard. He curled his fingers into fists and tucked them into the nooks in his elbows, before turning away from me. He was trying *not* to kiss me? That was the source of his anguish—the kiss.

Oh God. A chill ran down my spine. Suddenly I knew why my skin prickled when I was around him. I knew why he wouldn't kiss me. I knew why he tried to avoid me. *No. He couldn't be.* His emotions flooded the bond. Waves crashed into me. The sound of my voice, the curve of my neck, and the scent of my skin… His desire was so intense that he could barely control it. He wanted to press his lips to mine, and feel my silky flesh. Run his fingers over my cheek and thread his hands in my hair. But there was something raw under it. It wasn't passion, the way I'd thought. It reminded me of something else. Like the elation on a cat's face, as it paws a mouse to death. My stomach sank. It was like he wanted to…

"Oh God… " I stepped away from him. When I did, the bond tightened, holding me in place. My heart was racing. I wanted to run up the stairs, but I was frozen in front of him.

"I couldn't hide it forever, not with us like this." His hand pushed his hair back and I saw it. A scarlet patch of marred skin—the Valefar scar. Trembling, I tried to control myself. His intensity didn't change. The look of wanting on his face didn't fade. "And I already know what you are. It's why I didn't kiss you. It's why I had to stay away. But damn it! You did this!" He took a step toward me, blue eyes blazing. "I don't want to kill you, Ivy. Release me. You can't hold me like this."

I took a step back, but the bond tightened and became as rigid as steel cables. It held me to the spot, stunned. In front of me was my enemy. And my best friend. *Damn it!*

I suppressed the panic that wanted to dominate me. I was sick of being dominated. By grief. Fear. Lust—or whatever this was. In a steady voice I said, "I swear to God. I did not do this." My heart hammered in my chest. I smoothed my prickled skin, and wrapped my arms around myself. I looked up into his panicked face. "You're really one of them—a Valefar. Aren't you?" Saying it made the horrible truth solidify. I couldn't believe it, but the truth was staring me in the face.

His eyes flashed and a ring of crimson formed around the blue. He came at me, hissing in my face, "Yes, of course I am. What else would I be? And you! You're so new I can smell it. And you decided to ensnare me? Are you crazy? I can't function when you're around. What did you do?!" My thundering heart beat wildly in my chest. His heartbeat echoed through the bond. I could feel blood pumping, and wasn't sure if it was mine or his.

"We can fix this. We can." My voice was shaking. I couldn't help it. "We have to figure out what it wants. I didn't make the bond. Neither of us did. We just need to figure out how to break it."

"It'll break, if I kiss you." He pulled me to him. I froze in his arms. Fear surged through me. I remembered Jake's lips on me, and the way my soul screamed, as it was ripped from my bones. Memories of the pain flooded through me. A pained expression came over Collin. He released me and stepped away. I shivered, waiting for him to come at me again. But he didn't.

"I don't want to kill you, Ivy." His weary face looked at mine. He swallowed, "I've tried so hard to stay away from you, but your soul is so powerful. It can't be ignored. It calls to me. It's like trying to resist every lust you've ever suffered—all at once. I feel that every time I see you. The only reason I haven't given in, is because I was free to choose. I chose to let you live. But you trapped me." His face contorted, "Now the lust calls to me non-stop. I can't control myself much longer. Ivy, you have to break it. Now."

I tried to pull myself away from him. He felt my will resist his. I attempted to walk up the stairs and leave him behind. I pictured my feet running away, and leaving him here. But it didn't matter. The only thing that mental pictures did was show him I wanted to leave without him. The images seemed to settle him.

He finally sat down on the floor and leaned back against the wall. His fingers ran through his dark hair, and he closed his eyes. I sat on the bottom step and stared at him. The pull to kiss him consumed me, even knowing what he was. A stupid idea filled my mind. It was a way to snap the bond temporarily. "Do you trust me?"

He looked at me for a moment. His feelings flooded the bond. He was tired. I knew he needed to get away from me, and I knew that what I was going to do would make it harder for him. He tensed when he felt my intention. "That's not a good idea."

"I have to. It's what the bond has wants me to do. The more I resist, the worse it gets." Fear and longing were growing together. I couldn't think about it. I needed to act quickly before I lost my nerve. But I wasn't sure about Collin. It might push him over the edge. "Can you be still?"

His eyes shifted to mine. His voice whispered in my mind. *I think I can. But Ivy, I can't resist you much longer. If this works, if the bond snaps, don't stay. Run away from me.*

I nodded, and rose off the dirty step and kneeled in front of Collin. I moved slowly. My hands trembled. He could feel my fear. My breath caught in my throat. I tried to push the panic back into my stomach. I touched his face softly, feeling his body tense under my hands. I sucked in a scared gasp, as the tingling sensation I'd come to expect flooded us with a jolt of ice and heat. Once it subsided it felt like we were the same person. I felt Collin's fear, and his control was loosening. His primal needs were going to win. I could sense it. I kept my hand on his face and whispered to his mind, *Be still.* His inner urge to destroy me didn't respond. Instead the bond pulled me to him. All the way. I leaned into his chest, and my face went where the bond led me. My lips swept softly against his cheek. Collin's eyes closed on contact. The softness of his skin against my lips calmed me. The sensation flooded me like magic. It felt like pixie dust was poured into my veins. I felt powerful. Lighthearted. And more connected to Collin.

The kiss sated his hunger. He relished the sensation of my lips on his skin. I lingered for a moment before backing away. When I pulled back, I could feel the bond go slack. It felt like the steel cables that held us together unwound in a snapping motion. I knew I could leave. But I stayed wondering why he didn't destroy me when he could have?

Collin's eyes popped open. The blue was totally gone, replaced with eyes that looked like blood pooling with fire. He brushed one word against my mind. *Run.*

CHAPTER NINETEEN

"So. What happened?" Sister Al held a cup of hot tea in her hands.

"You were wrong!" I said hysterically. "The bond is *bad*. Like way bad. It's gonna kill me!" I didn't make much sense when I first got there. My hands were flying, my heart was ready to explode, and words were pouring out of my mouth in incoherent ramblings. Sister Al's remedy was to shove a steaming drink in my shaking hands.

"Hmm," she said. "I coulda been wrong. Cause you didn't tell me everything. What'd ya leave out, Ivy? Anything—important?" She looked calm, and pursed her wrinkled lips to blow on her hot tea. I shifted in my seat, and made an *argh* noise as I pulled my hair a little. Sister Al kept talking, "Anything about, I don't know, saying bad words? Lying? And stuff like that? I've heard dirty words before, ya know. Nuns got ears, girl."

My heart hammered in my chest. I couldn't stand it anymore. She beat me down. She won. I simply nodded and said, "Yup. Stuff like that."

A smile pulled at the corners of her mouth, and she put her cup down. "It's about time. Do you know how hard it is to think of metaphors for being what you are? Pies. Bah. I was down to nothing with that one. So spill girl. I swore to protect you—I don't lie. I will protect you no matter what words fly outa your mouth right now."

I looked around the room. Only one thought kept me from spilling everything right then. "What about Julia?"

Al straightened in her chair. "Julia means well, but she ain't here. And she ain't my boss. My boss hasn't been seen for over two hundred years. And no, I didn't see that coming." She laughed at her own joke. "I'm as high up as you can get in my branch of things. And no one is above me. So, what I say goes. And I say you have my protection. So you do."

I paused, looking at my teacup. "Julia scares me. But I need help. I'll be dead tomorrow if I don't get it. Julia will kill me the next day if she finds out." I paused. My face was pained, but I couldn't hide it anymore. "I'm tainted. I was marked as a Martis. It was blue that first night." I took a huge breath and blurted it out. "But now, it's not. It turned purple." I pulled my comb from my hair and pushed back my hacked off bangs, showing her the mark.

She lowered her cup to the table and said, "Oh my. I had no idea," totally deadpan.

I tried not to roll my eyes. I suspected she knew, but I wasn't sure until then. "You knew this whole time, didn't you?"

"Of course I knew! I'm old, not stupid." She smiled, taking a sip, and returning the smoldering drink to the table. "And when I saw you, I knew you were the girl in my visions. Dressed in solid black with a hole in her heart the size of... something really big. Of course it was you."

"Why didn't you tell me that you knew?" My thundering heart started to relax, since I wasn't going to die right then. "I thought you'd want me dead. I heard Eric and Julia talking about the prophecy and that they had to kill the girl in the painting—me. Eric doesn't know. I've been lying to him. I *hate* lying to him. And the bond. The bond!" I yelled as tears ran down my face. "It's linked me to one of *them*."

She snorted. "Well, he's really *not* blue then, huh?"

"It's not funny! How can you laugh? He wants to kill me." I wiped the tears off of my face. "The bond keeps throwing us together, and it's pushing us to do the one thing that will kill me. I don't want to die, and he doesn't want to kill me. The only reason I got away from him tonight was, because I gave the bond what it wanted—a kiss, but on his cheek. The cords that held me to him snapped, along with his self-control. So I ran. If I wasn't just a little bit faster, he would have killed me! For all I know he's waiting outside." I rubbed my hands over my eyes. "What am I supposed to do?"

Al looked at me. She left her steaming cup on the table while I ranted. My grief and fear floated to the surface and spilled out of my mouth. She extracted bits of info from the muck. "So, you're bonded—but not bound—to a demon kissed boy, who doesn't want to kiss you?"

I nodded. "Yeah. But it doesn't matter. His control is gone. I broke it tonight to get away from him." We sat in silence for a while. The emotions that flared through him that night were intense. He wanted to protect me. And he tried so hard, but he knew he was failing. I was his undoing. His thoughts flooded into me, and I could feel it. My voice was a whisper, "When his eyes flashed, it reminded me of Jake attacking me. But I wasn't afraid of this guy."

"What's your question, dear?" the nun asked.

I breathed in, trying to steady myself, "Eric told me that they can't feel - that they *don't* feel anything. Since I can sense his thoughts and emotions, I know he wanted to protect me. Is that possible?"

"Anything's possible," she sipped her tea. "It's unusual, but not impossible."

"What do I do?" I asked.

"Something is going to happen with the two of you. Do you have any idea what it is?"

I nodded. "I think so. But I don't know how or why. He's in the painting. The guy I'm pulling up—or the one who's pulling me down. It's him. I'm sure it is."

She sipped her tea. "Then you have nothing to worry about. With him anyway."

My incredulous eyes flicked to her face. "Yeah, right. Al, he was ready to rip me apart tonight."

"But he didn't," she shrugged. "And his self-control is remarkable. It almost as if... " her voice trailed off. The rest of the thought passed through her brain and she left me out.

"As if, what?"

"Demon kissed are selfish and self-serving. But you can feel his desire to keep you alive. You need to know *why*. The only way you'll find out is to use the bond."

I shrunk away from her. The thought frightened me. I felt my jaw tighten. "No. I can't see him again. I can't."

Her head snapped toward mine. "What do you mean, *you can't*? You aren't weak. I've seen you with Eric. And you have been resisting and breaking the bond with the Valefar boy. Unless one of us knows what caused it and what it wants, you're stuck with it. And if he's trying to protect you, there is something else at stake here. Maybe it's the prophecy. But maybe it's not."

"What else could it possibly be?" I slumped back in my chair.

"It might be the prophecy, but there is only one way to be sure," she said.

A yawn escaped me. I hadn't yawned in weeks. Suddenly my eyelids felt heavy. "Sis-er..," I said weakly reaching out to steady myself. Then the room spun, and I passed out.

My first vision filled me with horror. At first, I was surrounded by blackness. It crept in like fog before a storm. Coldness pressed into me. My body felt dreamlike, but I wasn't in my own body. I was watching *me*. When the black fog cleared, I saw myself sitting a few feet away. I watched myself. A cool breeze lifted stringy curls off my face. The moon hung low on the horizon. As I watched the vision, I looked around to take in my surroundings. There were shadows that looked like people looming beyond me in the distance. The ground was glistening red. I held a limp body across my lap. Buildings were in the distance, but I only sensed they were there. I couldn't see anything clearly that I wasn't focused on in the vision.

I watched as my sobs grew softer, as I was speaking to the guy in my lap. I cradled his head in my arms. I was unable to see his face, only a crown of dark hair. *That could be anyone.* But from the way I was reacting, I knew it wasn't just anyone. It was someone important to me. Desperate to know who it was, I called out to her, um, me, "What's wrong?"

But she didn't respond. None of them did. It was like I wasn't even there. I walked closer trying to see the young man in her arms. He was covered in his own blood, streaming from a large gash below his neck. It leaked out of his dying body in a steady stream, too fast to fix. As I neared, I could see that my hands were covered in scarlet, and there was a wound across my palm. The vision flickered as I watched my hand press to his head.

A scream, "Nooooo!" came from one of the shadows. It moved forward quickly.

I tried to see the boy's face. I had to know who lay dying in my arms, but I couldn't. Then, the darkness swirled and I was back at the old church. The musty smell of stale air filled my lungs.

Sister Al loomed over me, watching me lying on the floor. "Well, that was weird. You fell asleep." I rubbed my head, and found a dishtowel rolled up under my neck. I pulled it out and sat up slowly. Al grabbed it. "I didn't know how long you'd be out. The rest of us go into a trace when we see. None of us sleep." She put the towel in the sink and turned back to me. "Have you been sleeping?"

I shook my head and immediately wished I hadn't. The throbbing made me deaf. I held up a finger to let her know I needed a minute. Images from the dream were spinning in my head and fading fast. She spoke urgently, "Ivy, we don't have a minute. When you come out of a vision, you need to immediately write down everything you remember. Since you can't see straight, you gotta tell me. Talk girl, before it fades!"

I began to collect the scenes from the vision, but they were slippery like soap. When I tried to grasp tightly on one, it would slip out of my grip. I decided to just talk and see if that worked better. I told her what I saw, leaving nothing out.

When I finished, she said, "That's odd. No faces."

I noticed her tea wasn't on the table anymore and the kitchen was cleaned. "How long was I out?" I asked.

"About an hour," she replied.

"Really? It felt like a few minutes. That's not good." My brow furrowed.

"I'm glad you see the problem. The visions should become shorter, as you mature and learn to use this power. But, they may not. Since you are tied to the Underworld, because of the demon blood, I suspect it may be different for you. Especially since we already know that your visions result in sleep. The problem is that we can't do anything to control you falling asleep, to protect you. If a vision came on while you were in danger, there would be no way for you to escape. But, there was a warning before it came to you. Before you fell asleep. You yawned. As soon as you feel sleep pull at you, get somewhere safe. Force your body out of the vision until you are. You won't be able to do it at first, but as your powers get stronger, you will." I climbed off the floor and back up to the table. I rested my head in my hands, leaning heavily. She said, "Ivy, I doubt you're going to be anything like the rest of us. Don't mention what happened here to anyone. They will know you are different. And Ivy?"

"Hmm. Yes?" I said.

"You have to tell Eric, before he finds out another way."

My heart twisted, as my face echoed the sensation. "Sister," my voice faded to a breath, "I can't." My heart slid up my throat. The ramifications of telling him were horrible. The look of betrayal on his face would be unbearable.

The nun had a sad look on her face. "I know he finds out. I've seen it." She warned, "Control what you can, Ivy. Sometimes when things happen on their own accord, they need to. But, other times it's best if we set the events into motion. Eric will be with you and another, when it matters most. You will need *both* of them."

CHAPTER TWENTY

That night, I finished my homework, and jumped in the shower. Letting the scalding water beat down on me, I thought about what Al said. *You need both of them.* She wouldn't tell me who the other person was, but I knew that Eric had to help. If he didn't, it would be bad. While it was hard to accept Al not telling me who the other person was, I did understand her reasoning. During my Seyer lessons she revealed the importance of not telling the person who was in the vision too much information. If too much was revealed before the vision came to fruition an alternate future could happen—one no one saw. Seyers had the horrible job of choosing which visions to derail, and which to allow to progress. Right now, Al said I was too inexperienced to make those choices, but given the chance, I would derail my prophecy in a heartbeat.

As for Eric, I wanted to believe that he wouldn't destroy me. It made no sense for him to rescue me then, and slay me now. I didn't know what to think of him. I owed him my life. There was no way around it no matter how much I hated it. The debt made me feel trapped, because there was no way to repay him. It would linger forever… or until I told him what I was.

At the first crack of dawn, I got dressed. The house was still quiet. I padded down the stairs to the kitchen with a fist full of trash. Sifting through the papers, I found what I was looking for. It said CLASS TRIP on it. They were going to Albany, New York for a week to tour the state capital. A multi-hour, multi-day school trip—on a yellow school bus? No, thank you. The orange flyer crumpled in my fist, and I extended my arm over the trashcan. But, I hesitated before dropping it in.

My mom appeared behind me, and snatched it out of my hand. "What's this, Ivy?" she asked. As soon as she saw what it was she squealed, "Ivy! You can't throw this out!" She was fully dressed, and alert. She looked at me like I was nuts for not wanting to go.

The flyer was a reminder to pay for the trip so I could go—tomorrow night. The school needed the permission slip signed and returned, today. I bristled, knowing it was going to be a fight, "I don't want to go, Mom." Besides, if I left my house then I wouldn't have the wards to protect me. I couldn't go even if I wanted to, but I couldn't tell her that.

"How can you *not* want to go?" Mom asked, standing in front of me. "It's a seven day trip. And it fulfills your history assignment." She paused, hand on hip, and looked at me, "You'd really rather write a fifteen-page paper about the state of New York? Did you write it already? It's due tomorrow, if you skip the trip."

I sighed. *The paper. Crap. I forgot to write the paper.* "No, I didn't write it." Sensing that I already lost this battle, I gave in. I'd have to make sure Eric could come with me. I couldn't just disappear for a week. "Fine, I'll go. I need the money and the slip."

Mom smiled at me. Her cheeks were rosy. "You'll love this Ivy. They are going to theatre shaped like an egg. You'll get to see backstage too. I know that's only a small part of the trip, but that alone makes it worthwhile." Mom grabbed her purse, and took out some cash and a pen. She signed her perfectly scripted signature (that was impossible to forge) and crushed the cash into my hands. "Here is some extra to get yourself some snacks and souvenirs."

"Thanks Mom," I said.

Since I was officially the last student to turn in my permission slip, I had to walk it down to the office. I swung open the office door, and walked up to the counter. It was oblong, painted the unhappiest shade of yellow in existence. A honey-colored wooden swinging half-door was at the end of the counter. It held the secretaries in their pen, like zebras at the zoo. The women worked at their industrial gray desks, and ignored me. I walked over to the counter. The office was slatted in mid-morning sun as it shone through dusty metal blinds. The room smelled of musty cinder blocks and Xerox machines. I slapped my permission slip on the counter. The change in the envelope jingled, as it hit the blanched wood. I sighed, waiting to be acknowledged.

A pear shaped woman rose from her cramped desk. "Yes?" She snapped. Her fried red hair shifted as a mass. She immediately drew out her crimson claws and tapped the counter, glaring at me.

"I needed to turn in my permission slip for the class trip," I said and pushed the envelope and slip toward her.

"Kinda late to hand this in; isn't it, hun?" she scolded.

"Yeah, I was gonna write the paper instead," I mumbled.

She replied with a *humf*, and took my stuff and walked back to her computer. "You're in the system. Be here tonight by 5pm or they'll leave without you."

The day passed like all the rest. No sign of Jake. Eric was Eric. And Collin was absent. I told Eric that I'd be going on the trip, and he said he'd accompany me. He left after school to clear it with Al. At the final bell, I launched myself from my seat. I got home swiftly. Rummaging through my closet, I grabbed a few hoodies, jeans, and tee shirts.

I paused in front of the mirror. Apryl's necklace peeked out from under my shirt. Touching it, I wondered if I should take it with me. The thought made me look at Collin's ring. It had been sitting on the dresser since the night he revealed he was a Valefar. Suddenly, I wanted that ring on my finger. I didn't know what to do. The ring was on the dresser because I didn't know what to think. There was no way to tell if he was a friend or enemy. At a very basic level, he was my natural enemy. Just because he didn't act on it didn't mean he wouldn't. I hesitated. There was no time to think. I could do that on the bus, and for the next seven days. I stuffed the necklace under my shirt, and slid Collin's ring onto my finger.

It was 4:45pm. I had to haul ass to get back on time. Good thing I was a super awesome runner. I scrawled a note to my mom that I'd see her in a few days. Throwing my keys in my bag, I ran out the front door, slamming it behind me. My feet slapped the pavement in quick graceful leaps. Dappled light shone through the tree branches, as the crisp air swirled around my face. I ran across four lanes of traffic— during rush hour –managing not to get hit, which was something. *Two blocks to go.* It was 4:53pm. I shifted my duffle bag, and picked up the pace. *Almost there.* Turning toward the alley, I ran at full speed straight down it.

Five strides max and I'll be in the schoolyard. As my foot slammed into the pavement on my third stride, something struck me from the side. I let out a yelp, as my body smacked into the asphalt. I felt who it was before he spoke, because the bond snapped tightly into place on impact.

His words touched my mind with urgency. *They're tracking you. Be still.* I lay in Collin's arms, facing the brick wall. His hand was over my mouth, and the other was still wrapped around my waist. His heart was hammering. Something cold slid around my wrist and I heard a metallic *clink.* The protest died in my mouth, as I saw two guys run into the alley. They ran straight at us faster than humanly possible. Collin's arms untwisted from their protective hold around me, as he lunged at my stalkers. I pressed my body back into the brick wall, heart racing. Watching.

Collin was quicker than the attacker. Before the guy had a hold, he grabbed him and threw him into the alley wall. The second guy jumped on his back, and laced his arms around Collin's throat. He couldn't get the guy to release him. I started to step out of my hiding place, but Collin threw him off. The attacker landed in the dumpster next to me. Both of the unknown guys got to their feet quickly, acting like their injuries were no more than a stubbed toe. Maybe they were. I didn't see any blood or bruising on either of them.

Before I had time to consider it, Collin had one of the guys by the throat. "How dare you attack me!" His voice was unrecognizable, his face contorted with rage. He dropped the guy to the ground, and kicked hard. It was at that moment that I realized they were Valefar.

The attacker swallowed a scream of pain. He finally bit back, "I didn't know it was you. We were tracking someone. She came through here."

"She isn't here. Do you see her? Do you see her!" Collin yelled. The man shook his head. Collin's boot connected with stomach and the Valefar made a gurgling sound. He didn't try to get up or fight back. He lay prone on his side, as if begging for mercy. The second man stood there, saying nothing. "No one betrays me. No one attacks me! You know the penalty for such an error… " He slowly leaned down.

I was going to be sick. Did they really kiss their own kind? I couldn't watch him kill someone. I couldn't. I pushed my voice through the bond. *Collin. Don't. Please don't.*

Collin turned his face towards mine. His expression was animalistic. Enraged. His eyes were rimmed in crimson, and were pooling blood red. A shiver ran down my spine, as the bond surged through me. It was stronger than the last time I saw him. We weren't coming apart this time. I could feel it. Shoving my fear down, I stepped over the Valefar that had been chasing me, making my way to Collin. I held my hand out to him and said, "Let's go."

A jagged edged knife was in Collin's hand, lingering dangerously close to his victim. It was a brimstone-laced weapon that Eric had once mentioned. It was crude bearing a jagged edge that looked like it was bitten with pointy teeth. The edge of the blade was lined in solid black - brimstone. I walked away slowly hoping that the bond would help. And it did. The bond pulled Collin into step behind me. After a few paces, his eyes started to return to normal. A faint red ring remained, but his bloodlust eased as his breathing slowed.

He terrified me. Every urge in my body told me to run from him and never look back, but the bond wasn't the only thing holding me there. I needed to know he was alright. I had to see him again. My heart raced as we walked quietly. I forced my feet to maintain a normal pace, trying to suppress my fear. I was so going to need a shrink if I lived through this. Eric was right. I suppressed everything. I hoped that this wouldn't blow up in my face.

He cleared his throat. "They deserved to die, Ivy. They betrayed their own kind. And, I know what they were going to do to you." His face was contorted with anger.

I ignored his statement, not wanting to think about him killing them or anyone else. "Were you following me?" I asked. My heart was still racing. "And what's this?" I pointed toward the gold bracelet. It had three big rubies on it. It was really ugly.

He nodded, knowing he couldn't lie to me. "Yeah, I've been following you. And that will protect you," he gestured toward the bracelet. "Leave it." He began to pull me away from the school as he spoke.

I had no choice but to follow, as the bond tugged me along with him. Irritation shot through me. "We're stuck together, Collin. Tell me what this is. Now." I pointed to the bracelet.

"It'll hide you," he explained. "We use those to train our best fighters to track Martis. The rubies are infused with darkness—shadow. They mask the wearer, so they can't be seen. It makes the Valefar learn to rely on their other senses to track Martis." Stopping abruptly, he turned me to him. "They are looking for you. All of them. The Valefar want you, and the painting. They mean to take it by any means necessary. They think you have it."

My stomach sank. "What painting?" He looked at me, seeing the memory of the prophecy flash across my mind. He saw my hands take it, roll it tightly, and then throwing it. *Damn it.* I couldn't hide anything from him.

"I suspect you know which painting. And you have it?" Collin's eyes were completely blue. He looked sane again.

I nodded. "Why do they want it? And me?"

"Jake wants you. He suspects something. He can't be sure until he sees you. I'm not entirely sure of you either." He continued to pull me away from the school to a side street.

"Collin. Where are we going?" I asked. Worry pierced my stomach like a fishhook. I squirmed.

He pointed to a blue Spyder parked at the curb. "Car. We're not walking. And you're going on a different field trip today."

CHAPTER TWENTY-ONE

I was torn between feeling like I was kidnapped, and feeling like I was cutting school. Collin led me into a room. The bond pulled me behind him. The bond had tightened, so that we couldn't part more than a few steps. The images and shared memories intensified. When Collin remembered something it felt like I was there. The entire memory flooded me: color, taste, sound, touch, and scents. Nothing was his alone. This new development went two ways. And it scared me. There were no more secrets between us. Well, that's not quite right. There was still one. But, it was only because nothing prompted the memory, yet.

I followed Collin into a lush room dripping with rich dark colors. The walls, the floor, the desk even— they were all rich deep tones of amber, ebony, and mahogany. The carpet was that frieze shag stuff. It reminded me of a dog that licked a socket. He threw his keys down on the desk, and I slid into a chair. I asked, "So, what's going on?" I was silent on the drive to— wherever we were. It's much easier to shut up, when you can actually feel the person next to you short circuiting. Collin had driven us out east, passing by small farm towns, until we finally stopped outside a building surrounded by sod farms. It stood alone in the middle of a field. There was a spot of land behind it that rose up into a hill. It was odd to see it on the flat landscape, but there it was, covered in sod.

Collin looked at me. His shoulders slouched down, as he leaned against the desk. "They know the painting isn't on sacred ground anymore. And they suspect that something else is going on. Rumor has it that one of the Vatican blue's, an important Martis, was here not too long ago. Those folks only poke around when something big is going on. We thought it was about the painting. But that doesn't make sense. She wouldn't be here for that. She'd be irate if she knew it was missing, and she wouldn't have left. But, I'm not sure your people know it's gone. Which makes me think something else is up. Either way, it's attracting more and more Valefar to this area to find out."

I arched my eyebrow and folded my arms. Knowing he was dangerous and knowing he was Collin, was conflicting. "Why haven't you killed me? You've known what I am all along. You knew we were enemies and you let me live. Why?" My heart was pounding. I couldn't mask my rationale: *He couldn't be all bad if he didn't kill me, right?*

"No," he shook his head closing his eyes tightly. "Ivy, I'm not like you! I'm not good. I spared your life for selfish reasons." His blue gaze met mine. "Nothing more."

I felt something in the back of his mind. It wouldn't come forward, so I pressed. "What selfish stuff did you want me for?" He shifted. His confident stance became more boy-like and unsure. I wondered if he was playing me.

His blue eyes flicked up to mine. "I don't know. I just knew I wanted you around. If I took your soul, you wouldn't be around anymore."

"Why didn't you just bind me, then? You could have had me around forever." My arms folded over my chest. I tried to contain the panic that was rising in my throat.

"I could have." He walked toward me. Pulse racing, I watched him approach. His beautiful body slid down next to mine. His fingers ran down my cheek. His eyes closed, and I felt him fight for control over his flesh. His inner-demon wanted to destroy me.

But, Collin wasn't allowing it.

My voice was a whisper, "I know." I found myself leaning towards him. It felt normal, like a moment between a boy and girl, when they knew they liked each other. But we weren't a boy and a girl. We were natural enemies. I pulled back. "But you didn't. I have to know why."

He leaned away from me. The bond tightened, keeping him from moving away. "I wanted you." That was all he said with no further explanation. I had no idea what to say. I wasn't sure what he meant. He turned to look at me. "Ivy, you're the best thing that's happened to me in eight-hundred and forty-six years. Binding you would have lessened you. And I like you the way you are." He shrugged and looked away. He appeared relaxed, but the bond betrayed him. Collin's emotions swirled within him, making it difficult for him to think. I affected him that much.

"So, you won't bind me? You won't hurt me?" I asked, uncertain.

"No. But the bond is trying to force us to do the one thing that I want to do, but can't. I've never wanted a kiss so much in my life." His expression was pained. He began to pace as I relived his memories with him. "The first year I knew you, I wondered what it would be like to kiss you and hold you tight. Then death cracked you when your sister died. I could barely stand to watch it. I wanted you to come to me for comfort,

but you didn't. I watched you in the arms of others."
He shrugged acting like it didn't hurt him, but the bond
told me otherwise. "Then I found out you were blue—a
Martis—and I knew that we would be enemies. It was
too horrible to think. As a mortal, it would have been
easier to be around each other. But, when I saw you
with that skater, slipping back into old habits, I couldn't
stand it. I snapped. He had the one thing I wanted. The
one thing, I can't ever have."

His words sank into me. *Something's different about
him.* He had similarities with Jake, but he's different,
somehow. I could feel it, but I didn't know how.
"Don't think that," he warned. His gaze shot up to
mine. "I'm not safe. Never think I am. If I lose control
the way I did the other night. Damn Ivy... "

Sometimes I saw people who acted brave. To
everyone else it looked stupid. There was a fine line
between the two. I didn't know which side of the line I
was on when I walked over to him. I draped my arm
over his shoulder, and spoke from my heart. I figured
he'd see it anyway. At least this way I could be the one
to tell it. He flinched at my touch, fighting to restrain
himself. His blue eyes looked into my face as his fingers
twitched nervously at his sides.

"It wasn't that I didn't want you, then. I saw you
watching me—sink," the words were hard to force out.
They'd stayed buried in my chest, packed away from
everyone. "I felt like I was *dying.* I saw your face, and it
was like I was drifting away. And I had to. The pain of
losing someone. It broke me. I didn't want to feel it
again. I thought if I hooked up with random guys, I
wouldn't hurt as much. And it worked for a little while,
but it didn't last. The only real comfort I had then—

was you." It was quiet for a moment while my words sunk in. They felt raw. I'd never said it out loud before.

It felt oddly intimate to speak to him this way, but he meant everything to me. I couldn't lose him. I continued, "I know who I am. Even before I was marked. I'm dangerous, Collin. The people who cross my path are destined for heartache and despair. I didn't want to inflict that pain on anyone else. Especially not you." I laced my arm through his, and leaned into him. I could feel his senses warring within him. A soothing sensation came into my mind and passed through the bond, subduing his thirst for my soul.

Odd sensations licked my spine as I sat next to the boy who wanted to steal my soul. I never knew I even had one until recently. I didn't know it was mine to protect. Or share. Then I did something stupid. I acted before the thought could form in mind, knowing that if he saw it, it would never happen. But something pulled me, calling deeply within, and I had to. Looking up at his face, I leaned in and brushed my lips across his cheek in a single kiss.

The bond tightened and choked us both—then released. His heart was racing, and his senses were screaming as if he were being attacked. He turned on me. I jumped back knowing he lost control before he touched me. But I was too slow. He caught my left arm, as I watched his eyes pool crimson. Without thinking, I reacted, pulling my comb out of my hair. I slashed in a quick arc. Skin melted away where the tines scraped across his beautiful face. He jumped away from me. His hands shook and his eyes were wide.

"Ivy… " his voice trembled as he spoke my name.

I could feel the fear rise in his throat. "Don't. Nothing happened. I was stupid. I won't do it again." What the hell was wrong with me? Why did I do that? The bond was influencing me so much that I couldn't tell what thoughts and desires were my own and which were coming from the bond. My hands trembled as I pleaded, "Collin, look at me." His wide eyes took in my face. The crimson drained away leaving only the ring of fire surrounding his iris. The skin I had slashed with my comb had already healed. It was as Eric said; the only way to harm a Valefar was to pierce their heart. Collin had regained some control. Something else was consuming his attention, and it shocked him thoroughly. I could feel it through the bond. I could see it on his face.

My comb was at my side, and my hair hung over my face. I panted as my heart raced, thundering in my ears. My fingers held the silver comb tightly in my hand. Collin's hands tangled in my curls, pushing them away from my face. I sucked in sharply, as I felt his emotions flood the bond. His voice was a mournful whisper, "Oh my God. It's you." Collin stared at my forehead, clutching my hair tightly. When I started to peel his fingers free, he released me, and stepped away shaking his head. "How? How is it you? How did this happen? It couldn't have... " He shook his head, as confusion overtook him. He focused on me. I felt regret as it surged through him. "Ivy. You're the one they're looking for. They're hunting *you*." His gaze wouldn't leave my mark. He was mesmerized.

My heart raced. This piece of information seemed to change things. I wondered if I should trust him, or if he was trying to trick me—all doped up on bloodlust.

He smirked. "I do lust after you in every way possible. I just can't have you in any way possible. It royally blows." His words didn't roll off of me like false flattery. They felt real. I questioned my sanity, wondering what would become of us.

"Collin," I said. "You shouldn't say things like that to me." I turned away, wrapping my arms around my body, pulling tightly. *My mark. How did I become so careless that I showed him my mark?*

"I figured I might as well say it. You can feel it anyway." He walked up behind me, subduing his desire for me. His face turned more serious as he spoke, "Ivy, I'm sorry to be the one to tell you this, but you have demon blood flowing through your veins. It tainted your mark."

I nodded weakly, "I know."

He stepped in front of me, trying to see my eyes. "You know that you're part Valefar?"

I cringed at his words. It pierced me in a way that I didn't think was possible. I'd denied it so many times, convinced that I wouldn't be what my blood made me—a creature of darkness.

Sadly, I looked up at him and nodded. "I'm a freak. Trapped by blood, and destined to die because of it. I'm damned, Collin. I've tried to steer my path in another direction, but it doesn't seem to matter." I pulled my lips into a sad smile.

Collin watched me. "You didn't want this, did you?"

I looked at him, shocked he asked. "Who would? Did you want this? Did you want to be what you are?" He looked away from me, as the tension flowed out of his body. Memories swirled around him of a past that I'd never known.

"No," he said faintly, "I didn't want this, but I had no choice. I'm a slave. The Martis are slaves too, but you—I'm not sure if you are."

"What do you mean?" My grip loosened, as the tension started to ebb.

"The blood that binds the Valefar is demon blood. It gives us power, but it enslaved us. But you have both angel and demon blood. Are you dually ensnared? Or does the angel blood cancel out the demon blood?" I looked at him confused, unsure of what he was asking. "You can lie, right?" he asked. I nodded. "You're not supposed to. Martis can't lie—ever. Valefar have no souls, but you have one—and yet you have demon blood flowing through your veins. You're dangerous because your power is unbound, and unchecked."

"I don't have any Valefar power, Collin."

He smiled softly at my naiveté, "Yes you do. You can do anything that the rest of us can do—plus your most of your Martis stuff. I'll show you."

Shaking my head, I said, "No. I don't... I can't be like that. I don't want it."

He took a breath before speaking. I felt the weight of his words as he spoke. They were filled with regret. "Ivy, you're already cursed. Nothing will change that. If I could undo it, I would. I'd do anything for you."

I felt the blood drain from my face, as gravity threatened to pull me to the ground. I steadied myself, reaching out for a bookshelf. Accepting my fate meant that I lost. I wanted to fight it, and that meant not giving into the Valefar part of me. I couldn't lose. I had to fight. "I can't Collin. I don't want to be - this." I gestured at myself feeling disoriented. I didn't like that he could feel my emotions through the bond, but I couldn't hide them. I felt lost. Completely and utterly lost. "I can't afford to make a mistake."

He spoke urgently, taking a step closer. "But what if the mistake is ignoring part of what you are? What if the mistake is *not* knowing yourself? How can you fight to save your life, when you are denying part of you? It's not like our powers are inherently evil, Ivy. You might be able to use them differently." His words caught my attention. *They may be Valefar lies.* They had to be. His words sounded too perfect. Staring at his blue eyes I remembered that Valefar spun lies in beautifully elaborate webs. I wouldn't know that I'd been lied to until I was hopelessly ensnared. But I had to know.

My arms were folded across my chest. I took a few steps away from him and asked, "What powers do you have that would help me?"

"I won't teach you anything that will harm you." He smiled. "It's mostly little things, like this." Faster than I could blink, he was in front of me. Nose to nose, I sucked in air, shocked and took a step back. My hand covered my racing heart, trying to shrug it off.

I said, "So, you're fast? So are we. So what?"

"It's not speed." He stepped back, feeling the bond swirl around us encouraging him to touch me. He fought the sensation, and continued speaking. "I can go to any place that I've seen. I only have to picture it in my mind. I'll instantly appear there. It's called *efanotation*."

I blinked. "No, that can't be possible." Good God. No wonder why the Martis were losing.

"Why not?" he smiled. "It's magic. You and I are made of magic. We can do lots of things that aren't possible."

I thought about it. Efanotation seemed harmless enough, and not evil in itself. The idea intrigued me. "I can appear anywhere?"

The corner of his mouth tugged into a smile. "Only places you've been. You must have a specific target in mind or you risk not reaching your mark. Being caught between places isn't fun. Don't try it." He smirked, and a memory flashed showing me that he had, and that it was not fun. I shivered. Collin laughed. "Would you like to try it? You can come to me, like I did to you a second ago."

Unsure, my fingers pulled my arms tighter into my chest. "I don't know." Accepting it would mean accepting I was a Valefar. I didn't want to.

His next words baited me perfectly. He walked toward me, unblinking with his face turned down toward mine. "You would never have to worry about being attacked. Ever. You could do this, and escape. Every time." His sapphire eyes bore into me. "You would never have to live through another demon kiss again." I stiffened. My muscles tensed, twitching as they remembered the pain my mind refused to recall. Desire flowed through the bond. Although he mentioned the demon kiss to scare me, I knew he was afraid of kissing me himself. He was terrified that he would be the one to destroy me. I stared at his lips, wishing they weren't poison—wishing I could taste them.

Collin turned away sharply, clutching his head like he was in agony. "Don't," his voice was terse. "Ivy you can't. I can't… " He couldn't speak. Rage mingled with desire, as it crawled under his skin. He denied his flesh the thing it coveted more than life—my soul. His pale fingers clutched tightly, as he fought to repress the urge my thoughts provoked. The exact nature of the way Collin tortured himself to be around me flowed through the bond. There was no doubt how much I meant to him, and how hard he had to fight his instincts to make sure he didn't kill me. His body tensed. Welds of blood ran down his arms where his nails pierced his skin. His agony burned, threatening to consume him. One action would ease it all, but he refused to kiss me. He denied himself the very thing that would make his pain recede. He wouldn't kiss me.

Something in my blood ignited. There was no way I could watch Collin writhe another second. I had to do something. So, I said the only thing that I knew would subdue his agony. The idea terrified me, but I knew I had to do it. In that moment I accepted my fate—all of it. I straightened my spine, knowing what I was, and knowing I could no longer deny it. I had no choice. This was who I was—part Valefar, part Martis. I took a step toward him. My voice carried authority that was foreign to me. There was a power in my words that washed over me as I spoke, "I am Valefar. Collin, show me how to be a Valefar."

My words were like pouring boiling water on ice. His angst physically melted, as like called to like. It no longer felt like I was standing with an enemy, and the bond shifted recognizing an ally. It resonated inside of me, like something luscious and dark, seducing me silently from within. It was the part of me that I couldn't accept—the part I repressed. The part that terrified me. It was free.

Heat seared through my chest, as Collin turned to look at me. The insistent pulling of the bond remained intact, but the discomfort eased. He watched in awe as heat seared through my body from my fingers to my toes, arching my spine, leaving a warm trail in its wake. The admission transformed me, igniting my blood in a way words fail to describe. I felt stronger than I've ever felt in my life. Fear vanished as power flowed through my body, encompassing me wholly. The demon blood was awakened, making me feel invincible, as the Martis part of my being was repressed.

Oh God. What have I done?

CHAPTER TWENTY-TWO

Accepting myself in whole had changed me. It changed the bond, confusing it, though not sating its lust. It still wanted me with Collin and didn't loosen, though it was less agonizing to be so close to him. The Valefar part of me quickly honed in on something I'd never noticed before. My gaze jerked towards Collin. I could smell it all around him.

Salivating, I swallowed, and walked toward him. There was a scent in the air that reminded me of something delicious.

"What is *that*?" I asked realizing it was emanating from Collin. Looking into his face I asked, "Why do you smell like that?" I sniffed the air again, swallowing the salvia that was pouring into my mouth, awakening my hunger.

Mildly alarmed, he leaned away from me. "Smell like what?"

"You smell *delicious*." Embarrassed, I thought about it for a moment, slowly realizing what was happening. My mouth was watering like my mother was cooking my favorite meal and I hadn't eaten all day. The yeasty scent of fresh bread filled my head, accompanied by the aroma of my mom's roast turkey that was always perfectly cooked, crispy on the outside and juicy within. The cinnamon scent filled me last, reminding me of the apple pies that she only made during the holidays, and that I craved year round. I drew in a long slow breath, letting the scents fill my body and savoring them before I realized what it was. It was the expression on his face that snapped me out of it. I lost my daydream, but the scents still lingered and were strong. It was coming from him. But why? As I looked at Collin, horror poured into me, as I understood what was happening—recognizing what the Valefar blood had awakened.

I covered my mouth in horror, stepping away from him. Revulsion poured into my mouth like vomit. Turning sharply, I walked away and threw myself into a chair. I shut my eyes tightly trying to banish the sensation—the smell. But it wouldn't subside. It clung to Collin like he was food. *Oh God. What was this? What did I do?*

My voice was muffled by the pillows, but I knew he heard me. "You smell like food. Why do you smell like food?" I asked already knowing the answer. I felt the rant start to pour forth before I could stop it. "Oh God! It's because I can smell you—your soul." I shot upright in the chair, watching Collin across the dimly lit room. "You have a soul! Don't deny it, I can smell it. It smells like everything that I'd ever enjoyed eating all wrapped together." My brain started piecing things together. "You said I smelled *new*. You can smell us? Valefar can smell Martis blood. That's how you hunt us. But… that isn't what I smell on you." I sniffed the air again, and looked him in the eye knowing he could not lie to me. I would hear it through the bond. "I smell your *soul*. How do you have a soul, Collin?"

Collin leaned back onto his desk, looking at the shaggy carpet. "I don't have a soul Ivy. It's not what you're sensing." His eyes lingered on the carpet, as he tried to hide his shame and failed.

Why wouldn't he look at me? What made him feel like that? It was bad enough he smelled like a delicacy and I felt like I was starving. What else would have that scent

- the intoxicating smell of a human soul? What else would make a new Valefar react like this? It had to be a soul, but he didn't have one. So what did I smell?

"Oh God." My throat constricted as I uttered the words. Pulse pounding in my ears, I felt sick. The blood drained from my face, as ice slid into my stomach. I'd risen slowly, and stepped away from him, horrified. I knew exactly what it was. My cheeks pinched as my vision blurred with tears. I wanted to run, to run away from him and never look back. Instead my voice rasped, "That's what it is, isn't it? The remnants of your victims. How could you?" Shaking, I swallowed hard not wanting him to say what I already knew. The scent that lingered on him was the residual essence of those he'd killed, clinging to his flesh. I sucked my lips into my mouth biting down, swallowing bile before it could escape.

There was remorse in his voice, "Ivy, it's not what you think. Please listen. I don't want to be what I am. I wouldn't have done it, but to live, we have to feed. I had to. I had no choice." Collin touched my arm, shocking me out of my horror. I didn't hear him approach. His face was grief-stricken. "I thought that you knew. I don't torture people for fun—they're food. A body cannot live without a soul. It has to have something to animate it, and give it life. Valefar have no soul, so we steal others to survive. I had to." His hand was still on my arm when I felt him reach for my mind, trying to comfort me.

Repulsed, I shot away from him. Selfishness consumed me, and it wasn't the deaths of innocent people that horrified me, and it wasn't that Collin killed them - it was that I wanted them for myself. They smelled like heaven and I felt starved. Is this what it was like to be a Valefar? Shannon didn't have any clue when she told me how horrifying it would be. I couldn't control my own flesh. Desires were warring within me to do things that were despicable. Unforgivable.

The scent swirled off of Collin making me crazy. My mouth wouldn't stop watering, and I swallowed again feeling queasy. I looked at him, realizing that Collin did not appear as tense as he usually was. "How can you stand it? How can you live like this?" I wrapped my arms around my middle, and pulled tight to repress the horrors stirring in my stomach.

"I've had a long time to adapt." His face was serious, and tension lined his eyes. "Controlling the urges is the best I can hope for. I can go for weeks without feeding, but it's harder for new Valefar, which you are. Only the powerful ones can control themselves." He cleared his throat, looking uncertainly at me. I knew what he wanted to ask, but he wasn't sure if he should. His voice was faint, "Do I smell *human* to you?"

"Yes. You do. It's confusing—and unexpected. My lips want to lock onto yours to drink your soul." Taking a deep breath, I clenched my fingers, trying to restrain my body, and refusing to give in to its demands.

"I'm sorry. I know it's hard." After a moment he said, "Imagine how much harder it is to abstain when you smell a real soul, and not shadows of the dead. Ivy, I don't want to be what I am, but I can't help it. And you tempt me like nothing I've ever experienced before. There is something about you." His voice trailed off as he stepped away.

I never understood it before. I thought Valefar were evil—that they reveled in it. But seeing his face, feeling his emotions through the bond and having Valefar blood coursing through me—I finally understood.

"You're a slave..." I fully understood the implications. With my brow pinched tightly, I looked at him. The Valefar possessed my body, and I wanted to turn it off before I did something stupid. I didn't trust myself not to attack Collin, even though I *did* have a soul to suck out. I would lose my life with a mistake like that. Never mind if a human came near me now. I felt ravenous.

My voice shook as I spoke, "I want to undo this. I'll kill someone if I stay like this. Collin… " Terrified, I looked into his eyes, realizing that my natural urges would destroy both of us, "How do I undo it?"

Backing into the corner my hands slid behind me, as my back hit the wall. He walked towards me slowly. "Ivy, you don't have to kill anyone. You don't have to perform a demon kiss to live. You still have a soul. I can smell it. It's still there. Your Martis nature is still there. It's just dormant. Apparently you can't possess both traits at the same time." He studied me for a moment, feeling pained that I shared any part of his curse. "You should be able to undo it the same way— by focusing on being a Martis. But Ivy," his voice was urgent, as his hand reached for mine. He held it softly, "I can teach you how to defend yourself, but only if you stay like this for a little while. I won't let anyone else near you. I want to protect you. But, I can't do it any other way. I've tried. I was lucky I got to you in time today. The Valefar will kill you, and if the Martis discover you... Ivy," his words trailed off as his hand slid against my cheek. I couldn't help but lean into it. There was a desperate plea in his voice, "Please let me show you."

My heart raced, as his skin touched my flesh. The plea in his voice was too urgent to ignore. And the subdued state of the bond calmed him, although it confused me. Smelling souls like they were a succulent delicacy disturbed me deeply. I knew I couldn't control myself very well, and that scared me.

Collin's consciousness brushed mine softly, *Please, Ivy.*

Breathing deeply, I looked him in the eye and made the stupidest decision of my life. "Show me."

"Ivy," Collin scolded, "concentrate. Otherwise you'll split your skin from your body. You can fix it, but it hurts like hell." He grimaced.

I stared at the ruby ring Collin gave me for my birthday. Apparently Valefar liked to use rubies in their dark magic. As I stared at the blood-red stone, the edges of my vision filled with black mist and my veins burned with a garish intensity. The first time that happened I freaked out, thinking I was setting myself on fire. But Collin told me that meant that I was doing it right. If I wanted to appear next to him, I had to focus so strongly that my demon blood boiled, turning my body to mist. If I continued to think of him and only him, I would reappear next to Collin.

Efanotation hurt like hell if I did it right. I can't imagine the pain of doing it wrong.

It turns out that I felt like I was on fire, because I was. The heat coursed through my veins as I stared, imagining Collin's face in the ruby stone. I could see his cool blue eyes and long brown lashes as if he were standing in front of me. The ruby was used to hold my focus, insuring that my skin would reappear with my body. Flames engulfed me from inside, licking my stomach as the power manifested within me. I fought to keep my eyes trained on the ruby, picturing nothing but Collin's face.

When I thought I couldn't bear the pain for another second, it ceased and I found myself in Collin's lap, staring up at him. His eyes were as close as I'd imagined. A slow smile crept across his face, as he wrapped his arms around my waist, pulling me tightly. The icy hot shock was replaced with searing heat when he touched me. The intense focusing made it easier to tune out his delicious scent, so his fragrance was fainter.

I breathed deeply, proud of myself for finally getting it right. Doing it half way had been painful, and we'd been at it for hours. "I did it. Did you see? I finally did it!" I smiled at him, half blushing, as I tried to wiggle out of his lap.

His gaze made my stomach twist, as his arms held me in place. His lashes were dark and full. I stared at them to avoid looking at his mouth, not wanting to tempt either of us with things we couldn't have. "I noticed," he smiled. "That was perfect." His hands were still around my waist when his thoughts started to brush my mind. Soft caresses and lingering fingers occupied most of them. As much as he tried not to think of me like that, he couldn't—not while I was on his lap. He replaced the thoughts as quickly as they came, trying to hide them from me, but he couldn't. The bond wouldn't let us hide anything.

I leaned back into his arms, as they tightened around me. Surprise flittered through the bond, as Collin pulled me tighter into his chest. I laid against him for a moment, listening to his heartbeat. It sounded totally normal, masking the demon blood within. I breathed slowly, half remembering the last time I felt truly safe.

"Collin," I breathed, "what happened to you?" His body tensed at my words. I turned slightly, looking into his face. "How did you become a Valefar?" I didn't want his mood to come crashing down, but I wanted to know. I had to know.

CHAPTER TWENTY-THREE

There seemed to be some humanity still lurking within him. I just wanted to know who he was, half convinced it was the Collin I saw and adored.

"Ivy, the past is in the past. What's been done can't be changed. We should just leave it." He pushed me off his lap, and walked away, looking at a mahogany bookshelf that extended floor to ceiling. Old books with titles I didn't recognize lined each shelf.

I walked up behind him, sensing his sadness. "Was it that bad?" I suddenly felt heartless for asking. "Of course it was that bad. I lived through it. So did you. I'm sorry, Collin. I didn't mean to..."

"I know." He turned to me with that half smile on his face to mask his pain. "It's part of the curse, Ivy. I don't remember much of my past, only the pain of what I lost. And the pain of the conversion." His eyes flicked up to mine. "I felt the pain of your demon kiss through the bond, when I scared you the other night. I didn't mean to. Your memory of Jake's attack crossed the bond and reacted with my own nightmare—snapping it back to life."

His eyes gazed over, as his memories flashed through the bond, showing a past I couldn't imagine. Anguish flowed through me, as I saw his village stricken with poverty and illness. The cries of women and wails of men holding lifeless children in their arms flashed through the bond, illuminating the horror in my mind. While he spoke, his memories flooded me. It was like I was there, and the desperation and rawness of his situation plagued me. The pain of my attack was primarily physical, but his wasn't. I had no idea how much I asked of him until he started to relive the memory.

"I made a foolish mistake." He looked back at the wall, dragging his finger along dusty book spines. "Everyone was dying. My family. I already lost my parents and sisters. My wife and baby were infected shortly after. The illness invaded the village, killing more than war and famine combined. It didn't matter what we did, there was no way to stop it. It spread from house to house, slowly killing us. I watched my wife fade, as the disease destroyed her."

He smiled faintly, remembering characteristics he admired about her. She was strong-willed, cunning, and loyal, but the thing that drew him to her was her kindness. Turning to me he said, "She held our son, refusing to leave him when he became ill, and she got it shortly after. I couldn't blame her for trying to comfort him. I tried everything I knew of. Everyone had. And it didn't matter. Every day was the same - more of us died. The funeral pyre grew larger and larger, burning from dusk until dawn. Very few of us remained, and we did our best to comfort and provide for the sick. But it was hopeless, Ivy."

He folded his arms over his chest, mentally withdrawing, allowing the past to consume him. "One day a woman came into the village. She said that the apothecary in the next town had found a cure. She said it was even working on the little ones. The children died within days of contracting the illness. The babies were so frail then. My son was so close to death, and my wife would soon follow. I sat by unable to help ease their pain, watching them fade away. Losing them both would have been..." he paused, his eyes staring into the void.

"I took everything of value that we had, hoping it would be enough, knowing that I couldn't fail. I had to convince the apothecary to give me enough to save my family. Three of us from the village set out, following the woman that night. We were desperate, and failed to see what she really was. Her eyes glowed crimson as she led us into a Valefar den. We were stripped of our belongings, overpowered, and thrown into a pit." He looked up at me. "They used us for entertainment, Ivy. They said that the survivor would get the cure. I survived, but the reward was not as promised. Instead I had my soul ripped from my bones." He said nothing for a moment.

My eyes were brimming with tears, as I listened in horror. I didn't blink. I couldn't. Every sensation he felt flowed through me. His face was expressionless, like he was lost in a memory devoid of emotion. But I knew that wasn't true. He writhed internally, and felt so much pain that he'd gone numb from telling me.

He swallowed hard, "I killed the Valefar that made me. My rage gave me power that they lacked. The remaining Valefar of that den scattered. I went back to my village, running, hoping that I wasn't too late. I had to be there with them.

"I felt the warmth of the fire before stepping through the gate. It was constantly burning, but I still didn't expect to see what I saw. Her body was on the top of the pyre, lifeless. Our son was still clutched in her arms. His small face was gray and lifeless. I failed them. Completely. I brought no cure. I wasn't there when they died. I watched the flames consume what was left of my family. But, tears didn't come. Rage filled me instead. Before I could escape someone saw me. The orange flames illuminated his face, and as he reached to comfort me..."

Collin turned to look at me. Misery filled his chest like it was an endless chasm, and poured out of him in unrelenting waves. "I was starving, Ivy. No one told me that I had to kill to survive. No one said to be cautious or to stay away. I drained him without realizing what happened. Then I ran, destined to become the atrocity you see in front of you. "I'm a murderer. Centuries of souls were condemned to die, so I could live."

His shoulders slumped as he looked away from me, pressing his eyes closed to try and seal out the pain. When he looked back at me, his lips possessed the faint smile he wore so often—the one that masked his pain. "Demons like pain and misery, Ivy. They grant power to their slaves, phenomenal power. But, I would do anything to be free from them."

Stunned, I couldn't speak. I said nothing, staring at him, finally seeing the monster he told me he was. But I also saw the boy he was, trapped inside, suffering for eternity.

The Valefar curse was cruel, and unrelenting. Centuries had past, and I could feel the horror that flowed through his veins as if it happened yesterday. "You've never said that before, have you?" I asked.

He shook his head, turning his back to me. Shame washed over him. Weakness threatened his control, and his natural Valefar instincts flared. He closed his eyes drinking in my subdued scent, warring internally. The Valefar within him wanted my soul so badly, but he would not let his flesh concede. Collin was much stronger than me. I hadn't his control, and I couldn't have survived his losses, or accepted his fate. And yet, I was standing there with him, similar but different. I could suppress my Valefar so far that it was almost non-existent. He couldn't.

I swallowed hard, thinking he must hate me. Collin turned to me slowly answering, "Never think that. How could I possibly hate you? You are the only good thing that has happened to me in nearly a millennia. But Ivy, I must constantly fight to override my desires. Your scent is a hundred times greater than mine, because there is a live soul in your body. It blinds me at times. I'm afraid that I'll lose control - and kill you."

"You won't, Collin." I assured him, but he wouldn't listen.

"It's not like that. And now you know. I still own a tiny fraction of who I was. I fought to keep it, and it's what protects you. But the demon blood is all that flows through me, and it constantly wants to destroy you." He breathed in deeply, his saddened gaze locking with mine. "I'm teaching you how to use the Valefar's greatest strengths to protect you from your greatest enemy. Me."

Shaking my head, I walked toward him, "I don't believe you're my worst enemy. Jake is. Not you." There was no doubt in my mind.

He shook his head, and turned toward me. "No. It's me. Because you feel like you know me—you won't defend yourself the same way. If Jake attacked you, your rage will destroy him. I can feel it in you. It will protect you, but the ideals you hold up to me—they will kill you. You can't trust me, Ivy. You must always think

I might turn on you at any moment, because I might. And if I do, I won't be able to stop."

Heart pounding at his admission, I swallowed hard. I didn't want his words to be true, but I felt them resonate inside of me. It wasn't a matter of belief or will power. It was the way things were. Reluctantly, I agreed. "I believe you."

We stared at each other, saying nothing for several moments. His tormented past allowed him to understand me in a way that I didn't think was possible. He lost everything - his loved ones and his freedom. His fate was so similar to my own. I would lose everything when the prophecy came true. Knowing his pain and all he survived made me feel like I could survive whatever was ahead of me.

"Teach me what's next," I said with more conviction than I felt.

CHAPTER TWENTY-FOUR

Shaking, I rose from my seat, and said, "I could use a pizza. And a lot of soda. No diet crap. Regular Coke. Will someone deliver it all the way out here?"

Collin's eyes turned to me from his chair across the room. "It's still too early. We worked through the night and nobody's open yet." We'd worked all through the night and I still couldn't do the next thing he was trying to teach me. "I'll get you whatever you want, as soon as you get this. You have to at least pull the shadow into your hand."

My tired body slumped upside down in a chair with my head hanging upside down. My feet dangled off the back. "I can't do it. It's too hard." I clawed at my hair, beyond feeling frustrated, and righted my body. The blood flowed away from my head making me woozy. I almost fell out of the chair, but didn't. Collin smiled, leaning back into his seat. His dark hair fell across his eyes as he tried to hide his amusement. He liked my flaws for some reason. Clumsy wasn't the new sexy, so I wasn't sure what he was impressed with.

Irritated, I shoved my hair out of my face. Everything else had been so easy for me, but this wasn't. It reminded me of my failure to call light. Maybe I just sucked at all this stuff. I didn't understand how shadows would come to me. That sounded impossible; until Collin reminded me that the shadows bound me to the ground the night Jake attacked me. If I could call them, I could control them, and free myself.

I hated that I couldn't get it, but I wasn't making any progress.

"Try again," he said as he leaned forward, gazing at me.

"Fine." I pouted. I held out my hand, palm up, pressing my other hand to the ruby ring. Apparently this was the remedial way of calling shadows. I felt the sharp edge of the stone beneath my skin, and rubbed my finger slowly over it. With my mind, I reached for the nearest shadow not really understanding how I was supposed to make it move. It was attached to a lamp and melded with the bookcase shadows. Pressing my eyes tightly closed, I saw the blackness and felt the coolness fill my palm.

Collin's voice brushed my mind, *Now tell it where you need it to go. It has to obey you. Demons are not slaves to shadows.*

Opening my eyes, I gazed at my palm. A frigid sensation started to crawl up my spine and I startled, almost losing the shadow I'd been coaxing.

"That's what it feels like. Shadows are ice cold. One is responding to you. Now call it into your palm." Collin walked over to me, shivering, feeling the cold through the bond.

I nodded, trying to do what he asked. The cold enveloped me, finally licking at my throat with frost and chilling my eyes, forcing me to blink. I felt molten snow in my palm, but couldn't see anything yet. It felt as if the shadow slid through me to go where I commanded. Why did demons insist on doing things this way? Their powers were great, but they made sure pain was associated with the power. As I gazed at my palm, I saw something pooling in the center like liquid night. I held it there, asking, "Now what?"

Collin stood over my shoulder, excited that I'd gotten this far. "Hmmm. Let's do something easy first. Can you mold it? Make it change shape?"

The coldness licked my throat, grossing me out as I commanded the shadow into sphere. It floated above my palm, as I separated it into a sphere within a sphere—the thing Eric asked me to do with light. "Like that?"

He sounded excited, "Yes. Good. Good. Now shift it back to its natural form."

"What would that be? The pool of ink?"

Collin nodded, "Yes. Shadows are fluid, so they look like liquid when you call them." The sphere melted back into an inky pool. My fingers were numb. The shadows coldness was an unearthly coldness—like a creepy sensation that spreads over your skin, giving you goose bumps when you get creeped-out. It was like that, but a hundred times worse.

I held the pool, not looking away from it. "How do I get rid of it?"

"You can release it, but I want to try something else. See if you can make it affect me."

I looked up at him, startled, "You want me to hurl it at you?"

"No," he smiled, "I want you to see how much you can control it, and how much a little shadow can do. You can call larger shadows, but you need to have an idea of the strength of the one you are holding. It will allow you to judge how much you need." He paused for a moment, waiting for me to glance at him. "Ivy, attack me."

I scoffed, "Yeah, as much fun as that sounds—this is a puddle. What can it do?"

"It can do anything you want. You can't hurt me with a shadow that size. Come on. See if you can restrain me if you're too chicken for a full on attack." The corners of his mouth curved sharply up. I could feel his pulse increasing through the bond.

"I don't know." I wanted to release the shadow, but I didn't want to hurt Collin.

"You won't hurt me," he waved me toward him. "Come on. Start small. Try to restrain me. Push me away from you, and then do something creative." His eyes were sparkling.

"How do I release it? In case stuff goes screwy?" I asked, liking the idea of doing something creative.

He took a step towards me, and whispered in my ear, "You release it. Just let go, and it will retract to the thing it was originally attached to." His breath was warm. My stomach flip-flopped, as I pressed my eyes closed. Breathing deeply, I reopened them to see him step away.

Protecting my cupped hand like it was holding liquid gold, I looked at Collin wondering how to make liquid push him back. It would just slide all around him. He stood there, smiling, waiting for me to act. His blue tee shirt was untucked from his dark jeans. His leather jacket was hanging over the chair. His arms flexed, waiting for me.

Unsure, I stepped toward him so that we were nose to nose. I gazed into his eyes as I tilted the liquid out of my hand, pouring it over his hands. His wrists suddenly snapped together like they were bound by two huge magnets, as he was dragged backwards to his chair. I flicked my wrist, still holding the shadow like a piece of string and pulled hard. Collin laughed as his chair spun like a top, with his wrists still bound together in his lap. The chair spun so fast and hard that it made me sick to watch it. Smiling, I stuck my hand out to stop the violent spinning. The shadow slid back into my palm, even though I was no longer cupping it. It clung to my skin like it was my own flesh.

Collin was laughing as I kneeled in front of him. Smiling, I asked, "How'd I do?"

He tried to look up at me several times, but his eyes were flicking around the room like he was still spinning. "That was pretty good."

"So what else can I do with this?" I asked as I made the shadow slide under the hair that obstructed his eyes, and push it back so I could see his face.

"Anything you can think of. The only thing it can't do is attack another shadow." He shook his head, trying to see me. I could feel his head still spinning through the bond, and sat down quickly. He laughed.

"So, how will it help me if someone pins me the way Jake did? I mean, if the shadow can't attack the other shadow, how would I get free?"

"You'd attack your assailant. If you are both pinned, that usually stops the fight." He leaned forward. "Shadows can take on the qualities of air, liquids, or solids. They are only trapped by your imagination."

"Really?" I asked, an idea forming in my mind before I knew what I was doing.

"Yeah," Collin looked up at me his smile fading as he pieced together what I wanted to try to do. "Ivy, don't... !" He shot out of the chair, still raked by dizziness and staggered forward trying to stop me.

I held my ring hand out, the way I did when I materialized in front of Collin last night. But instead of transporting me to him, I wanted to make the shadow bring him to me.

Before he said another word, the shadow covered his body in a glistening black mist. I pulled my hand gently and Collin's body disappeared into the air, though I still felt him moving toward me. I opened my palm and the black mist poured out of my hand into the sparkling shape of Collin Smith. His body shimmered and I felt his palm solidify in my grip. He looked stunned as I smiled at him. I assumed that I was doing baby Valefar tricks, which didn't match the look of shock on his face.

"What?" I asked not liking the way he was looking at me. He took short ragged breaths and stared at me. I released the shadow, and it shrank back, taking the cold with it. Collin's hand felt warm in my grip. I squeezed it gently. "Collin, what's the matter? I thought I did good?"

He nodded, "You did, it's just that... Valefar can't do that." Stunned, he stared at me, not releasing my hand. He breathed in again, catching my scent now that the shadows receded.

"But, I just did? I don't understand." I said shaking my head. I pulled my hands to my chest, a nervous tic to subdue my pounding heart, but Collin's hand was still in mine. Instead of steadying myself, I made my pulse skyrocket. I trembled.

What was happening? Why was his touch affecting me?

His scent filled the air, making my mouth water. I closed my eyes, attempting to release his hand, but he wouldn't let go. Taking a step closer, he covered my hands with both of his hands.

His eyes shone, "If you are the Prophecy One, then you have unique powers, and abilities that I lack." He smiled at me, not breaking my gaze. "Ivy, your eyes are rimming. They're violet." He leaned his head down, as his breath washed over our tangled hands.

"Rimming? What do you mean?" I asked. I couldn't look away. I couldn't release his hand. I couldn't move. The bond felt like it glued me to him, and the sensations flooding between us were increasing. I was too dazed, enjoying it too much to realize I should be concerned.

He pressed his forehead against mine. Smiling he said, "It means you want something. Very badly." He watched me as he drank in the euphoria that surrounded us. "What are you lusting after Ivy?"

Startled by his words, I flinched. "Nothing," I lied. "I don't want anything."

Collin smiled lazily. His grip loosening as he slid his fingers down the inside of my arm. My body responded to his touch, melting as his fingers pressed the soft flesh.

"Liar," he whispered. "Our eyes rim when we can't… " suddenly Collin seemed to wake up. His spine straightened and he tried to step away from me.

Still dazed and euphoric I asked, "When we can't what?" My heart was beating slowly in loud thuds making me feel warm all over. Collin's scent filled my lungs as I took a deep breath. A foreign sensation slid within my stomach, as I stepped toward Collin, holding his face between my hands. He breathed deeply, closing his eyes. His skin seared with heat under my touch. When he opened his eyes, a ring of fire surrounded his irises. It should have meant something to me, but I felt like I was floating.

His voice was so soft, "Control. They rim when we can't control ourselves much longer."

I threaded my fingers through his hair. My thoughts felt distant, suspended by sheer bliss. But, I could still hear the internal warning that something was wrong. My body felt like it was lost in a dream. It felt warm and happy, happier than I'd ever felt. Collin's breath flowed softly across my lips, causing my pulse to race. Confidence that wasn't mine held my hands on his skin, and kept my fingers tangled in his soft hair.

Something's wrong. Collin's voice brushed the back of my mind.

I tilted my head to the side, ready to press my lips to his. The sensation of his soft flesh on mine was all I could think of, but I froze when I realized neither of us was moving.

Straightening my head, I tried to release him, but couldn't. It felt like I didn't want to, although I did. There was a reason why I wasn't with him. There was a reason we couldn't be together. As I tried to remember, my eyes locked on his lips—his perfect smooth lips.

Collin's voice broke through my mental haze, "Your eyes are almost completely violet. Tell me what you want Ivy. I'll give you anything you want." The allure of his words and the seduction in his voice enticed me further. His words made me feel seductive. Powerful. He felt it too. My mind registered a warning, but I couldn't think. It was so warm and Collin was so close. His eyes drank me in a way that felt sensual, like he desired me in every way possible. My breath caught in my throat as our lips lingered dangerously close. *If I could taste his lips, I'd die happy.*

Something in the back of my mind awoke with the thought. It began to break through the haze. My pulse quickened, as if my body were fighting for its life. The thought resonated with something deep inside of me—an instinct. Words tumbled out of my mouth, whispered so close to his lips. "I'm not Valefar." The words penetrated the haze. I snapped out of it, realizing where my thoughts where. I was about to kiss him. "I'm not Valefar!" I cried. "I'm Martis and I can't! We can't! Collin, don't!"

I yelled trying to push him away. My heart thundered in my chest as I realized what was happening. His eyes were pooling crimson. My heart lurched, as I tried to wiggle out of his grip. "Collin, you have to let go of me. We can't do this. You don't want to do this." I managed to pull my wrist away, but he was still lost in lust.

His crimson eyes raked my body. His movements were jerky, like he was trying to control his body, but it wouldn't let him. The bond was a jumbled mess, part Valefar, part Martis. I couldn't catch his scent anymore, which meant mine was much more potent. I wondered if I could call shadows as a Martis. I tried, but they didn't respond. I needed to figure out how to possess both at the same time, but now wasn't the time to learn. Focusing intently, I realized the bond wouldn't break as a Martis. I shifted my focus back to Valefar to subdue my Martis scent. Heat surged through me, and I fought back the lust that claimed me before.

Collin's eyes saw me, but were still rimmed in red. I called the shadow back to me, and made it cover my body, hoping that it would seal in my scent and allow Collin to regain his composure. The shadow covered my body like a sheet of ice. It was disgusting, and felt like corpse fingers were stroking my flesh. But, I held the shadow in place and it sealed in my soul.

Collin closed his eyes hard, and stepped away from me. Clutching his head between his hands he asked, "What happened?"

CHAPTER TWENTY-FIVE

I was looking at my shimmering body, holding my arm in front of my eyes, when I answered. "I don't know. We were talking, and then things got weird. Are you all right?"

He nodded, and turned to look at me. His eyebrow shot up as he cringed. "What is that?"

Proud of myself, I said, "It's an Ivy suit. It seals in my wholesome goodness so you won't try to eat me. I feel like I'm wearing dead people though, so I'd really like to take it off as soon as you can stand there and not eat me."

Collin nodded, turning away. His eyes were still rimmed in fire. He leaned against the bookshelf, looking at the floor. "We have to break the bond."

"But I told you already," I couldn't believe I was saying this. Again. "I didn't do this to us. I can't break the bond. I didn't make it."

The door crashed opened with a loud crack. I startled, backing away as three guys walked in. One was Jake. They didn't see me. I backed away faster, wishing I could shrink into the shadow and disappear as my heart lurched into my throat, gagging me. Collin's voice brushed inside my mind, *He can't see you.* The shadows that formed my Ivy suit held in my scent, and my body was hidden by the massive bookcase. I didn't move.

"We looked everywhere for her, but she's gone. It's the same as last time. And there is no sign of the painting. Are you sure...?" Jakes words were cut off. I watched in wide-eyed horror as Collin addressed him.

"I am. Keep looking for the girl. It's *not* like last time—at all. Continue the search." He glared at them. "Leave." The three quickly left and closed the door. The roar of my pulse thundered in my ears. I shrank into the corner, as far from Collin as I could get. Collin was authoritative. It almost seemed like they were making a report.

The truth crashed into me. "You're their leader!?"

Collin didn't deny it. He nodded sadly. "You see the mess we're in? You weren't supposed to be wrapped up in a girl I wanted to keep." He shook his head.

"Yeah," I said. "So, you sent them to look for me?"

"I had to. When you got away from Jake, he thought there was something about you—something different. He was right. It just wasn't what I expected." His fingers pushed his silky hair out of his eyes.

"What'd you expect?" I folded my arms.

"I don't know. Just—not this. Ivy, I thought you were Martis. I had no idea you were the girl in the prophecy." His hand gestured at me.

"So, what do we do?" I shifted as I stared at him, wondering if the past twenty-four hours had been filled with lies, a complex plot to ensnare me and steal my power. He said nothing, rubbing his head in his hands. When he looked up at me, his eyes were impossibly blue. He didn't accept what he was. Just like me.

Walking toward him, I said, "Something inside of me is—it's wrong. It doesn't fit. That same odd piece, it's inside of you, too. I can feel it." He said nothing. His eyes tracked my movements in a wolf-like manner. I started to walk over, ready to push the point, when fatigue pulled at me. I pushed it down, but a yawn escaped my mouth. I uttered, "Collin, help me… " as I crashed onto the carpet.

This vision was as sucky as the first. The black mist swirled, reminding me of the shadows I conjured. Three figures came into focus. I emerged from the mist and moved toward them. The three were in a frantic discussion. They stood outside a stone building. It was night. As I watched myself in the vision it was clear that I was only concerned with the two people in front of me.

"We need six," a familiar voice said. "It's suicide with less than six to hold the circle. Even so, someone has to seal the portal."

The other slim figure nodded. "He's right. It has to be six."

In the vision, I was covered in sweat, despite the chilled air. There was a gash on my cheek, and I paced in place. My hair was pulled tightly into a frizzed out ponytail, and I looked like I'd been rolling in dirt. Nervously, I shot looks at my two advisors. Julia and Eric.

I watched as the vision version of me asked, "What happens if we do nothing?"

"Then they come," Eric said, as the wind howled louder. They were standing in the center of a storm that hadn't formed yet. The pressure was uncomfortable. It kept shifting, making my head ache.

"And the terror begins," Julia raised her voice, "and there'll be no way to stop it."

"And if we try without six?" I asked.

Julia yelled over the howling wind, "It doesn't matter anyway. We need six to hold the circle, but there is no way to seal the portal. We don't have what we need." Her words unnerved my resolve. Seeing fear flash in the eyes of a totally confident woman made my stomach sink. Wind whipped through the clearing. I could almost see where we were, but I couldn't make it out.

Al said as I matured that I could force the visions to reveal the information I wanted, but right now, the vision wasn't cooperating. I didn't know what had us outside during a wicked storm, where we were, or why things felt so dire. I tried to focus on the blurred area behind where I was standing, seeking some distinguishing landscape, building, or something. But there was nothing there. The blur wouldn't lift. The main thing I noticed was that the longer I was in the vision, the more panic I absorbed from the people around me. Suddenly, I was ripped from the vision, as cold slid over my skin.

I sat up dripping. I sucked in air, shocked. "What the hell!"

Collin stood over me with a huge empty cup in his hand. Kneeling next to me, he said, "I couldn't wake you. I tried." His breath was choppy. Brown hair stuck to his pale face. "What happened? What was that?"

I pulled at my wet shirt and glared at him. "I'm a Seyer, Collin! You pulled me out of a vision!" I stood up, and smashed my fist into the wall, desperately fighting the urge to freak out. "I needed to see the end! Now I just saw a world of crap being thrown on me—without the ending."

"I wouldn't have wakened you. It looked like death tried to claim you, again. I'm sorry."

Again? What did that mean? I shook my head, sopping wet, all the fight drained from me when I saw the terror on his face. "It's fine. You didn't know. Apparently I can't see the future without fainting." My fingers frantically pushed my hair out of my face. I sat down hard on the floor.

Collin sat next to me. "What'd you see?" I told him. But I still didn't know what was coming. Or how to stop it. "Six is a doomsday number. The portal gets opened. Huh?" Collin's expression was odd.

"Spill," I insisted. "What are you talking about?"

"If you're doing something really big, you need six people to form a circle. Everyone always thought that you—the prophecy chick—would rule the Underworld from below, not above. Maybe you called them up here?" His eyes were wide as he looked at me. "That would suck."

"Collin, I didn't call them." I shook my head. "Well, I don't know who called them. I just know something was happening. What makes you think the Underworld was called up here?"

He shrugged, "It's part of the prophecy. Probably not a part you heard. When the purple one rises to power, she kills me, and rises up the Valefar. Apparently, that's literal. You call them *up* here." His uncertain gaze was lingering on me, and the expression on his face told me that he didn't totally trust me.

"Don't look at me like that! I'm not going to kill you. Damn it! How does this happen?" I held my head in my hands. Panic wove tightly through my muscles, landing in my stomach. I wanted to run away, and leave this nightmare behind, but I couldn't. I was trapped. Breathing deeply, I tried to steady myself. I couldn't fall apart. I swallowed, asking a question I didn't want answered, "What did I do, Collin? I had to do it, right?"

His blue gaze held mine. "The prophecy says you *will*—it doesn't say you *want to*." His words hung in the air.

"Damn." There was nothing else to say.

Collin's ideas about destiny didn't mesh with Al's. If it didn't matter what I did, then the prophecy would just come true. But, she said visions showed paths, so I should be able to change it by choosing another path. I just needed to know how and when. Al had more details that she didn't tell me. If she gave me the information, I could derail my future. I had to try.

I jumped up. "Get up, Collin. I have to go talk to a nun."

CHAPTER TWENTY-SIX

I pushed Collin within inches of his sanity to snap the bond. As soon as I felt the bond slacken, I launched my body through its hold. Pain shot through me. It felt like bone was ripped out of my skin in one big chunk. I screamed. Breaking the bond left me breathless, and writhing in pain. I knew I had to get to my feet and run before Collin's animal instinct to kill anything that hurt him woke up.

I ran before he came after me. But, I wasn't stupid enough to think I was safe. My feet beat the ground. My lungs sucked in air, aching. I didn't stop. I focused on the ruby and saw the church building in my mind— its dreary brick façade, and the trees that faded into the distance behind it. I imagined it from across the street. I felt my blood boil as heat surged through me. *Efanotation sucks.* My body felt like it was on fire and disappeared into the air. I had no idea how far I was from the church, but it felt like forever. The burning didn't stop. I wanted to cry out, but had no breath to scream. The fire licked my stomach, searing my insides. When I wished I would die, the mist dropped me on my knees in front of the church.

I clung to the grass, coughing as my body protested being hurled through space and burned. I fought the urge to lie down on the cool ground, and pushed myself up. My thoughts raced. I had to get to Al. I needed to know what was happening. Pain shrieked from my shins, and stabbed at my ribs when I moved. I was almost there, but transporting my body had weakened me. I was safe though. I'd made it to the church, one of my safe spots.

A wave of relief flooded over me. It ended as an ear-piercing scream echoed behind me. Spinning on my foot, I saw Eric remove a silver sword from the chest of a man with a red scar above his right brow. The sword flashed in the light, slicing through his throat. The night was quiet again. The ground around him was glistening scarlet.

My hand covered my mouth, as I fell to the lawn. The man's blood and his entire body turned to thick black goo. It looked like tar mixed with molasses. It sunk and was reclaimed by the earth. My body reacted without my consent. I dry heaved onto the lawn. Eric grabbed my underarms, dragging me toward the church. He was talking to me, but I couldn't hear him. Nothing registered. I don't know why it shocked me, but at the moment being around Eric was the worst thing I could imagine. He angled my uncooperative body through the door, and sat me on the nearest pew.

"Ivy. Ivy!" his voice crashed through my haze. "What happened? Where were you?" I sat there mute, wiping my mouth. The death of the Valefar danced before my eyes. Suddenly, I realized that was also my fate. No, wait. My fate was worse. I felt myself blanch. My head felt light, as it swayed with unseeing eyes.

Eric's warm hand was on my neck before I fell. He forced my head down between my knees. Warmth flooded my skull. The pounding of my heart thundered in my ears. His gentle voice said, "Breathe. Just breathe." His hand remained firmly on my back, waiting for me to pull it together. "Ivy, what happened to you?" Eric whirled in front of me and lowered himself to his knees. "I swore I'd protect you, and I will. Tell me what happened."

My long hair fell forward. It obscured my face. My throat stung. "I have to tell you something. It's not good." My heart hammered. I fought to control my voice. "Do you trust me, Eric?"

He recoiled. "Of course. I just risked my life for you. I'd do it again." His hand was on my forearm. He gave me a gentle reassuring squeeze.

"You mean that? It's not just because I'm a Martis?" I asked.

He sounded offended. "Of course not. Ivy, I'm your friend. I was your friend before you were blue."

"Sometimes people can't be friends. Sometimes they're just on the wrong side of the line. Sometimes they can't help it." I swallowed, hoping he'd see where I was going, "Sometimes blue is just a color."

He looked at me like I hit my head too many times, "What are you talking about?"

"I can't lie to you anymore," I breathed. My heart raced and my muscles tensed. I felt sick.

"Lie..?" he asked. "Martis can't... " Shaky fingers pulled the long silver tines from my hair. I sat back in the pew with the comb on my lap. My curls fell away from my face. My bangs hung in tight, wet ringlets, revealing my purple mark.

His sword was loosely gripped, as his jaw fell open in shock. He backed away from me, appalled. I breathed softly, "I know you're looking for me. I tried to tell you before, but... " My pulse raced. I could taste the salt on my skin when I licked my dry lips.

His gaze was wide, as he stared unbelievingly at my mark. "It can't be you..."

"It is." I swallowed hard, "I didn't ask for this. I don't want it. It *happened* to me. I don't even know why. The only thing I know is what I saw in my visions." I tentatively reached my hand out, but he backed away. I stood, giving him more space. "I need *you*. None of this stops unless you help me. Killing me doesn't change things either. The demons still come. Soon. I saw it." I placed the comb into my jean pocket. I wouldn't hide who I was, and I wouldn't fight him.

Eric's face was white. His fingers twitched on the hilt of his sword. Anger seared his words. "I've been tracking the purple demon—the Prophecy One—for nearly two millennia. She's supposed to become ruler of the Underworld. How did you… ?" His muscles tensed. "How is it *you*?" Betrayal burned behind his eyes.

I shrugged. "I don't know. Shannon thinks I swallowed demon blood the night I was attacked, but I don't remember. I didn't do it on purpose, and I can't change what's already happened. Eric, the visions I saw… "

"They match Al's?" His brow pinched.

I nodded, "They were the same vision. The demons are coming here. The only way we stop them is with *you*." He breathed in deeply. His eyes shifted from my face and then to my mark. His hand rested on his sword.

"What are you supposed to bind me with?" It was a morbid question, but I wanted to know what he was thinking. The silence was killing me. I was tired of hearing my heart thundering in my ears, waiting to die. Al was right. I should control what I can. If he planned on killing me, I had to know.

His gaze snapped to attention. "You knew I was hunting you? This whole time?"

I nodded stepping toward him. "Yes. I freaked out with good reason. I know you're the Seeker—the Regent Polomotis. I know you were working with Julia and Al to try and find me. I know what you're supposed to do when you find me, too. I heard Julia. I heard *you*."

He shook his head and stared at me. His brow was pinched tightly. "How is it *you*? The prophecy—it was supposed to be someone inherently evil. You were supposed to be a demon."

"Yeah, I'm not." I rubbed my arms, trying to calm myself, swallowing hard.

"I can see that. But still. You can *lie*. You lied to me this whole time. How can I believe you?" And that was it—the moment I'd been dreading. The look of betrayal infused his entire face with disgust. But the worst part was his eyes; his amber eyes were wounded, disappointed, and disgusted. I swallowed the lump in my throat. I had nothing to say. There was absolutely no reason why he should believe me. None at all. I lied to him this entire time—about everything. Ashamed, I couldn't bear to look at him anymore and turned away.

That's when Al spoke from the shadows, "Because I say you can." Her voice echoed through the hall.

Eric spun around to see her. His jaw dropped in surprise. "Sister, you knew?"

An odd smirk crossed her lips. "Of course, boy. I'm a Seyer. I saw what she was as soon as you brought her here. Thank God she told you. Now don't mess it up and kill her." Her candor was awesome. If she was afraid, I couldn't hear it. She continued, "If you do, the prophecy happens anyway. What's been done can't be changed. She's the catalyst, but she's also the key."

"But she's the enemy!" His face contorted with rage, as his finger flew up to point at me. "She's the force that rapes the world of good and ushers in a demonic age. Humanity will be enslaved. We'll lose. Sister, I can't... " Eric's words were cut off.

Her old voice barked. "Think boy! Don't let the laws cloud your brain. If things have already been let loose, then what happens if you kill the gatekeeper?"

His lips pressed tightly into a straight line, as his jaw locked. He stared at me with burning hatred. I wanted to die. Seeing him look at me like that was more horrible than I'd imagined. It took every ounce of strength to stay, and be ruthlessly judged by someone who was my friend—but was now clearly my enemy. His amber gaze burned holes in me, but I wouldn't look away.

His voice was gruff, "We can't close the gate." The words came out grudgingly.

Al said, "That's right. Now if you want to be an idiot and make the prophecy come true, kill us both. If you want to stop this—let us live."

I finally spoke, "Al, you can't... "

Her old bark cut off the rest of my words as she turned to me, "I can so. I said I'd protect you, and I have to, otherwise everything I've worked to prevent happens. It *happens* Eric." She turned her haggard body back to him, shaking her head. "I can't let it happen, no matter the cost. If you kill Ivy, you'll have to go through me first."

Eric eyes were wide as he looked at Sister Al. His hand gripped his hilt so tightly that his fingers turned white. For a long moment Eric said nothing. Then he pressed his sword to his mark. It became the cross I'd seen hanging around his neck at the diner. Grudgingly he said, "Sister, I respect your vision and will do as you ask. Ivy. Come with me."

I reached for the comb slowly, unlacing it from my hair. My curls tumbled forward. I sat down on Eric's couch. I held the cold silver in my hand. He dragged me across town, not telling me where we were going or why. His gaze rested on my mark. I knew that he didn't trust me. "Touch it to your mark." I pressed the silver filigree against my mark, and then lowered it. Eric's gaze shifted to the silver. He told me that celestial silver would melt to a weapon that suited its owner. He wasn't sure what mine would do since I had a ravaged soul and was part Valefar. But whatever he thought would happen, it must have been worth the risk of removing me from the church.

We watched as the intricate ivy on the comb became larger. It grew down and embedded into the silver. The tines increased in size. The ivy pattern shifted to look like it was etched into the silver. The tines became razor sharp as they grew. They curved like the blade of a reaper. The butterfly melted into a hilt wrapped in purple leather. It looked like a big sharp pitchfork. A single hysterical giggle escaped me. Eric's eyes were narrow, as he watched the comb turn into a really big comb.

I felt gypped. "I thought it was supposed to turn into something useful? This is just a bigger comb."

"Don't question the shape of your weapon," he scolded. "It chose you. And it chose that shape for some reason. You will need it to survive." He moved around the apartment like he was sitting with a demon.

"Eric… " I began.

But he stopped me, "I'm not talking about it Ivy. Al said you needed to know this—or we lose. I believe her. She can't lie. So I'll show you. That's it." He folded his arms and regarded me coldly. "You're on your own after that."

"Whatever," I sulked back into the couch.

Eric moved through the room like he was looking for something. But, if he was, he didn't tell me. His fingers finally scraped along the wall, and pulled a wooden panel forward. It looked like the rest of the wall, but it was hollow. When the panel opened, a book raised out of the space. It slid into his hand.

He walked over, with the book open, thrusting it into my hands. "This is what you do." He hated me. I snapped the old thing away from him and looked at the pages. The book was so old that the spine barely held the pages intact. It was a handwritten book, older than any book I'd ever seen.

"What is this?" I asked.

Narrow eyes stared at me before answering, "Just look at it."

I sighed, my eyes scanning the page, unsure of what I was looking at. There were words I couldn't read, in letters that were foreign to me. Drawings lined the edge of the page—not pretty ones meant to enhance the contents. No, they were more like technical drawings. One was a circle; the other was a building with no windows that was surrounded by tombstones. The drawing that made my stomach lurch showed layers on top of layers with a demon at the bottom of a pit.

Something inside me reacted to the images, knowing I propelled them into motion, but not knowing how. I turned the page and recognized a drawing before Eric snatched the book out of my hands. It was the pendant on my necklace—on Apryl's necklace. But I couldn't read the words around it. Why was it in his book? I didn't have time to ponder what I'd seen.

Eric yelled, "Do you see! This happens because of *you*. Centuries of notes, studying what would prevent you from doing this, and it was all for nothing!" He bit his lip and hurled the book down on the table in front of me. It landed with a loud thud, and I flinched.

My eyes narrowed, as I stared at him, hating the person I saw. He was the ruthless warrior. The one Shannon warned me about. The fact that Eric could act like this pissed me off. It made everything we shared meaningless. Even if I was the one who laced our relationship with lies, I did it because I had to. He didn't have to do this now. He didn't have to hate me so much.

I sneered at him, as the words slid out of my mouth, "I knew you were full of crap."

"Me?" he sounded incredulous. His hands flew to his chest, as his fingers pressed down. "You think I'm the problem here?"

"Damn straight." I nodded and jumped up, walking toward him. He backed away, avoiding contact. Anger surged through me. "Like that. What the hell was that? We use to spar, wrestle, and be normal—but not now. Now that you know what I am."

Rage painted his face red, as he fought to control himself. "You didn't tell me what you were! I would have never… "

I cut him off, "Yeah, I know. You would have never done any of that if you'd known. Damn it, Eric. I'm not bad!" The fight went out of my voice as I looked up at him. I couldn't take the venom in his voice and the pain in his eyes. "I didn't *choose* this. I don't even know why it happened." I whispered, "Why can't I just be Ivy?"

He shook his head. "Because, you'll never *just be Ivy*. You'll always be the one who damns us all; the one who destroys everything good. Everything I protect. Everything I've worked to keep safe." He turned away from me, running his fingers through his hair. "I can't forgive that."

His condemnation pissed me off. "But I didn't do anything! I swear to God! I don't want demons here. I don't want any of this!"

He shrugged. "It doesn't matter. It's already done."

I watched him shrug, like I didn't matter. Like none of this mattered. He'd already written me off. Anger boiled in my mind, and made my body tense. "What a bunch of shit." He flinched. "Stop acting all pious. You're full of crap! You act like you care, and if you really cared about making sure this doesn't happen, you wouldn't give up on me." My brows pinched tight, as I felt my muscles twitching ready to fight.

He folded his arms into his chest. "I didn't give up on you. It's not like that. You have demon blood. You're one of *them*. There is no help for you." Disgusted I turned away. What could I say to that? There was no in the middle for him, even though I was trapped there. "I'm going to teach you how to use your weapon. I waited too long, assuming you were normal. The silver can make Martis bleed if it hits us, but it can't kill us."

He showed me how to use my comb. It was basically a multi blade knife. The tines curved, which he told me would help rip open flesh. Ewe. He spoke to me with a frigid tone and unsmiling glare.

When I couldn't stand it anymore, I turned to him and threw my arms up. "I was right."

He straightened obviously ready to fight with me again. "No. You weren't. Things changed." He held his sword loosely in his hand. It was the only clue that he might still trust me - a little.

"It shouldn't matter! I told you. I knew you'd turn on me! You swore that you wouldn't. And here we are." His amber eyes were intense. He walked slowly toward me. His jaw locked tight, and the vein in his temple was throbbing.

"We're enemies Ivy. It's the way it is. I can't protect you. My previous promise is void. No matter what I want."

CHAPTER TWENTY-SEVEN

I looked up at him, gnashing my teeth. "What do you want? Cause it seems like you want me dead, but you can't hold your hilt tight enough to do it." I took in a breath. My anger faded. I looked up at him, not wanting to fight, and wishing I could undo everything. If I could go back to the night Jake attacked me and Eric saved me… oh God. I'd rather die than live through this again. Sadness covered my face. I didn't try to hide it from him. My voice was soft, "I didn't want this."

His face softened for the first time, since I told him my secret. His mouth opened, but I never got to hear what he was going to say. The glass windows shattered, pouring into the room like a crystal carpet. I screamed as it seemed like everything played out in slow motion. Jake's body passed through the flying shards. I sprung backward. Jake came at me quickly. Blood ran down my cheek. I smeared it away, as my body tensed. I touched my comb to my mark, extending its tines.

"Give her to me and you won't die tonight," Jake breathed heavily. Eric answered him with his sword.

Four more Valefar poured into the room. They swarmed Eric. Jake refocused his attention on me. A sadistic smile spread across his face. I darted across the room, heading for the door. My body lunged for the knob. I turned back to the room slashing. Jake jumped back. Pulling the door opened, I swiped the silver in front of me. My blades cut through two more Valefar. They crumpled onto the carpet. I wounded them enough to slow them down, but I didn't give the deathblow. I couldn't. I darted into the hallway, with Jake right behind me. I could hear Eric's voice spill out into the hallway, but I couldn't make out his words. I backed down the hall, keeping the curved blades in front of me.

Jake's face was contorted, as he snarled, "Ivy, you bitch! Do you have any idea what you've cost me?"

"Cost you! Are you insane?! Cost *you*?" I yelled. Hatred spewed out from me. I suddenly didn't care if I lived or died. The urge to kill Jake was too strong. I couldn't control it. I ran at him. The sharp tines slashed through the air. I wanted to feel the bite of my blades move across his flesh—to feel the sensation of his body ripping open. The feeling consumed me. And I let it.

Jake paused, then withdrew his attack before I could pin him to the wall. Backing down the hall, he twirled the brimstone chains in front of me. It kept him just out of reach of my blade. He jumped down a flight of stairs, and looked up at me. He didn't think I would follow him. He was wrong.

As my feet sprung off the ground a body collided with mine, and I fell to the floor. I turned growling. My hand slashed the creature that downed me. The silver pierced his flesh. Fury blinded me until it was too late. The curved blades ripped into Eric's chest. He fell back. Scarlet poured out of the sliced skin. Clutching his chest, he dragged me away from the stairwell, moving stiffly.

"There are more of them down there," Eric said, "He was baiting you." He walked into his apartment and clutched the counter. I stared at him. All that crap about how he wouldn't protect me. I never thought he'd try to save me again. And I'd slashed him!

"Eric. I'm... I thought you were one of them." I tried to help him, but he held up his hand, waiving me away. I stayed back.

Shannon was moving quickly through the room. "Shannon?" I asked, dazed. When did she get here? I couldn't take my eyes off of Eric. She moved around me shifting through the debris looking for something, "Al told me what happened. Listen, we have to get out of here. Now. There will be more coming."

My focus fell on several patches of black goo smeared on the carpet. My stomach twisted. Shannon pushed her hands through a pile of wreckage and pulled out Eric's book. She dragged me out the door. Eric followed. I could hear movement below, but the only Valefar left alive was Jake. He wasn't stupid enough to come after me with two Martis at my side.

We went up the fire stairs to the roof. Shannon kicked open the door. Crisp night air hit my face. The wind bit my tear-stained skin. I didn't remember crying, but my face was wet. We ran down the rooftop of the building. Fear clutched me so violently that I wanted to use my ring and turn to mist. I could leave them behind. I could evade Jake and the rest of the Valefar. Then it occurred to me that he might be doing the same thing. I was the only Martis who realized what they could do. Shannon urged us onto the other buildings. They connected to the apartments. We went to the end of the block. She went down the fire escape. Her eyes shifted over the area.

"Keep moving," Eric's voice came from behind me. His hand pressed my back. I pressed myself forward. I decided to stay with them. I had to. Eric saved me. Again. Damn it! The wind cut into my burning face. We emerged in front of a darkened church. Shannon opened a door. We didn't stop until we reached a kitchen in the back of the building. Shannon ignored Eric's wounds. He opened a few drawers, until he found a dishtowel. He held it under a faucet, and then pressed it under his shirt.

"Say something to me." I looked up at him. "I didn't know it was you. I wouldn't have… "

Eric said nothing. He removed his flannel, tossing the stained shirt into the giant garbage pail. I stared at his smooth chest. There were faint red lines where the tines slashed his skin. "I'm fine." His jaw was locked, and his muscles were tense. Barely breathing, I reached for him with my fingers outstretched. I ran my fingertip over a red welt. He closed his eyes at the touch. Eric remained perfectly still.

I stuttered, "How? How did this heal so fast?" I stared unblinking, not believing what I saw or felt.

His face regained its hardness. His fingers wrapped around my wrists, and gently removed my hands. "Celestial silver can't kill us. Everything heals. It's demobilizing, not deadly."

I stared at him. I didn't move. "I didn't know it was you." I wanted him to believe me.

"You said that."

I took in a deep breath, "I'm sorry. And… Thank you." He nodded. *Crap*. There was no way to fix things between us now. Shannon moved to the door. She was ready to shove us out.

I asked, "Where are we going? I thought they couldn't come into the church. Why are we leaving?"

"Throw them off," Shannon answered. "They'll stake out the church as long as they don't see us leave. Eric's blood will make them think we stayed in the building. And they can't come in to find us. It should give us a head start." She knew the Valefar could smell their blood. I knew she was right. That bloodstained shirt would smell like a buffet to them.

"Unless they split up. So let's move," Eric put his hand on my back, pressing me out the door, and into the night.

I followed Shannon blindly through a maze of streets as we ran away from the building. Eric was on my heels. We ran for long spurts. Then crept whenever they heard something. My lungs burned. The cold night nipped at me. As we crossed into the woods, I felt it. It came on fast. Raising my hand, I tried to call out, but the vision engulfed me. I never felt my body hit the dirt.

The vision began. Black silk flowed from my body, cascading into a ball gown. The skirt was larger than anything I'd ever worn, yet it was light. The bodice was lined with tiny diamonds that shimmered in the dim light. The fabric on the silky skirt flowed lightly through the air as my ethereal body moved through the room. I felt weightless, as I floated across a room toward a chair. The air crested under my feet, never allowing me to touch the floor.

The room was empty at first. Then it began to fill. They were things I thought were pretty, but never had any ambition to own. They were fine golden rugs woven with intricate detail. Vases formed from the darkness. The sweet scent of Star-Gazer lilies filled my senses. I inhaled deeply.   I lowered myself onto an intricately carved chair. My back rested against silk cushions. Ivory steps flowed in front of me. They cascaded away, and spilled into the room. The pale marble met with black and gold starbursts. It was a throne room.

The thought jolted me. I stood, looking around the room again. It was filled with more riches. Piles of gold and silver emerged from shadow. Gemstones glittered in vivid colors on the piles of wealth. My feet felt like lead. My heart felt cold and numb. I was alone. I stepped off the dais and onto the glassy floor. My feet did not touch it. The wind carried my footfalls across the room. A windowpane appeared in front of me. I rested my hands on the cool sill, and gazed out.

Expecting to see green pastures, I recoiled. My hands covered my mouth, as I swallowed my scream. Darkness surrounded the land. There was almost no trace of light. Twisted dark forms toiled in shadows. Demons were slaving below. Flames licked their charred skin. I was in the Underworld.

Jagged cliffs rose and fell, making the land look equally ruthless. But the worst horror was under my window. Three marred forms impaled on stakes were long dead. The demons deposited gifts at their feet. Unable to tolerate what my eyes revealed, I looked away. Tears wanted to fall down my cheeks, but I didn't cry. I didn't shake or sob. The numbness soon overcame my fear. I had to see the three stakes, again, to be certain. The first held the remains of a man. Tatters of clothing clung to his bones. A silver sword pierced the ground at his feet. My chest lurched as I recognized the intricate design on the hilt. That was Eric's sword.

Horrified, my eyes took in the second body—a woman. Patches of long golden brown hair still dangled from her head. A silver dagger, just like Shannon had, was lodged into her chest. The third form was male. I looked for the silver that would clue me in to who the third person was, but found none. My eyes finally landed on the skeleton's clenched fingers. Something dangled in his bony grip.

I stared down, too numb to cry, and too shaken to move. My hand instinctively touched my ring finger, but my ring was gone. Where was Collin's ring? I couldn't imagine talking it off. Instinctively, my hand reached out the window. I wanted what was in the skeleton's hand. I had to see it. A sensation tickled my palm. The dark air swirled in that spot. I extended my arm and the wind left my hand. The currents changed into a crow. Its feathers emerged from darkness, gleaming deep purple. The crow flew to the skeleton. Its beak pierced the bony hand, before flying back to me. The creature landed in front of me on the sill, and dropped its treasure with a squawk. It flew into the darkness, and was absorbed into the night.

My fingers wrapped around the metal, lifting it to the light. I didn't breathe. I didn't blink. My fingers scraped across the square blood red stone of the ruby ring Collin gave me. A scream died in my throat, as I recognized the final corpse as Collin. I staggered back across the room. My body collapsed into the throne. Panic was lacing my thoughts. My heart thundered. *It couldn't be them. There was no way.*

My head shot up as two demons skulked into the room. Their posture was bent so that their upper bodies almost scraped the floor when they walked.

Their angular heads were bowed. Their blackened hands looked like prehistoric claws.

"You there!" I screamed at them, as I rose. My black dress billowed around my ankles. They stopped. I asked, "Who did that to those people?" My hand pointed out the window. "Tell me now! Tell me!" I screamed, but could not feel my voice.

The creatures' gaze remained downcast. One responded, "It was you, Majesty. You are the most powerful, most beautiful, most vengeful Queen." Its voice was like gravel escaping from tar. The words gurgled in its throat.

"Stop lying to me! Tell me the truth! Who did this?" I yelled. My fists balled as I screamed. I felt my voice heave from my lungs in rasps.

The second creature gurgled, "It was your Majesty. She tricked them all. They did trust her, and she led them here. They followed her. They swore to protect her." A contorted expression leaked across his face as he continued, "But she took power and killed them all. She kept power for herself. She left their bodies under her window to remind her not to trust anyone but herself. They took what was not theirs. Queen does not pardon the treacherous. None is a more powerful, more beautiful, more vengeful Queen than you, Majesty Ivy." The creature bowed so low that his head touched the marble floor.

I felt my eyes roll back. My body crumpled. The cold impact crashed against me, as I hit the floor. My mind screamed, as my body felt like it was trapped in tar. It clung to me and robbed me of breath and life. Suddenly, I sucked in a sob, and shot upright.

I heard Eric's soft voice. "Shhh. It's all right. I've got you. You're safe." His hand traveled softly across my hair and down my back. "You're safe."

The world swam back to me, and I knew I was sitting in the woods we were running through before the vision pulled me under. My feelings crashed into my chest. I closed my eyes tight as I waited for the violent impact to pass. I knew it was only a vision. At the same time, it scared me to death, because it *could* happen.

"Ivy?" his voice whispered. I shook my head. I couldn't look at him. The images of the bodies on stakes and the silver sword gleaming in the ground, I knew that it was him. I betrayed him. Utterly. I betrayed all of them. Somehow all three of them followed me.

And I killed them.

Trembling at what I would become, I said, "You were right."

CHAPTER TWENTY-EIGHT

"I was right about what?" He was acting normal, and not treating me like I had demon blood flowing through my veins. Somehow, that made it worse.

"Me and the prophecy. It'll happen, whether I do anything or not. I saw it. Oh my God. I saw it." Sitting up, Eric's hands fell away. I told him about the vision. He was stunned. Saying nothing, he sat next to me, utterly silent. This was worse than having demon blood. Way worse. Horrified or not, the vision showed my future. I didn't know how I would get to that point—the point at which I felt nothing and killed all my friends.

Thinking of what Al told me, I remembered that one decision is going to trigger a chain reaction. I didn't know which decision was the trigger. But Collin told me that it didn't matter. It wasn't the action that was the catalyst—it was me. The fact that I breathed was enough to cause it. I trembled.

Eric's head shook slowly. His amber gaze bore into me. "Do you want it, Ivy? Do you want the life you saw?"

My arms were folded tightly, as I stared between the dark trees. I shook my head. "No. God, no."

"Then choose," his voice sounded like the old Eric. "Your dreams are premonitions... warnings. They are nothing more. If you choose a different path, they won't happen."

"But, Eric, I don't know which decision put me on that path. It could be anything. It could be me—the fact that I breathe."

Eric said, "I know, but I suspect, you'll know what decision it is when you come to it. There is one thing we do know—something that will keep you *off* that path."

Hope filled me, as I looked at him. "What? What is it?"

"You need me," he said. "You and Al both said it. I'll stay with you through this. The vision you saw won't happen—it can't happen—if I stay with you, right?" I nodded, not entirely certain anymore. It was difficult to be certain of anything. I thought I knew who I was, or at least some inkling. But, the future version of me that I'd seen scared me. I didn't want to be that person.

Conviction flowed through Eric's voice. "I'm not leaving. Like it or not, we're on the same side for a while." He dusted himself off, and stood, turning away from me.

I sat in the cold dirt and wondered when I should tell him about Collin. Then I noticed it was just the two of us. "Where's Shannon?"

"She's scouting the area," he answered. "She heard something and you were out cold. She should be back… "

"Shhhh," we heard her whisper. Shannon emerged crouched from between the low brush with a silver dagger drawn, crouching low. The shadows masked her approach, and somehow she moved silently through the crisp leaves. It was the same dagger, lodged in her chest, from my vision. My gaze shifted to see what she was staring at.

Across from our spot there was a little clearing. It sat dark and empty in the cold night. Eric shook his head, putting his finger to his lips to cut off my question. I sat quietly and watched. Across the street, a figure moved between the shadows. We weren't alone. Shannon stalked forward abandoning the cover that the woods provided, and crossed the street quickly. She kept out of sight until she came up behind her target, with her dagger drawn. Right before she was in striking distance, the figure twisted, and sprung at her. There was a flash of silver, as her blade flew out of her grip.

"No!" I screamed. Panic shot through me, propelling me into motion.

Eric's fingers just missed my shoulder. "Don't!" But it was too late. I was running full speed at Shannon. My heart was deafening, as anger surged through me. My fingers pulled my comb from my hair, but before I could extend the deadly tines, I was knocked to the ground. When I managed to get back on my feet, I didn't have my comb.

A blond emerged from the group. She held my silver comb in a gloved hand. "Hey virgin. Funny how life works out, isn't it?"

"Nicole," I spewed her name, shocked.

She laughed. "We have your buddies, so unless you walk with us, we're gonna shred them. What are you gonna do?" Her gloved hands held up my comb, as she examined it closely. Her perfect skin wrinkled as she frowned. "This looks like the same weapon we took last year. Jake!"

My stomach dropped. I looked around the small park. Shannon and Eric were outnumbered. They were still fighting, battling too many Valefar at once. We were screwed.

Jake stepped forward. "It is. The girl had it. How'd she get it?"

They all looked at me. "It was my sisters."

"That was almost a year ago. That girl we were chasing in Italy? Ha! That's funny." Jake laughed, "We were chasing the wrong girl."

That was when the pieces started to click together in a horrible deafening slam. Taking a menacing step towards Nicole, I asked, "You killed her?" Raw hatred shot threw me. "It was *you*?" Not knowing what happened to my sister ate me alive for over a year. To learn Apryl was involved in all this made me sick. All the hatred surged within me, and I wanted to unleash it on the one responsible—Nicole.

Nicole laughed. A wicked smile curved her lips. "It wasn't me. But I do know the person who is responsible." A sardonic smile covered her mouth as her gaze shifted towards Eric. She pointed. "It was him."

I blanched. My knees buckled. *Eric killed Apryl?* And that was all it took. That moment of shock undid me. The Valefar were on me in seconds. I heard her command them to kill everyone but me. I slumped, trying to catch my breath, but failing. My knees wouldn't hold my weight. The Valefar wrapped my wrists in black chains, tugging me to follow them. I couldn't move. The shock wasn't fading. Everything that went wrong was connected. The Valefar, Apryl, Jake, Eric, and Collin. The only one who seemed to know nothing of it was Shannon, who was fighting for her life—and losing.

The thugs holding my arms moved to kick me, but Nicole said, "Carry her." One of the Valefar thrust me onto his shoulder, like a caveman. They carried me away, watching my friends—or whoever they were—fighting to the death.

Suddenly there were two Valefar with oozing red scars in front of me. The next thing I knew, I was waking up and looking at Collins face.

CHAPTER TWENTY-NINE

His scar was glowing scarlet. I'd never seen it do that before, no matter what had happened. It unnerved me. My gaze shifted off of his face as I sat up. We were at his place, back in the same posh room. My jaw dropped as I looked at him for an explanation.

"We only have a minute," he said. "The others will be back. They brought you to me to bind you. Right now they are fighting over who can have you if I allow it." Seeing the startled expression on my face, he quickly added, "I won't let them have you. And I already told you that I have no desire to bind you. I want you the way you are, but I have to do something to protect you. Ivy," his sapphire eyes were wide, "I need to fake a demon kiss with you. That's the only way. They'll think I bound you and will leave you alone."

My forehead scrunched as I his words washed over me. "How do you fake a demon kiss?" I swallowed hard.

"I can't, really. I have to kiss you. It has to look real, but I'll only take the smallest piece of your soul. You have to writhe like I'm tearing all of it from you."

My stomach lurched at the thought. It was the one thing we'd tried so hard not to do. It was the one thing that would kill me. I stared at him, unblinking. Even if he wanted to save me, I didn't believe he could break the kiss. The bond would lock us together, and I didn't know if Collin had the will power to pull apart.

His blue eyes were rimmed in red, and remorse flowed from him knowing what he had to do. It was heavy, filled with regret. His voice brushed my mind again, *I promise I'll protect you, Ivy. This is the only way.*

The door opened and several Valefar came in. They were all speaking at once, and staking their claim for my soul. Jake argued that he found me; Nicole said she captured me, while some of the others said they lured me out into the open. They looked at me with ravenous eyes while they argued. Collin sat behind his desk listening and made no indication he had other intentions.

Finally, he cut off their words with a single gesture. They fell silent when he raised his hand. "You all want this Martis because you believe you've earned her. But, I believe there is more to it than that. Her scent is different—more powerful. She would make her master strong. I've made my decision." His lips curled into an evil smile. "I will bind her. She will be your gift to me."

The Valefars' rage was clearly written on their faces, but not one of them protested Collin's decision. They obediently began doing as he requested. Two Valefar grabbed my arms and pulled me onto Collin's desk. Jake produced the black chain he attacked me with earlier. Wildly I looked to Collin and started to try and fight my way out, but it was pointless. There were too many of them. The Brimstone chains bound me to his desk. I couldn't move. Collin stood over me. I could feel his attempt to control his lust, but the bond was making it difficult. It pulled on both of us ruthlessly, threatening to destroy everything. There was no choice for me. I had to let Collin kiss me or die at the hands of his Valefar. They wouldn't leave until they knew I was bound. Jealousy seethed from them as Collin smiled above me. My heart pounded in my chest as memories of Jake's kiss came to the front of my mind. A scream erupted from my throat. The terror made it impossible to silence.

Before I knew it, his lips landed softly on mine. My body arched in response. I tried to push him away. All the noise around me faded, sucked away as a small piece of my soul was slowly being stripped from me. I expected a rush of pain, but it was mild. It wasn't like Jake's at all. Tears streamed from my eyes, as the kiss continued. Desire shot through Collin, as he tried to repress his innate need. I wasn't sure he could stop, but I knew that he wanted to. He held his face above mine, breaking the kiss, holding my face between his palms blocking our lips from everyone else. It looked like he kissed me longer than he really did.

His skin was covered in sweat. His mind brushed mine, *Repeat what I tell you. They'll think I bound you to me. They'll think you're mine.*

His sapphire eyes were rimmed in red. He spoke loudly, but never took his eyes off of me. "Ivy Taylor, you are mine for all eternity." He prompted me to say words that made me cringe, but I said them anyway. My expression was blank, despite my racing heart. He removed the ruby ring from his pocket, sliding it back on my finger before anyone noticed. I didn't realize they'd taken it. Collin said a few more words. Then he turned and left the room. I followed two paces behind like he told me to, with my gaze to the floor, totally shocked that I was alive and still in possession of my soul. We walked away with eyes burning holes in our backs. I willed my feet to walk slowly, easing the tension out of my legs.

We're almost there. No one will hurt you now. They cannot touch you. His voice reassured in my mind.

We walked out into the night air and were surrounded by sod fields. A sliver of moon hung above us, too thin to light the ground. The Valefar remained inside. I guess when the boss walks off with a new slave no one follows.

"That was risky," I said, breathing in the night air. My voice trembled, as I wrapped my arms tightly around me.

Collin pulled me to him. "It was. And I'm sorry. It was the only way I could make sure they don't bother you again. I just hope the price wasn't too high." His fingers pushed away my bangs, revealing my mark. He studied it.

"What do you mean?" I asked.

He threaded my comb back through my hair. "You lost some of you soul once already—when you were attacked. And I just took another piece. It was risky, because I didn't know how much soul you had left, not because I wasn't sure if I could stop. I would have never done that if I didn't think I could stop."

"My soul?" I asked, looking up at him. "It's turning into Swiss cheese, isn't it? What happens if it's totally gone? Will I even know if that happens?"

"I'm not sure how fast you'll know, but if you ever lose enough of your soul, the demon blood will overtake you, and you'll become fully Valefar." I cringed. I knew my soul was damaged, but I had no idea how much, or what I risked when he kissed me. I failed to realize pieces of it were actually missing.

We walked on, crossing the sod farm on foot, headed towards Collin's car. I was stunned into rare silence, as Collin maintained his master lead a few steps in front of me. Things were more precarious than I'd thought. As we approached Collin's car, two figures emerged from the darkness. Recognizing the threat, I ran at Collin.

"No!" I screamed, shoving Collin to the ground.

CHAPTER THIRTY

Collin's body went down quickly. That was my mistake. If I hadn't shoved him, he wouldn't have been such an easy target. Everything else happened quickly. It wasn't until later that I realized what I'd done.

Shannon emerged from the shadows. She stood with her silver dagger in hand. Tear streaks ruined her otherwise perfect complexion. Agony furrowed her brow tightly. Her eyes flicked from Eric back to me. Her indecision was transparent. I don't know how they found me, but they knew I'd been brought here. They thought I was bound. Their faces said it all.

Eric's amber eyes were fierce. His muscles tensed, as he reached for his sword. His head was tilted down, and his jaw was locked tight. With unblinking eyes, he stared at me with condemnation. As if on cue, Eric swung his sword. It gathered momentum, and he thrust it down. Not thinking, I threw myself in front of Collin. But I was too slow. The silver blade sliced across Collin's chest, inches from his throat.

Collin's body writhed. Liquid pain shot through the bond, engulfing me. Scarlet flowed rapidly from his wound. Collin's eyes fluttered once, then closed as the ground became drenched with his blood. The bond slipped, fading quickly. Collin lay in front of me covered in demon blood. It was blood like this that damned me. It was demon blood that tainted him, and ensnared him into a life of servitude.

The unseen cables that bound us together were loosening. The pain that flowed through the bond and into my body was slipping away. It made it so that I could breathe again. Crawling to him, I clutched his body not caring that his blood touched me. I watched helplessly as the boy who saved me bled to death in my lap. My heart was screaming, watching as the boy I loved die in my arms, and I was helpless to stop it. That was the first time I recognized it. *I love him.* I couldn't let this happen. There had to be something I could do. There was only one option, and it would be gone in seconds.

Before I could contemplate exactly what would happen, I moved. The glint of Shannon's blade caught my eye. I reached for the blade, and lunged at her. The sharp edge bit into my palm, ripping my flesh open. My blood pooled in my hand. I pulled away, barely noticing the shocked faces. Eric and Shannon were poised for an attack that didn't come. I held up my wound. Blood flowed freely, cascading down my wrist in red ribbons. Eric and Shannon stood there with unblinking eyes. Shocked.

Ignoring them, I cupped the blood running from my wound. I opened my fist, placing my hand flat against Collin's scar. The blood pooled into the crescent shape that marred his flesh. I rubbed my bloody palm into the wounds on his chest. The bond tightened. I knew I was doing what it wanted, what he needed to survive. Collin stirred slightly. *Let me go Ivy. It's too late.*

My heart caught in my throat, "Shh. It'll be all right." His head wobbled, and fell back into my lap. His pain was ebbing. The horrible burning, the seared flesh, the writhing—it was all fading. But, he wasn't healing. The wounds still flowed. The bond was breaking.

Although I did what it wanted, I was losing him. I could feel it. He was barely there.

I pulled Collin higher into my lap. Damn it! I did what it wanted. The bond wanted blood. I gave it! And he's still... Oh God. What else did he need? He's demon kissed. The only other thing he'd need is... *a soul*. With complete certainty, I knew what to do. I took a quick breath to steel myself to the pain. I pressed my lips to his, not caring if I gave the last bit of me.

Eric shouted, "NO!" But, it was too late. The bond swirled around us forming a translucent barricade. A tingly sensation covered my skin, as my lips brushed against Collin's slowly. His lips were warm. The sensation filled my entire body with tingles. His scent was perfect, like the boy from his memory—not the demon slave. And he tasted so sweet, but not like food.

The Valefar part of me didn't surface. The part of me that longed for him didn't want to let go. My body didn't reel in pain, as I anticipated. I knew I was giving him part of my soul. It should have hurt, but it didn't. The longer my lips stayed on his, the stronger he became. The bond had changed. I didn't really notice when, but it had walled us off. Violet and black mist swirled around us, blocking out the noise. Protecting us. A surge went through me, forming a blue light between us.

Ignoring it, I knew that I wanted more of him— that he needed more of me. I slid my tongue over his lips, feeling his soft flesh against mine. Recklessness overtook me, as my hands threaded into his dark hair, and I kissed him deeper. The bond took on a life of its own with the deeper kiss. I felt it mending him with long threads of living silk. Then it wrapped around something inside his chest. Something he wasn't supposed to have. He told me he held onto a fragment of his old self, but I didn't take it literally. And when I'd asked him if he had a soul, he said no. But he did. His soul was scarred and miniscule, but it was there buried deep within him. It was too small for him to be anything but Valefar, but it was there. His wounded body healed, as I held him tightly against me. Finally, his breath steadied, and I felt his strength flow back into him.

His hands found my face, and his fingers tangled in my hair. His breathing was deep and ragged. He kissed me softly, as he cradled my face. When the tingling stopped, I pulled away slowly. Our eyes locked, breathing raggedly, we gazed at each other. I smiled at him. "So that was why you... seemed so mortal at times. You did have a scrap of soul left." My fingers gently stroked his hair away from his eyes. The bond felt good now. It was warm, and happy.

"I guess so," he answered. As I stroked the hair back from his face, I saw his Valefar scar. I sucked in a shocked breath.

"Your scar changed color. It's violet." I paused for a moment, my eyes going wide, realizing what that could mean. I may have turned myself Valefar. "Did I give too much? What color is my mark?" I swallowed hard. "Is it red?"

Smiling at me, he said, "No. Still purple." The reality of what I'd done, of what I chose, didn't hit me until the mist faded. I saved him. He had a piece of me inside of him. And the light. Somehow I called light and it helped heal him. I saw it. My Martis and Valefar powers fused, and gave my best friend his life back.

Happiness washed over me. The euphoria from the kiss left dopey smiles on our faces. The two of us stared at each other utterly love struck.

But, angry voices broke my bliss. Shannon's voice snapped at me, "Ivy, what did you do?" She was ghostly white. Her hands trembled. "You chose them? I can't believe you chose *them*!" She looked like I punched her in the stomach.

Eric stood next to her with a similar expression. "My God, Ivy! You made another one."

I scowled at him. "Don't judge me! A life is a life. I may not have your sense of right and wrong. And I'm glad I don't. They told me, Eric." I glared at him with hatred. "I know. I know what you did to my sister. I know you killed her." My brow pinched tightly, as I spit words at him, "If you didn't save me from Jake, I'd kill you now. Prophecy or not."

Eric's shock intensified. He didn't look away, apologize, or try to explain. He simply stared at me, unable to speak. Maybe it did look like I could make an evil army. They had every right to be afraid of me. But the reason he should have truly feared me was because he stole her from me. Apryl died in vain—because he was hunting her when he really wanted me.

Eric's face pinched. He didn't respond the way I thought he would, "I *didn't* save you from Jake. You were alone when I found you. No one was there that night. It was just you, half dead in the dark." His words shocked me. All this time, I thought he saved me. And the reality that I didn't owe him anything left my anger unchecked, boiling inside of me.

My body started to shake with rage. "It *wasn't* you?" I repeated. The disdain in my voice was so thick, no one moved.

He shook his head, amber eyes narrow. "I found you. I took you home. I trained you. I wasn't the one who stopped the attack."

Something inside of me broke, and shattered into a million sharp fragments. Anger made every muscle in my body shake, as my eyes creased into little slits. I wanted to attack, but something held me back. I had to know. "Why'd you kill her?" I hissed.

His body was tense, poised for attack. His muscles flexed as his fingers clenched slowly around his weapon. He was fighting every instinct he had. He wanted to attack. If I gave him a reason, we'd fight to the death. Eric's voice was callous, "I was tracking her, and trying to confirm who she was. She was in the wrong place at the wrong time."

"You told me that the best part of being a Martis was getting to live a life that wasn't lived in vain," I spit the words at him. "You stole that from her! She wasn't even a part of this! She was a tourist. And you slaughtered her like she was the anti-Christ."

He tried to explain. "If you were blue. If you were a pure Martis…"

"I'm not," I snapped. "I'm not blue. I'm not like you. I'll never be like you!" I stood, and Collin moved behind me. "I don't kill innocent people. You do!"

"Ivy, you don't understand." He sounded reasonable, like I should see his point. "You saw what happens in your visions. If one life could prevent it…"

"NO! That's the point. It's a damn prophecy! Nobody's life can prevent it. It's going to happen no matter what! It doesn't matter what we do—or who you kill. It's coming." My eyes cut into him, as I shook with rage. "You stole the one thing from me that mattered most. I thought she died for no reason. Just some random accident. You let me think it. You watched me crash and burn for over a year, trying to get a grip on her dying for no reason!" Tears streamed down my face. "*You are the reason.* I hate you! If I ever have the chance to repay the pain you caused me—the innocent life you took—I will."

I felt my eyes rimming moments before. I knew they would pool violet and that I wouldn't be able to control myself. A distant thought echoed through the back of mind, reminding me that I needed Eric to help with the prophecy. I wished I didn't, but I knew he had to be there. I grabbed Collin, wrapping my arms around him, focusing on the ruby ring. His voice called out, "No!" as soon as he realized what I was planning to do. But it was too late. I'd already decided. I couldn't stand in front of Eric without killing him. And I couldn't leave Collin behind. I only had one choice—to attempt to efanotate both Collin and myself.

I focused all my rage into the stone, and felt the surge of heat lick through me. We were instantly engulfed in burning black mist. Shannon and Eric disappeared from sight. I could see nothing, but I could feel Collin searing along with me. Suddenly, we lurched forward, stumbling on the carpet inside the church, gasping for air as the heat dissipated. I transported both of us. Collin and I gasped for air, doubled over. When I looked over at him to make sure I didn't weaken him further, his eyes were wide.

"Ivy!" She was shocked to see me appear in front of her.

"Al. I'm sorry." Brushing the tears from my eyes, I forced my heart to regain a normal thumping. "I had to see you. Something's wrong." Collin settled into a chair looking leery. Al seemed uneasy that he was there, but didn't throw him out. I don't know how insane it was to bring him with me, but leaving him with Eric wasn't an option.

It took me a moment to sense that something wasn't right. She had a pile of tissues next to her rocker, scattered across the side table. Her face was blank, but her eyes. Something was wrong. Very wrong. Al looked at Collin, dabbing her nose. "So this is what you've been after?" She tilted her head toward me. He looked at her, but did not respond.

I couldn't wait anymore, "Al. What's happened? What's wrong?"

Her voice was somber. A sad smile spread across her face. "They found out what you are, Ivy. They know. The Valefar *know*. It's going to get bad now."

"What do you mean?"

She slowed, reaching for me. "Dear girl. I wish I could have stopped it." She rubbed my hand between hers, and it seemed like time stopped. "But by the time I saw the vision, it was too late. When they found out what you are, they searched for you. I suppose some of them found you, and dragged you away. But, the ones that went to your home... they were looking for something they needed. Something you took. When you wouldn't bring it out to them... " her voice trailed off. Her grip on my hand tightened.

My stomach dropped, as my throat tightened. "What? What did they do?" My voice was so faint, I wasn't sure I spoke.

"I'm sorry, Ivy. Everything is gone. They destroyed your home, and everyone in it. Ivy, the Valefar killed your mother." It took a minute for me to process what she said. Surely I hadn't heard her right.

"No. That can't be true. It can't be." I backed away from her. Pity was strewn across her face. Suddenly, my legs gave out from under me, as my chest was crushed by an unseen force. I dropped to the floor, barely able to hold my head up. Collin kneeled down and threaded his arm around me, propping me up. I saw nothing. Felt nothing. Voices continued around me, but their words were meaningless. I was utterly alone. After suffering for a year, not knowing what happened to her daughter, my mom was dead. *I was alone*. Only one questions hung in my mind. It leaked out in a whisper, "How?"

Al leaned forward and put her old hand on my shoulder. "The Valefar couldn't enter, because of the wards. I think they meant to drive you out. They used fire, trapping your mom inside, trying to force her to turn you over. But, you weren't there."

I nodded. Stale air swirled around me. I felt strange. I'd lost everything. My family. My home. They were all gone. And at this point my only friends were a demon kissed boy, and a nun. A hysterical sob bubbled out of me, as I leaned into Collin. His arms wrapped around me. He asked Al, "What did you see? Are they going to call him?"

Al replied, "Yes, they are. They need two puzzle parts that they don't have. One is the prophecy—the painting. You know what the other piece is. Where is the key?" She looked at Collin, waiting for him to answer. She obviously expected him to know what she was talking about.

He said, "We don't have it. No one knows where it is."

The conversation caught my attention. The thing that they assumed was in my house, the thing that wasn't there. It didn't burn. "They want the painting? What for?"

"It shows some things in detail," Al said. "Some things that were forgotten, and rightfully so. If they had the key and the painting, they could summon Kreturus." There was fear in her aged voice.

Collin answered my question before it was asked, "He is the most powerful demon there ever was. He created the Valefar. But he's imprisoned. No one can summon him—well, if they do, he can't come."

"But once they have the prophecy and the key," Sister Al added.

"He can come. Here. And that would be—really bad." Collin pulled me to him. The bond changed, but I could still sense things. I knew he cared about me. And it felt like he was afraid he'd lose me.

I wrapped my arms around his waist, and looked up into his eyes. I wanted to reassure him. He was the only thing I had now. The only thing I cared about. "I won't leave you. I promise."

His lips pulled into a soft sad smile, as his dark hair fell over his eyes. He kissed the top of my head. "I know you won't."

Al watched me interact with Collin, but she said nothing. I finally looked at her and admitted what I'd done. "I changed him, Al. I didn't mean to, but he's not all Valefar anymore. I can tell you know each other, and I suspect that the reason you know each other isn't good. But he saved me, Al. The Valefar did attack me. He pretended to bind me, but he didn't. When we escaped, Eric," I choked on his name, feeling enraged at the thought of him, "attacked us. Al, I'm sorry. I just wanted to save him."

"Don't be silly child. A life is a life—no matter what. And although you turned him purple, he's not like you. He doesn't have your power and ability. He is part Martis because you are, but the amount of angel blood he received from you wasn't what did this—it was because he was given a piece of your soul." She paused for a moment. "I just hope that your trust is well placed." She stared at Collin.

"It is. I know it is. Al, he is the only person— besides you—who doesn't want to use me or kill me." I said.

Her eyes flicked to Collin as I spoke. Her expression was rigid. "Is that so? Collin. You don't want anything from her?"

His voice was a whisper, "No." He kissed the top of my head.

I smiled weakly at him. It felt safe and normal. I scooted away from him, realizing I was covered in dirt and sweat. "I need to take this off." I turned to Al as I indicated my shirt. "Any chance you have a sweater or something I could borrow?"

The old woman rose, and went to the closet. She disappeared behind a door in search of a shirt. I lifted the sweatshirt over my head, revealing the black tank underneath. The tank top was soaked through with sweat, but I had nothing else. Apryl's necklace clung to the flesh at the hollow of my throat. I picked it up, wiping away the grime and sweat that accumulated under it. Collin stared at me, his eyes fixated on the pendant hanging around my neck. One hand lifted a curl and tucked it behind my ear. The other hand picked up the pendant. He held it for a moment, before releasing it.

When Al returned, Collin dropped the pendant and stepped away. Al handed me a navy blue sweatshirt that said ST. BART'S BASEBALL. I pulled it over my head quickly.

Al said, "You need to get the painting. We can't let them get it."

"They can't," I replied. "It's still on holy ground. It's in an old church."

Al's face pinched together. She approached me slowly. "What old church?"

"I'm not sure if it has a name. It's an old one out east. I found it the night I took the painting." I was getting nervous that she hadn't sat down yet. She always sat down.

Her eyes were growing wide. "Ivy, do people still worship there?"

"No one goes there anymore. It's a relic, in-between some farms." Al paled. I asked, "What's the matter?"

"It's not protected. The wards only work at churches." Her wrinkled face was pale. She froze in front of me.

"But it is a church," I replied.

Collin cut in, reminding me he was there, "Not if no one worships there—it gets demoted to a building—

like any other. There are no wards. The Valefar can go inside. They can get it."

Al's eyes cut between Collin and me. She didn't like him, that much I could tell. Her gaze shifted back to me and softened, "You have to get it. You have to bring it back here. Ivy, if they get it, then they only need the key to call Kreturus. You can't let them get it."

Panic flooded me at her distress. "I didn't know. I'll get it. I'll bring it back here. I promise, Al. They won't get it. It's hidden, and not in plain sight. I can get it right now, and be right back." I looked at my ruby ring.

Collin slid his hand over mine. "There are other Martis in this building. I can smell them. They will sense us if you use Valefar magic here. We need to go outside."

Al looked unsure. Her gaze shifted between Collin and me. She finally said, "He's right, they will sense you, but I am sending Shannon and Eric after you." I groaned, and started to protest, but she cut me off. "No, Ivy this is too important. If something happens," she looked at Collin, "I want them there. You need them. You have no choice."

I locked my jaw, knowing she was right. "It's the old stone church out by Cutchogue. It's between a bunch of farms. It's the only building—you can't miss it. But Al, I'll be back by the time they get there."

She took my hands in hers, "I hope so."

CHAPTER THIRTY-ONE

"I can't believe you can do that," he said. Collin and I efanotated, and appeared in front of the old stone church.

"Do what?" I asked, looking around to ensure we were alone. We were much closer to the Valefar now, and I didn't like it.

"I've never seen anyone do that. I can't move two people. It's amazing that you can, that's all. You amaze me—in every way possible." His voice sounded odd.

I turned to look at him, unsure of his sudden mood. "It'll be okay, Collin. We'll get the painting and leave." He nodded, taking my hand and walking towards the stone building.

The humidity clung to my flesh like droplets of honey. If the wind picked up more, it would feel better. Collin followed me as we walked up to the little room. He said nothing, but I could tell something was bothering him. I chalked it up to nerves. When we were up in the room inside the church, I walked to the spot I'd thrown the painting. I dug through the piles of books, feeling my way around between the dusty stacks, but I didn't find it. The painting was rolled up. It could have rolled under something. The dust shifted and tickled my nose.

"So, how does this work?" I asked. My butt was in the air, as I reached through a stack. "Does it have a chant on it, or something?"

"Something like that." His voice sounded weird.

"Well, that's a nice vague answer," I laughed. My hand dug between more stacks. I could have pushed them over, but I thought it would crush the painting if it was back there. I sat up. "Huh. I thought it was over here."

Collin's eyes went wide. He looked around the room. The bond shifted suddenly. He was doing something. Something I couldn't fathom. It was like some animal instinct. He was training his senses on the air—looking for signs of previous visitors, besides me. I sat up and watched him, perplexed. His body tensed. "Come!" The room filled with Valefar. They came through the stairwell and poured into the room like roaches. There were too many to fight or run.

I looked at Collin, but he wouldn't meet my gaze. My stomach lurched. "Collin?" I breathed with my heart pounding in my chest. "What is this?" I heard the doubt in my voice. I stared at him unblinking until a familiar voice caught my attention.

Jake. He handed Collin the painting. "You were right. We found it right before you got here."

My gut twisted as severely as my mouth. What had he done? He loved me. He wouldn't do this to me. But, he did. He called the Valefar, and they appeared. They took the prophecy on his command. My doubt suddenly curdled into betrayal. "You didn't… " My eyes went wide, as anger filled me. I knew he could feel it, but I didn't care. "Tell me you didn't tell them to come here and take the prophecy!"

He looked at me, as he took my hand in his. They were rimmed with violet. "I did. I told you that I would do anything to lift the curse, and gain my freedom. I made an agreement with Kreturus a long time ago. A trade. My life, for yours."

Collin's gaze shifted away from me, to the rest of the Valefar. He was stoic, like the rest of them. Repulsion overtook me and I couldn't stand to look at him. I wanted to scream, and felt a surge of angry words building in my mind. All that time we spent together, was what? A lie? A brilliant lie, orchestrated by a cunning being that would do anything possible to gain his life back. I jerked my hand out of his grip. But he tightened his fingers, and stripped the ruby ring. I was stripped of my Valefar power, and trapped.

He turned back to his Valefar and said, "Take her. And two others are coming. I'll need them too."

I screamed, hoping that the others could hear me if they were there. But it was too late. I walked them straight into a trap. "COLLIN!" I screamed at his back. "I saved you! How could you do this to me!" I flailed, as strong Valefar hands restrained me. Collin ignored me, and stared barking orders to people. The Valefar dragged me outside into the night.

There was a circle on the ground. Someone cut into the frozen earth with a shovel. A trail of tiny white crystals marked the edges. Salt. Shannon and Eric were tied and staked at different points along the edge of the circle. My heart sank. They got here and were captured. The thug dropped me on the ground, jolting my tailbone. Despite the sting, I jumped up. Every muscle in my body flexed, ready to run—ready to fight, but I didn't get the chance. They restrained me, gashing my cheek as I tried to fight them. It didn't matter how much I twisted and turned. I couldn't get away. There were too many Valefar. Too many to overpower or outrun. With a jerk, my wrists were bound behind my back and my ankles were tethered to the third stake. My lungs heaved in cold air. I strained against my bonds, but they didn't give. Rage shot through me, burning with fierce intensity. I screamed, thrashing, doing anything possible to free myself—but it did nothing. When I gave up, it felt like the veins in my forehead exploded. I heaved in ragged breaths, still refusing to accept it, knowing that we were going to die. And it was my fault.

Blinking back tears, I looked around. The Valefar were frantic. I watched them, wondering what they would do since they didn't have the key to open the pit. Collin said they didn't have it, and I didn't feel him lie. That meant that he was telling the truth at the time. Damn it! How could I be so foolish? Why didn't I see this coming? I reached out for Collin through the bond, wanting to scream at him. It felt like reaching out through water, and masked his thoughts. I couldn't hear him.

A breeze blew through my hair, cooling my skin. I looked across the circle at Eric. His face was sorrowful. He didn't scream *I told you so* at me. He appeared sad, defeated. Shannon's long hair was whipping around her stake, caught in the wind. It flashed red in the moonlight. Her face was pinched in fear, realizing better than me what was coming. While the Valefar made preparations to free the most powerful demon alive, we helplessly watched them unable to stop it. My only hope was that Al knew I should have been back by now. She had to know something was wrong.

The Valefar began to close in around the edges of the circle. Jake stood triumphantly next to me. He pulled a knife from his pocket, and cut me free. I fell to the ground and punched him in the kneecap, ready to fight. His hands reached down, pulling me to my feet, by my hair. I yelped, rising swiftly, feeling some of the roots snap away from my scalp. Collin's voice growled behind me. "Drop her."

Jake said, "But, we're just going to… "

"Drop. Her." Collin stood with every muscle in his body flexed. When Jake's fingers didn't release me, Collin slashed something silver into his stomach. Jake fell to the ground. Blood flowed out of his abdomen, as he crumbled onto the grass. The smell of sulfur filled the air, as his body turned to tar, and the earth reclaimed him. I started at Collin, horrified. I froze in place with my throat so tight that I could barely breathe.

"No one touches her. I have to do it," he said glaring at the Valefar, pointing at them with my comb. There was a desperate intensity in him. His mind was wound so tight, he was about to crack. But, the thing that concerned me most was his eyes. They were filling with crimson, not violet. He was still a Valefar. The angel blood wasn't enough to overpower his demon kiss. Al said we weren't the same, even though I turned his mark purple. But, I didn't see what she meant until that moment. Collin was still Collin the Valefar, despite the coloring on his head. My soul hadn't changed him. My stomach sank. *What have I done?* Out of all the stupid things for me to do, out of all the choices I made, this one was beyond redemption.

Collin turned back to the circle, acting like he had done nothing more than step on an ant. There was no indication that he just killed a man, or that it bothered him in the slightest. Unrolling the painting in his hands, Collin's eyes hungrily devoured it. His face lit up as he gazed at the canvas. Those intense eyes were still blood red, rimmed in violet, and moving across the painting, like he was reading something.

The wind whipped harder, howling, making the night feel more sinister. With a locked jaw and throbbing temples, Collin looked back at me. His eyes gazed over at me once, and then he rolled the painting back up and shoved it in his waistband. Certainty washed over him. I shuddered in response, and tried to hide how terrified I felt. My pulse didn't slow; my chest felt like it would explode, and if my jaw locked any tighter it would crack. All traces of the boy I saw, of the Collin I knew, were gone. There was nothing left of him. Callous indifference lined his face, as he looked over the many Valefar under his command.

Nicole sauntered up behind him. Her arms wrapped around his waist. He didn't shake her off. He let her stay there, holding him. Bile rose in my raw throat. *No.* I thought, *I couldn't have been that dumb. He was still with her? All the time I spent with him, and he was still with her?* I wanted to be one of those girls who filled with rage, the kind that didn't feel the betrayal or the pain. But I wasn't. I felt every last drop with agonizing clarity.

He turned his face toward Nicole and said, "Go take it from her." She smiled, unslithering herself, and walked over to me. Collin watched her do as he commanded. His crimson eyes traced her body as she moved through the darkness. Nicole stopped in front of me, cocking her hip, and stared. I had no idea what she was looking at, until her sharp nails bit my skin, and the chain on my necklace snapped. My pendant fell into her palm. Her long tapered fingers closed around it, before she smiled at me. Then without a word, she tossed it into the middle of the salt circle, laughing at my shocked face.

When the pendant hit the grass the ground churned like it was alive. A ripple spread from the edges of the salt circle, and raced toward the necklace. I watched in horror as the ground ate the pendant, leaving a black hole at the center of the circle where the necklace disappeared. A shiver of shock spread through my shoulders. By the time it reached my heart, it had deformed into utter hatred. She took Apryl's necklace. It was gone. Forever.

My hands started to shake as I balled them into tight fists. Collin knew how much that meant to me. He took her comb, and now the necklace was gone too. I stood there frozen, unable to move, unable to comprehend the level of his attack. It was like he wanted to destroy me completely.

Nicole turned back to me smiling, reveling in my agony. "Thanks for the key, Virgin. We were looking for that." She looked smug.

Collin averted his gaze, no longer watching me—only the circle. I looked at the ground, and sucked in a breath. My hand instinctively flew to my mouth, muffling any sound I might make. The ground inside the salt circle was swirling slowly, like it was liquid. The edges were white, rimmed in salt, and stationary. The ground was still hard on our side of the salt line. But the other side was turning into a mixture of earth and rock pudding. The swirling mess was becoming darker with every turn.

"What'd you do?" I asked Collin as my voice cracked. Disbelief grabbed hold of me, and I couldn't shake it. This was the portal. It was open. That meant that the necklace... My words came out drenched in disbelief, "My necklace—it was the key?"

Nicole laughed, "Yes! We couldn't have done it without you, Virgin!" She walked over to me, her golden hair blowing around her face. "See, every reason why this portal is here now is because of *you*. The prophecy was right—*you* are the reason that everything goes to Hell."

I looked at Collin, trying to wipe the horror off my face. His words haunted me—it wasn't something I decided, the prophecy was something that happened *because I lived*. Dread churned in my stomach, allowing my agony to rip through my body in an unimaginable way. Collin's body tensed, but ignored my gaze. He stared unblinking at the growing hole. The wind whipped his brown hair around his eyes. He looked like a god, in a black tee shirt and jeans. The earth sank and spun before him. The wind and water swirled around him.

The Valefar began saying words that I didn't understand, at Collin's prompting—words that lined the edge of the painting. The spinning pit grew deeper and darker. I'd expected it to be open space—like the sky—but it wasn't. As the thing spun and took shape, it looked more and more like the painting. The pit became deeper, as the walls shifted from brown to black. As the hole widened from the center out, the ground cracked and fell away, revealing slimy black stone. The only sounds that could be heard were wind, and the noise of rock and dirt falling into the chasm. Shards of shiny black glass clung to the walls. The hole would trap whatever fell into it. Fingers would have to fight the slippery slime to escape, and then if you did get a hold, those chunks of sharp black glass would shred you.

The wind howled, biting my face. I stood there, stunned, and too shocked to move. My eyes flicked to Shannon, who stared at me pleadingly. She wanted me to fight back.

But I didn't know how. I had no weapon, no ring, and no way to channel my power. I broke her gaze, feeling ashamed that I didn't know what to do—that I was letting this happen. I glanced at Eric—he wouldn't look at me. There wasn't any time to consider that because the bond filled with searing heat. Collin broke his gaze, and looked at me. He nodded at his Valefar. They moved in around me swiftly, and grasped my arms, moving me toward the edge of the pit.

Heart racing, I dug my heels into the ground, refusing to be thrown in. The wind whipped my hair out of my face, carrying faint noises from a distant farm. The air grew colder, as the pit grew deeper. I straightened my legs, locked my knees, and dropped to the ground screaming. The Valefar watched silently. Collin said nothing. He ignored my cries for help. He ignored the fear that penetrated the bond.

As they dragged me closer to the edge, all eyes were on me, ignoring what was occurring behind them. It took everyone a moment to recognize what was actually happening. It wasn't until I saw several flashes of silver that I knew.

Al sent help.

The three Martis who watched me spar with Eric in the gym were suddenly in front of me. The two men slashed the Valefar who held me, killing them, while the woman, Elena, dragged me away from the edge of the pit.

Urgently she spoke in my ear, as the Valefar realized they were under attack. "We have to destroy them and close the pit. If they throw you in, you must—you MUST—kill yourself before Kreturus gets hold of you. He will absorb your power—power he needs to fulfill the prophecy. Don't give him the chance." She shoved me back, throwing a piece of celestial silver at me.

I touched it to my mark, and it turned into a single reaper blade. "Oh, what the hell!?" Why did I need the Grim Reaper's blade? It felt more like an omen, than the silver choosing the weapon shape that was right for me. The farmland that surrounded the church turned into a war zone. More Martis shot out of the shadows. Eric and Shannon were freed during the first wave of Martis. When they cut Shannon free, she jumped into the fray, taking her dagger back from the Valefar who stole it. Shannon's hair flew wildly, as she screamed, slaying Valefar after Valefar. My stomach clenched, making me sick. The smell of sweat and blood spread on the wind. I stood there unsure of what to do. I had no choice. I had to fight, but I couldn't throw myself into the battle.

Julia ran beside me screaming, "Fight or die! If we don't push back the Valefar before the pit opens completely, we can't close it." Her graceful body moved through the Valefar, slashing her short silver swords like a ninja.

I did as she said, not because she told me, but because I had to. Valefar ran at me, trying to drag me back to Collin. At first, I tried to hang back. I didn't want to kill them. They were slaves. They had no choice in what they were. But when it turned into me or them—I swung my weapon without remorse. I could cry later. My blade cut through Valefar after Valefar. There were an unending number of them. They just kept coming. Eric's cry caught my attention. He was making his way toward Collin, who was fighting Elena next to the pit. Collin and Elena seemed equally matched.

Silver flashed against the inky sky. A Martis cried out, as a Valefar sucked out her soul. The ear-piercing scream made me lose my focus, as my stomach lurched in response. My muscles trembled, reliving the moment of my demon kiss with Jake. The pain was so vivid that a Valefar almost caught me. At the last second, I swung my arm, and my blade ripped through his throat.

Slowly, I realized I was making a path toward Collin. The rage that filled me was because of him. His betrayal was worse than any I'd experienced. I couldn't contain my pain. I lashed out, ripping flesh from bone, not bothering to bury my blade in the Valefar's flesh to make sure they died. They cried out, as I left a wake of blood and screams behind me. I had to get to him before Eric. This had to end now, and I knew how. Elena told me if I died that they couldn't use me anymore. My instincts told me that I would not survive anyway. As I slashed through two more Valefar, I knew they would never stop coming for me. I knew it would cost me every person I loved. They would never stop. That creature in the pit wanted *me*. I had to throw myself into the pit, and pierce my heart with my silver. The demon blood in my body would not allow me to live with celestial silver through my heart. It would kill me. That was the only way to end this and make sure all the things that I'd seen would never happen.

Morbid determination propelled me through the crowd. More screams went up around me, as Martis were drained of their souls. It chilled me, but I kept moving. My resolve thickened, as the meaning of the prophecy emerged in my head. I felt certain. All this time, this was what I was supposed to do. This is where I fulfilled my destiny.

I glanced at the pit. The sharp stones shone against the slick black walls. The lack of moonlight made it no less frightening. The hole was a portal to the Underworld.

With every step I took towards Collin, my determination increased. I slashed my weapon, not noticing the blood on my hands, not feeling the wind cutting my face.

This was my destiny. I had to fight. I had to defeat Collin Smith. As I approached him, his eyes locked on my moving figure. They had the familiar sadness that I saw every time he revealed something about his past. But now I knew that wasn't grief, it was a lie. He planned this. And I walked right into it. With each step, a new thought flew through my mind, convincing me that I was wrong about him—that he was beyond redemption.

I'd trusted him. He made me think that he loved me. It was so easy to believe him. Eric called out to me, but I ignored him, lost in my own thoughts. I slashed the Valefar in front of me in two strokes. His blood washed over my hands, and I walked away leaving him screaming behind me.

Soulless creatures cannot love. Collin didn't love me. The only real piece of soul he had now was mine. Hatred seared through me, making me feel invincible. I hated that he had a piece of me inside of him. It was a piece of me that I gave willingly to save his life. It linked me to him with an intimacy that I couldn't tolerate. Not now. I felt the sting of my naivety, as my blade collided with another Valefar. Three moved in around me. Rage flashed in my eyes. I had no doubt they were completely violet, as I was consumed by bloodlust. I moved quickly, taking them down in rapid succession. All this time, Collin said I made the bond, and that I put the bond between us.

I slashed another Valefar across the face, and continued walking. I was a sucker, and I chose wrong. Again. Everything I thought about Collin was wrong. It wasn't like I picked a bad guy—he wasn't a bad guy— he was a Valefar. He used me, manipulated me in every way possible. My eyes burned with intensity that was singly focused on Collin. I knew he could hear my thoughts. *Good.* I was coming for him. I was going to kill him.

Eric yelled behind me again. "Your anger! Snap out of it, Ivy! Control yourself!"

His words finally registered. I stopped, turning to look at him as he fought a Valefar. His body heaved as he fought; slashing down Valefar, but more took their place. I turned my attention back to Collin. I didn't know what Eric was talking about. Why should I contain my anger? We were in the middle of a battlefield, fighting to the death.

That was when I saw it. Lifting my blade in front of my eyes, I saw the silver was glowing bright white. I stared at it, but that wasn't what made me pause. It was my reflection. I could see it in the blade. The glowing blade illuminated my face, revealing raging eyes that pooled deep violet. I could see the ends of my hair were glowing. They were illuminated with purple flames that did not burn. My hair had come loose from my ponytail and was whipping my face. I had no idea it was engulfed in violet flames. I couldn't feel the heat. It neither burned nor smoked. It was just there, showcasing my rage in a way unique to me—the Prophecy One.

I sucked in a deep breath, unsure of what it meant. My heart thundered, pumping blood through my body, as my muscles flexed. I twisted the blade away from me so I couldn't see my reflection and wondered if it mattered. *Control my anger? Was my anger doing this to me?*

Elena's scream shattered my thoughts. She'd been fighting Collin the entire time, holding her own. I knew Eric trained her, so she was good. When I turned, I saw her body go limp, as she fell past the edge of the pit and into the chasm below. Blood was running down Collin's right arm where her weapon pierced his skin. He beckoned my forward. Eric's warning was quickly forgotten, and I allowed the rage to consume me. I couldn't contain it. I stopped before him, just out of reach. Hatred flowed through me like fire. I didn't recognize my own voice as I spoke to him, "A life for a life. A heart for a heart. A soul for a soul. You took all those things from me, and now I'm going to take them back."

Before I finished speaking, before my words had time to sink in, I thrust my blade at his chest, expecting it to pierce his flesh. But, it met his Brimstone knife with a metallic clang. Collin's eyes were wide. "Ivy, stop! It's not what you think." He didn't strike out at me with his blade. He only blocked.

I swung again, and he blocked. Another cry pierced the night. I repressed a shiver that sent ice down my spine at the sound of Martis being demon kissed. Sucking in air, I continued to advance on him. I thrust my blade at his body, aiming for spots that were vulnerable, and finding none. "Stop lying to me!" I screamed. I swung at him again, only to feel my blade crash into his. "I lost everything because of you!"

Every ounce of fury went into my next swing. I knew it would make contact. I knew it would be his death. It would end the lies, the pain, and the look in his eyes; the look that caused me to believe him when he said he loved me. He twisted sharply at the last moment. The blade came down hard, missing his torso, but it pierced his arm. His shaking hand dropped the knife, as blood flowed over his arm. I kicked the black blade into the pit. It hit the side, clattering, as it fell into oblivion.

Rage filled my chest. I sucked in air, and drew my weapon over my head, as the wind whipped my flaming violet hair. Fury and power flowed through me, numbing everything but the revenge I so desperately needed. Collin fell to his knees, raising one hand over his head, as I was about to end his life. Pinched between his pale fingers, he held up something for me to take. Something I wanted. Something I never thought I'd see again. Apryl's silver comb gleamed in the darkness, as he held it out to me.

I hesitated. His gesture threw me off, causing me to falter. I stood there poised to strike, but didn't move. *If he had the comb, he could fight. But he wasn't. He surrendered.* Certain I was over-thinking this, I reached for the comb, intending to rip it out of his hands. But when I reached out, his other hand flew up and caught my arm. He jumped to his feet, jerking me toward him. Looking down at me, his chest swelled with ragged breaths. A shriek tore out of my lungs, as I tried to pull out of his grip. I tried to twist away from him, using anything I could. But, he didn't let go. Before I realized what was happening, the icy hot sensation from the bond shot through me. It came to life injecting images, memories, and emotions into me. I stood there paralyzed, with him clutching my forearm tightly.

He was forcing me to relive one of his memories. I fell into the memory, and a blood curdling scream came from somewhere in the distance. Collin ran toward the sound, not finding the girl who screamed. There were too many trees. *She isn't where she's supposed to be.* His heart beat violently, threatening to tear apart his chest. His feet crushed the earth, and dirt flew into the air, as he ran. Anxiety consumed him whole. He repressed his fear, but it kept trying to surface as he ran. He thought he was too late. As he ran into the clearing, his stomach lurched. He found the girl he was looking for.

Her pale form was lying lifeless in Jake's arms, while his lips pressed to hers, striping her soul from her body.

The girl was me.

My eyes were closed and I knew that was when the golden light was leaving me. Collin saw it spilled on the ground like puddles of liquid gold. A tangle of emotions shot though his body—fear, dread, rage, revenge—but he never slowed. His body rammed Jake's, knocking him away from me. Jake's body flew through the air.

His head connected with a tree in a loud crack, and his body slumped to the ground, motionless. If he weren't a Valefar, the impact would have killed him.

At that moment in the memory, I tried to pull away and break Collin's grip. I didn't want to see this, but the bond held me tight—Collin held me tight—forcing me to relive the rest of his memory. As it continued, Collin watched my broken body, as I lay still on the dirt that night. My chest didn't rise or fall. He slid his fingers carefully under my neck. His strong arms trembled, as he lifted me into his lap. My body was limp. I didn't respond. I didn't cry. There was no expression on my lips.

He pressed his forehead to mine and whispered, "No. No. Ivy… " He held me in his lap, but didn't respond. I was ashen faced, and cold beyond possibility. Images of his wife flashed through the memory—gray faces and funeral pyres. His gut clenched in response, terrified. The memory of my laughter, my smile faded in and out, as fast as lightening streaking across the night sky. The joy I made him feel, shot through him and vanished. He realized death already had hold of me. The turmoil within him threatened to tear him apart. In his mind, I could feel that he made a decision that pained him, though I didn't know why.

Tears streaked his face, as he took his black blade and sliced his thumb. Scarlet flowed from his cut. He rubbed his blood into my mark—demon blood. My mark absorbed it, burning bright red, and then returning to pale blue. Words echoed in the memory, *I'm sorry Ivy. There is no other way.* His sliced finger touched my lips, as scarlet blood flowed into my mouth. I watched the memory, feeling the same horror that raked Collin's body. *He was the one who gave me demon blood. Oh my God!*

But the memory went on. He wasn't done yet. After the blood entered my mouth, his lips came down on mine, softly—gently. His lips took the kiss he always wanted but could never have. The result saved my life, and damned me at the same time. I could feel his thoughts. The demon blood granted the power to sustain life without a soul. It would allow me to live even if too much of my soul was taken. But, he risked me turning Valefar if he gave blood alone. So he didn't.

Something inside of Collin screamed, as his lips were pressed to mine. His tainted scrap of soul was torn, and a part flowed into my body, with the hope that I would not be Valefar. He hoped the angelic Martis blood would latch onto his putrid piece of soul and heal me. He took his thumb, spreading it over my lips as he backed away, using his blood to seal his soul inside of me. He watched my face. Waiting. His hand gently wiped the tears off my cheeks, and tucked a curl behind my ear. Quietly, he held me waiting and hoping. So many thoughts flew threw his mind, but they tangled together. The only coherent thought I heard, laced between the regret was, *Come back to me Ivy. Come back to me.* He held me in his arms, stroking my hair. Terror and remorse consumed him.

My eyes fluttered opened, staring up at him. Relief washed through him. All the heated rage washed out of him. His blue eyes wouldn't leave my face. His mind brushed mine, as he assured me, *You're safe.*

I couldn't watch the memory anymore. I gasped, pulling away from him. The bond released me. I was out of the memory and stood there, in front of him with my mouth hanging open—trembling, and still enraged. I knew the bond could only show the truth. Collin's eyes were the unreal vibrant blue that I saw after the attack. They were no longer red with bloodlust. Gasping, I stepped away from him. My voice was a whispered shock, "It was you? *You* saved me the night Jake attacked me? You were there?" My hand clutched my throat. I could barely breathe.

He nodded once. "Yes, but it's my fault. The whole thing is my fault. I asked Jake to watch you, suspecting you'd change. I could sense it was imminent—the scent of your blood combined with your suffering—you were prime Martis material. It wasn't a lucky guess that he found you. I led him to you. He was supposed to protect you, but that was never his intention. He betrayed me, and tried to take your power for himself. Ivy, I'm the reason you were attacked. I'm the reason you're tainted. I'm the one who changed you from Martis. It was my fault. All of it." He paused unable to look at me. "I couldn't lose you. Not when I could save you. And I didn't want to bind you to me. I already told you that. I wanted all of you, unhindered." He smiled faintly. "I knew Jake drained your soul, and that you didn't have any left. All living beings must have enough soul to sustain them. I tried to return your last piece of soul, the one that drained onto the ground when I ripped Jake away from you, but it didn't work. It wouldn't return to you once it was free, so I took it and combined it with a piece of mine. My putrid scrap of soul wasn't enough to release me from being a Valefar—but when combined with your last fragment of soul; it was enough to restore your life. I used my blood to seal it inside of you, but my blood changed you."

He sighed, pushing his hair out of his face and looking me in the eye. "When I left you that night, I thought you were fine. Your mark was still blue and Eric had you. I thought you'd be okay. It wasn't until I saw your mark had turned purple that I knew what happened. I'm the reason you're the Prophecy One. It's my fault." He stood there, looking at me.

My emotions were so wild that I had no idea how I felt. I knew the bond couldn't lie. And I believed his words. But something was still off. I said, "So why did you open the portal? Why were you going to sacrifice me?" My fists were gripping my weapon so tightly that my hand shook.

He shook his head. "I wasn't. Once I saw you were tainted, I tried to derail the prophecy. I taught you how to use your Valefar powers and you started doing things I've never seen before. Things that weren't part of the prophecy. I thought it would counter it, and maybe the prophecy would change course—like you'd hoped. But it didn't. It just kept moving towards this portal opening. The Valefar were still looking for you, the painting, and the key. They wouldn't stop until they had all three. I saw the key around your neck at the church." He swallowed hard, looking around him quickly at the fighting, then back at me. "I knew we had all three. I told them to open the portal."

Rage shot through me, "How could you do that to me?"

He held up his hands, speaking calmly over my yelling, "Ivy, I made a pact with Kreturus."

"I know!" I yelled back.

"No, you *don't* know," he said. "I told him I would bring him the Purple One. But he doesn't know it's you." His eyes locked with mine, half hoping I would understand, but also hoping I wouldn't. I could feel it through the bond.

"If you weren't giving me to him, then... ?" *What is he thinking?*

A soft smile spread across his face, and he said, "Ivy. My mark is purple, too. I'm taking your place." My jaw gaped, as I stared at him, horrified. That was his plan?

He smiled weakly at me, taking a small step back. "Like you said—a life for a life. I failed to protect you the night you were attacked." His blue eyes bore into me as his foot dragged slowly backwards. "I was too late. And I can't make up for what I did to you. I can't change it." He stepped back, a final time. His eyes were filled with remorse. "I won't fail you now." He was at the edge of the salt circle before I realized it. I stood there too stunned to move, not really believing what was happening.

He saved me. He cursed me. And I changed him violet. He was a freak like me, even if he didn't have my powers. He no longer fit anywhere either—he was a Valefar with part of a Martis soul. I shook my head taking a step towards him, still not realizing what he was about to do. Collin looked at me one last time. His eyes never left mine, "I love you, Ivy Taylor." He breathed in deeply, turned his back to me, and launched his body into the pit.

Fear shot through me as I screamed, "Collin!" watching him fall. All the breath rushed out of my body, as I lunged for him. The ground collided with me as my arm shot out, narrowly missing his hand. Anguish rose from deep within me, as I screamed, helplessly watching him fall to his death inside the inky pit. Sobs heaved from deep within. I hung on the edge of the rim half hanging into the pit, with vision blurred by tears, and unable to accept what happened.

He sacrificed himself for me—he took my place.

CHAPTER THIRTY-TWO

Collin's sacrifice shifted the battle in the Martis' favor. The remaining Valefar scattered into the night, after seeing Collin fall into the chasm. They thought I defeated him. They thought I threw him in, even though I hadn't. It didn't matter what really happened, not after watching the flaming-haired girl killing everything in her way. They feared me.

The wind howled as it whipped my hair over my head, and I clung to the edge of the pit. The ends no longer glowed with a false flame. I stared into the pit, seeing nothing, barely breathing. Shannon's arms tugged me to my feet, dragging me away from the rim. I let her. I was too weak to protest, or to think. The confused shock was rippling through me in unrelenting waves, as I watched the portal's power increase.

More dirt fell away as the rim grew even wider, hitting the edge of the salt circle. It was complete. The portal was open. The ground churned, grumbling so loudly that I could feel the vibrations through my shoes. Julia ran toward us, a grave expression on her panicked porcelain doll face. Other Martis, including Al, swiftly came up behind her. The pit cast a faint glow on their faces from the illuminated salt line.

Al turned as she took in the portal. "We have to seal it up."

Julia's hands flew frantically through the air while she spoke, "We can't. I knew this would happen! The portal will not close now. It's reached its full size. Only a Valefar can close it."

"We can't close it yet," my voice squeaked with shock, "Collin… Collin will come back." My eyes were wide and unblinking, as I turned slowly toward Al, wanting her to agree with me.

But she shook her head. "He couldn't have survived that, Ivy. He knew what he did before he did it. He saved you."

Julia's panicked voice cut through me, not allowing me any time to process anything, "If we don't seal it soon, they will start to come out. How else can we close the portal, if she won't do it?"

Stunned, I looked into her worried face. What will come out? Her brown eyes were wide, pinched together, and ready to have a nuclear-sized panic attack. What had her so freaked? Kreturus wasn't summoned, or he'd already be here. So why was she freaking out?

Shannon's hand was on my arm, "We can't save him. I would. For you, I'd do anything. But if we don't close this, God knows what'll come out."

"What?" I asked, not understanding. I shook my head and stared at them. The wind and cold pelted my body, but I didn't feel it.

Julia gritted her teeth, snapping at me, "She knows what'll come out!"

And I did. Deep inside of me, I knew what was in there. It was a gateway to Hell. Those things I'd seen in my visions—the servant demons where down there. Waiting. Trapped. They wanted their freedom as much as Collin wanted his. If there was a way out, they would take it—no matter the risk.

Al came up behind me. "You know what you need to do, girl. Do it before it's too late. You're the only one who can close it."

Tears flowed freely down my cold cheeks. "Are you sure there's no way he's... It's not possible he survived, is it?" The desperation was so transparent, even Julia noticed.

Julia unfolded her arms. "It's possible. But Ivy, it's not probable. If the fall didn't kill him, Kreturus did."

I don't think she meant to be cruel, but my bottom lip quivered involuntarily. I bit it to hold it still. I couldn't think. Why were they looking at me? "I don't know how."

Al said, "Dark magic opened the pit—it has to be the same magic to close it. Valefar magic."

Thoughts ran wildly through my mind. It was too much. This was too horrible. All this time he was protecting me, trying to make the prophecy change course. Then he threw himself into the pit. He saved me twice. *And what if he's still alive? I'll seal him in.* It would be worse than burying him alive.

My stomach twisted in knots and it threatened to purge itself. Swallowing hard, I looked around, not knowing what to do. My eyes fixated on the dimly lit rim. It cast an odd shadow onto the pitch-black walls. Patches of slime took on an odd shine under the light—a shape almost. My heart soared, as I ran to the edge, falling on my knees. Something was moving. I called down, "Collin?!"

The sound of its voice was like gurgling gravel, "No. Not him." My stomach dropped, as I recognized the demon's voice. It was one of the demons in my vision. My heart raced, as I peered over the edge. Movement made my eyes jump to different places on the wall, and then deep into the pit.

"Demons! The demons are climbing out!" I yelled, pushing away from the edge.

Frantically, I shot to my feet, backing away with my heart pounding in my ears. Those things terrified me. They were the reality of my visions. I didn't want to be the girl I would become. Fighting the growing terror within me, I looked at the others. They were helpless, but none of them were crying the way I was. Tears streamed down my face. I was the only one stupid enough to love a Valefar.

Eric ran to the edge confirming to the others what I saw. He was shouting, "We have to seal the pit. Now!" Terrified, I could barely think. The only thing I knew was that I wanted nothing to do with the black creature covered in dark slime, its glowing red eyes, or its gravelly voice. And I never wanted to meet their master. Ever. Even though Collin took my place, this wasn't over yet.

"What do I do?" I asked. My body felt frozen, as the wind chilled me to the core. Julia shook her head, muttering under her breath in Italian.

Al said, "Do what you learned. You're part Valefar. You gotta see if it's enough. Call the darkness to seal them in."

"The darkness?" I asked, unsure of what she meant. Al nodded. The other Martis started to back away. They had looked at me without really noticing what I was before, but now they saw it. I was half Valefar. I was their enemy. They slowly backed away, physically showing how alone I actually was.

I called out, knowing that I needed him. "Eric. Don't leave." He nodded, staying near me. With my lips pressed tightly together, I choked back a sob, and focused all my attention on the ruby ring. I commanded the shadows to come to me, but nothing happened. The night was dark. The dim light from the salt ring wasn't bright enough to cast even a small shadow, and I needed a large source of illumination. My eyes raked the area for a shadow, for anything, but there was nothing. The farms were engulfed in darkness.

"What's the matter?" Al asked, immediately noticing the look on my face.

"There are no shadows. I need a large shadow, but there aren't any." I turned to Sister Al. "I can't call them if there aren't any to be called."

Before I could say anything else, Eric had conjured the dual sphere of light into his hand. It glowed with a dim blue. "Will this help?" he asked.

I shook my head. "It's too dim. The only thing that will cast a large enough shadow is the church building."

Closing his eyes, he cupped his hands. The sphere started to grow. The orb of light quickly outgrew the size of his palm, and floated above like it was a balloon. It cast a blue light on Eric, as sweat dripped from his temples.

Julia gasped, "I didn't know he could do that." Her eyes were wide, as she watched him. A few other Martis mumbled that they could not call that much light, and wondered how he was doing it.

The shadows stretched out from the stone building, forming a silhouette of the church on the ground. As Eric's light grew larger, the shadow increased in size and clarity. Reaching through the darkness, I connected to my inner Valefar, and I called the shadow to me. I'd never called something so large. It was the size of a building, and I knew it would have to travel through me to be of any use. The idea repulsed me, but I had no choice.

The shadow obeyed and flowed through my body. It felt like icy fingers stroking my soul. I shuddered trying to hold it, as its death-like chill ravaged my body. I physically shivered, trying to hold it inside of me. Out of the corner of my eye, I saw Eric's strained face. Sister Al trembled as she watched the edge of the pit. Some of the demons were nearing the rim. I felt the shadow flow out of me and directed it to fill the hole, but something was wrong. It just flowed into the pit like water, splashing down the sides. It didn't affect the demons.

"Is that enough? Or can it at least hold them off?" I asked in gasps.

Julia laughed crazily, "Hold them off? This is a hole into Hell. No. There is no holding them off. They want out." I really didn't like her. Shaking, I held the shadow in place, not understanding why it wasn't working. The shadow had to be large enough. But, it wouldn't seal the top. It just flowed down the walls.

Eric glanced at me, and said, "They used the key to open it, right? Maybe it doesn't just open the portal, but holds it open?" Nodding, I agreed. But I couldn't even see the key to know if his idea were true. Trembling, I could feel my body wanting to give out.

Al's frantic voice brought me back, "The demons are too close the rim. We are going to try to push them back. You two hold your positions. Whatever you do, don't stop!"

I watched as a demon climbed closer to the mouth of the pit. It had the deformed figure of the demons in my vision. Its eyes burned red, and his skin was slick.

He crawled to the edge of the hole, like darkness creeping from a grave. The demon neared the edge, slowly climbing the slick walls with its taloned fingers. A snake like tongue protruded from its reptilian face as it stopped near the edge. "My Queen. You released us." Its tongue flicked, and licked its burning eye. "A life for a life." His eyes looked behind him, and then flicked back to me. His breath smelled like cabbage.

"You can go back to where you came from," I said, trying to sound more confident that I felt. Sweat beaded, and ran down my spine.

Its tongue wet his other eye, and then slid back into its mouth. "You will serve us, whether you accept today or we force you on another. You've no choice." My heart raced. The cut on my cheek burned. Ignoring it, I reached for the place inside of me, and pulled out every drop of strength I had left, trying to hold the massive shadow. The demon slid back several feet, and flashed his teeth at me. They were several rows that were pointed like kitchen knives. Some of his previous meals were still stuck in the crevices. "Ivy Taylor will be queen!" I shivered when it said my name, fighting every instinct to flee.

Looking at the group of Martis, I was wondering what was taking them so long. Eric conjured light into a massive sphere in seconds, but the lot of them didn't have enough light to make a street lamp. My heart fluttered. I couldn't call light to push that thing back down. And it wanted me. I felt my face grimace as I looked at it, and couldn't hide my disgust.

Her perky voice made me think I was hallucinating. "Ivy Taylor will *not* be queen today." Jenna Marie, clad in solid pink, walked up next to me like she was at a picnic.

Frantic, I said, "Jenna Marie! Run! Run away from here! Now!" I strained, weakening under the shadow's massive weight. Jenna Marie put her hand on my shoulder. Then she stood next to me. I urged her, "You can't stay here! Leave! They'll kill you!" I shouted at her, but she tisked me. She friggin' tisked me!

"Ivy, calm down," she said. "Let's send these things back to where they came from." She smiled her pink lips at me, and withdrew a silver ring from her finger. The blue mark instantly appeared, glittering above her brow. My jaw dropped. She was a Martis! *Why the hell is everyone around me a Martis or a Valefar!* I glared at her. She ignored me, still pleasant and perky. "Hey Althea! Long time no see!" She threw her power into their circle of dimly lit spheres. When Jenna Marie added her sphere of light to the rest, it was enough. The orbs slid down the side of the pit, illuminating the horrors below. Demons clung to the walls of the pit like roaches, crawling swiftly to the top. When the light passed over them, some slid back down, while others lost their grip and fell. It bought us a few minutes.

I yelled to Eric, "I'm going to try to get the key. No matter what happens, do *not* stop. You have to hold the light where it is or I'll lose control of the shadow."

Eric nodded, looking concerned. "Ivy how are you... ?" His sentence trailed off as he watched me.

Pressing my finger to the ruby ring, I held the shadow in place. It was leaving me breathless to hold something so large for so long, but I knew I had to get the key, or everything would be in vein. It worked before with a person. Now, I hoped I could do it with an object. I rubbed the ruby stone concentrating on the ivory peonies surrounded by the shining black disc. I saw the black chain that held the pendant in the hollow of my throat. I could almost feel the smoothness of the black stone on the back of the pendant slide into my palm.

Reaching out, I felt for it with my mind. Through the shadows, and glistening slime in the pit, I saw it in the wall at the top of the rim. Swallowing hard I focused. The cold corpse-like fingers of the shadow didn't like the flames licking my stomach, as I attempted to efanotate the pendant into my hand. The shadows tried to recoil as the flames traveled through my body, but I fought to hold them.

I screamed out as the two manifestations of evil warred within me, but I released neither. They were slaves, like all Valefar, and had to do what they were told. I bid the necklace to appear in my palm. As the feeling of being burned alive and consumed by cold death covered my body, I doubled over, clutching my stomach. I was combining things that didn't want to go together, forming a new kind of torture. Pressing my eyes closed as tightly as possible, I held onto the heat knowing that in a few seconds the pendant would be in my palm. I just had to be strong enough to call it and hold the shadows at the same time. Fire burned through my bones and icy death stroked my twitching muscles. I cried out again.

Soon. I'll have it soon. Don't let go. The voices around me no longer made sense. It sounded like I was in a tunnel and they were far away. I could no longer hold my palm open, waiting for the necklace. My fists closed, as my body was raked with pain. I crouched on the ground refusing to release either power. A scream rose up from my throat as the fire seared, white hot, and then faded. The fist that I had clenched so tightly that my nails pierced my flesh was holding something. I forced my fingers to uncurl. Apryl's necklace was in the center of my palm.

I felt my body failing fast. The shadows had been fighting the heat so intensely that they did not stop when the heat receded. The shadow's frozen nature threatened to consume me whole. My body shook as I tried to stand. Holding my trembling body upright, I open my palm and commanded the shadow, "Go." It knew what to do. The shadow left my palm in a wide black ribbon, as cold traveled up my throat tore out of my mouth. Although it looked like the shadow flew from my hand, my body felt like it was being ripped from my stomach, slicing its way up my throat, and out of my mouth. Demon power was painfully cruel.

I tried to push back the hurt, but the shadow had grown so intense that I couldn't. I closed my eyes, as it wound its way around the pit, starting at the center. Ribbon after ribbon was laid down forming a black barricade. When I opened my eyes only the rim was left open uncovered, and the shadow was quickly closing it. The last black ribbon touched the edge of the salt circle on the far side, beginning to seal the portal.

The ground shook, as the demons raced faster to the top. The walls of the pit began to crumble and fall in. Each time the outer edge crumbled, it was replaced with solid ground, and the salt circle shrank. The portal was closing itself. Breathing raggedly, I held the shadow until the circle collapsed. I had to be sure.

The demon that had spoken to me before was at the rim, trapped under a black film. "Queen. Collin Smith lives. And you will be Queen." His gurgling voice was hushed when the ground covered over him, and sealed the hole.

Shaking, I swallowed hard, and opened my palm to release the shadow. Its frigid hold on me was stripped out of my throat, making my spine arch in a painful at the response. It left my body and flew back into the ground in front of the church. I collapsed. It was so cold. I was barely aware of the others around me. Haze filled my vision, as I tried to hold my eyes open. My face lay against the frozen earth, and a nearby light faded into a beautiful pale blue. Then the blackness engulfed me.

Slowly, I opened my eyes, trying to figure out where I was. I was no longer raked with cold, although my vision was still clouded. I sat up slowly, and groaned as my body protested.

"Easy, Ivy." It was Eric's voice, although I couldn't make out more than a shadowy outline of him.

"What happened? Where am I?" My voice was raspy and it hurt to speak. It felt like I was lying on a hard cot.

Eric's blurred form sat across from me. "We're at Al's church. We took you back here when you didn't come to."

"How long? How long have I been out?" I rasped, rubbing my eyes. Why wouldn't they focus?

"A few days." He said softly. "I was worried you weren't going to wake up. Are you all right?"

I didn't know. Quietly, I sat there for a moment, blinking, forgetting that I would never forgive him. My vision wouldn't clear. I swallowed hard, "I can't see. Everything is hazy."

Eric sat next to me. His hands were on my face, as he said, "Let me see."

His face was very close to mine. I could feel his warm breath, but I couldn't see him any better. My heart raced as I started to panic because my eyes refused to focus. Finally I asked, "What happened to me?"

Eric said, "You saved everyone. It's making Julia's head spin, since she thought you were supposed to be evil."

I gave a little hollow laugh. "I'm stupid. Not evil."

"No, you're not. I told you already. You're smarter than anyone I know." He paused, and took my hand. I didn't pull away, although dread pooled in my stomach. He said, "I need to tell you something, but I want Shannon to take a look at your eyes first. Please Ivy. I need to talk to you. Okay?" I said nothing, turning away from him. He sighed, and walked away. My heart sunk. He wanted a chance to explain what happened with Apryl. I wasn't sure if I wanted to know. I couldn't take more heartbreak. It wouldn't undo what was done. She was dead, and somehow he was responsible.

Shannon and Al came into the room, followed by Eric. Julia snapped for Eric. He left, following her down the hall. I said, "She doesn't sound happy."

"She's never happy," Shannon said softly. "Let me look at your eyes." Shannon's hands were on my face before I could say anything. She turned my head, shining a tiny light into my eyes. The pinpoint of light cut through the haze, slowly melting it away. I sat very still, wondering how she did that. I expected to see a laser in her hand, or something similar, as the haze that distorted my vision melted away. But, instead I saw a tiny orb of pale blue light. She prodded the light, moved it, and poured it onto my eyes. When she was done, my vision was restored.

I blinked at her, stunned. "How did you learn to do that?"

She shrugged, "I didn't. It's innate. When someone needs healing, a Dyconisi knows what to do." She smiled at me, and threw her arms around my shoulders. "I'm glad you're here."

I hugged her back and said, "Me too."

When she released me, she said, "That thing lied, you know?" Her green eyes looked worried. I nodded, unable to answer. I wanted to believe that Collin was alive. But I couldn't. The sadness of that certainty clung to me.

CHAPTER THIRTY-THREE

I sat at the St. Bart's with Sister Al. In the past month, she'd helped me adjust. Most of the Martis left, Julia went back to Rome, and life resumed. I grieved as we buried my mom, and sorted out what was left of my life. It wasn't much. Mom had left me some money, so I didn't have to live in a box. But I lost everything.

And everyone.

All the memories, the things I had from my mom and sister—they all burned. There wasn't even a photograph remaining. The only thing I had left was the necklace, and comb that Apryl gave me. Shannon had saved them the night of the battle. I was so consumed by shock when Collin went over the edge that I didn't notice he'd left them behind.

Everyone I loved was gone. My family was dead. I was alone. I suddenly had no past, as well as no future. The sting of death was trying to catch up with me. I didn't want to think about it. I didn't want think about shirking off my mom, or my last angry words to Collin. Guilt gnawed at me constantly. I kept moving, trying to push it away.

Sister Al held a steaming teacup in her hand. She'd given me one too, but mine held steaming cocoa. I inhaled the vapor. Al's wrinkled skin had a rosy complexion again. She looked worn after the battle, but seeing Jenna Marie—who was her missing boss and best friend—helped her rebound quickly. Jenna Marie's task had also been to find me; the Prophecy Girl. She determined the location that I would originate almost two-hundred years ago, and waited until I showed up.

She had the patience of a saint. No wonder why she was so perky. It turns out that is why the area had so many Valefar and Martis. They were all waiting for me, the Prophecy One to show myself. As if I'd wanted the job.

After Shannon healed me, everyone left quickly. They had to report what happened to the Tribunal in Rome and decide how to proceed. It was clear that I fought for the Martis, but after expecting to destroy me for over two thousand years, it required a lot of paper work to get everyone on the same page. Julia disappeared, taking Eric with her. I didn't get to hear what he had to say. I assumed he'd be back, begging me to listen. I wasn't sure if I wanted to, but after what happened with Collin, I was willing to admit that I didn't know everything. Actually, I was willing to admit that I knew less than I did before all this started.

Al's voice cut the silence, "So, are we gonna keep ignoring it?"

A sad smile tugged at my lips, "Ignoring what?" It'd been like this every day for a month. I didn't go to school. I didn't have to once they found out my Mom died. No one noticed that I'd ditched the field trip, either. Social services left me alone since Al claimed me. I let her. I had no other family. The school didn't expect to see me again until after Christmas, which was fine with me. So, I spent my afternoons like this; sipping hot liquid with an old lady.

"The prophecy," she said.

I leaned back into my chair. "I hadn't thought about the prophecy." I didn't want to.

"Well, here's something you may want to think about. What if everyone was wrong? What if the prophecy didn't mean what we thought it did?" she asked.

My mouth hung open, as I put my cup on the table. "What are you talking about? Of course it was right. That thing even told me I would be its queen. I know you heard it." I shivered. That demon scared me. A vivid memory of the sound of its voice, and the smell of its breath, hit me. The realness of that creature made my vision of being the demon queen way too real.

"Yes. I heard it. It said you will be queen." She paused, sipping her tea. "You know, there is only a single ruler in the Underworld at a time—a king or a queen. The only ruler that I have ever known is Kreturus. His reign spans my lifetime and more. He's cruel—vile beyond words. Since you have Valefar abilities, you must have noticed the price of his power. Everything is paid in pain, misery, and agony. There is no rest, no peace for his kind.

"But, right now I sit across from a girl, who is part of his lineage, and is more powerful than he ever was— even though she is still young." She smiled at me, "And the things that have been laying the path to your dark fate are not things that were malicious or evil—they are actions that originated from love and kindness. Ivy, we thought the Prophecy One would be more powerful and more evil than Kreturus. But, how can that be true when the child I see sitting in front of me is you?"

I didn't know what to say. Tears stung my eyes, and before I could blink one away it rolled down my cheek. "It doesn't matter what I do, does it? That's still my fate. There is nothing I can do to stop it. I tried and failed."

"Ah," she said, "but perhaps stopping it shouldn't be the goal?" I wiped the tears from my face and stared at her unbelievingly.

"You think I should just *accept* my fate? How can you say that? You know what it means. I'll be trapped in the Underworld, with no friends and no family. I'll be alone forever, becoming something that I don't want to be." My chest felt hollow as the words poured from my heart. My destiny cost me everything. Accepting it meant Mom and Collin died in vain. No, I couldn't accept it.

"That's the part that I think we got wrong. It was assumed that you would continue in Kreturus' footsteps, but the prophecy doesn't explicitly say that. And I can't see you becoming the Destroyer, not when you've fought so hard to protect the ones you love. Perhaps your destiny involves this dark place, but the person you become is still in your hands." She sipped her tea.

I stared into my untouched cocoa, "It doesn't feel like it. It feels like I have no control over anything. And how is a good person supposed to live in Hell? That's not the way things are."

"No? Are you sure?" she looked at me through ancient eyes. "I've seen some things that make me believe things aren't as clear as you might think. I recently heard of an evil Valefar boy who saved a Martis girl, twice. Everything we know says that his actions were not possible, but that mark on your head says otherwise. Ivy, would an evil person give his life for you?"

I looked up at her. "No. And I don't think Collin was evil. He was a slave, forced to do things he didn't want to. When he resisted, when he refused to hand me over to Kreturus, it cost him his life." My throat tightened as I spoke. I hadn't spoken about Collin since the night he sacrificed himself for me.

"And what if he is still alive and waiting in the Underworld?"

My heart pounded. I couldn't believe she was suggesting it. "You mean... what if he's still alive? He couldn't have survived that fall. And if he did... " I closed my eyes. There was no way he survived the beast at the bottom, if the fall didn't kill him.

"If he did, you have a good boy in an evil place. You see what I mean? Things aren't so simple. You for instance, people will say you are evil because you have demon blood coursing through your veins. But, I know you to be a good person. Some may say Collin was a Valefar and evil. But, you also told me that you were bonded to him. There is only one way for that to occur. You both have a bit of the other's soul. You both performed the selfless act of saving the other by giving a piece of yourself. Selflessness is not evil." She sighed heavily. "Ivy, what I'm trying to tell you is that your destiny may not change, but the path that takes you there has not yet formed. I suspect your heart will pave your path, and take you where need to go."

I heard every word she said, but I fixated on one thing. She thought Collin may be alive. "He can't be alive, Al. I saw the pit. You don't need to sugarcoat things for me. I know I won't see him again."

"I don't know," she answered. "When Shannon comes in, ask her about the pit. Ask her what she thinks."

I shook my head. Shannon was very logical. Her answer would be obvious. "I know what she'll think. She'll tell me it's not possible."

"What's not possible?" Shannon dropped her book bag on the floor. She grabbed a bag full of Oreos and a cup of milk. She was still wearing her school uniform. I looked at her, not wanting to say it. My palms were slick. I wanted to ask her. The uncertainty of his death was making me nuts. It was like he disappeared, but I knew better. He was dead. My eyes saw him fall. There was no way he survived. A breath caught in my throat. I couldn't say it. I couldn't hope it.

"Do you think Collin could be alive?" Al blurted out.

Shannon straddled a chair, and pulled the Oreos and a glass of milk in front of her. "Well, it *is* possible. The pit allows things in, but it doesn't let them out."

"What do you mean?" My voice shook.

Shannon looked at Al, as if to ask permission to speak of such things to me. Al nodded and Shannon continued, "The sides were black slime and spikes—I know they looked bad. But the story about the pit says that it was made to hold that thing—Kreturus. He had to get down there somehow—without dying. So, it *is* possible."

That was the logic I dreaded. Right there. Uncertainty made me restless. It stole the sense of control that I so desperately needed. The clock ticked in the room. For a while it was the only sound I could hear. I stared, seeing nothing, dropping the cookie, floating it in my cocoa. I wished I knew for sure what happened to him. Jagged rocks were bad. But add the big demon at the bottom of the pit as a factor, and there was no hope. Holding out false hope almost destroyed me before. I kept waiting for Apryl to come home, but she never came. This felt so similar. I just couldn't believe it.

"Being a Seyer sucks," I stood and dumped the rest of my cocoa in the sink.

"And why's that?" Al asked.

"I can't see the one thing I want to see. I just want to know for sure." I leaned against the counter and looked at Al. "I didn't get to say goodbye to him either. I wish I told him... anything. The last words I said to him were something along the lines of you suck. I didn't believe what he said." I grimaced, trying to hold back tears. I could cry later. "I didn't know what he was doing. He hid it from me. Even with the bond. It was easier to believe the lies."

Al answered, "Seyers don't get to see what they want. Or what they wish. It's a blessing and a curse. And you're not just a Seyer. It's time someone told you that."

I nodded. "You told me that before. That I had a little of all three."

"Yup, I did," Al said, as she cracked her arthritic knuckles. "But it's more than that. You have strong traits of all three types of Martis. You healed someone who was half dead. Add to the fact that his soul was almost non-existent, and the tiny piece you found was covered in centuries of evil, and it's amazing that you healed him at all. But you did. You are a powerful healer." My heart sank. I didn't want to hear this. It didn't matter now. "And then during the battle—I watched you fight the Valefar. You hesitated at first, but then you became luminescent as you cut down anything in your way. And I know the demon kiss haunts you. You managed to attack while hearing the Martis cry out around you. Nothing distracted you. You fought like a great warrior."

"No, I didn't. I hesitated, because," I took a deep breath knowing my next words would sound insane. "I didn't want to kill them. They're slaves, Al. They have no choice. Every power they were given is laced with pain. Even their conversions—their demon kisses— were scarring on so many levels. No part of them remained unscathed. The demons stole their lives. They got an eternity of servitude with never ending agony. I didn't want to kill them."

The room was so silent I could hear Shannon and Al breathing. I swallowed hard, not looking at either of them. Al finally said, "Ivy, you see things we can't. It's who you are. There's never been one like you before. Just be careful that your anger doesn't get a hold of you again. I can sense it beneath your sadness."

I hung my head. "I'm fine. It's just… too much happened too fast. My life was ripped out of my hands, and people that I trusted turned on me."

"I know who you're talking about," she said. "Eric didn't do what they told you. I don't know why he didn't correct you, when you repeated it to him."

"No," I shook my head, "He killed Apryl. He said so."

Al answered, "I know what he said. I also know he didn't do it. I saw who killed her, and it wasn't him."

Shannon leaned forward, asking, "You saw it? Who was it?"

"I don't know," Al answered. "I haven't seen the person before. I'm sorry, but I don't know. I just know it wasn't Eric."

I pushed my hair out of my face and let out a whoosh of air. "Where is he?"

Shannon spewed cookie, saying, "Julia assigned him somewhere awful for disobeying her."

"But he saved everyone... He had to help me to close the pit. Without him, we would have died." What the hell was wrong with her? I couldn't believe she would punish him for saving everyone.

"Doesn't matter," Shan patted the crumbs from her lips, "She doesn't do things that way."

"What way?" I asked. "The sane way? How hard is it to notice his disobedience saved her? Is that the way Martis are thanked? What is wrong with that woman?" My shoulders slumped as I deflated. I didn't understand Julia. I didn't want to either. I asked, "Well, how do I find him?"

"Through Julia," Al said.

"Figures," I huffed. "And she's in Italy. Swell."

"I'm going," Shannon licked the cream off her fingers, "You should come."

I blinked at her. "Why are you going to Italy?"

"To report the prophecy stuff. I witnessed it and was one of the only Dyconisi there. You should come. You can hunt down Eric. You can also find out what happened to your sister." Al shot her a look. "If you wanted."

I looked at Al. "What aren't you telling me? Does Eric know what happened to Apryl? Did you see something?"

Al shook her head. "I didn't see anything that would help. Just faces. And I don't know what Eric knows. Sometimes that boy says nothing, trying to get around the lying thing that binds us to tell the truth." She leaned back in her chair, "I suspect he knows more than he said."

Thoughts spun in my head so fast, I felt like I was going to hurl. Giddy excitement that Collin might be alive was trying to rise to the surface, but I couldn't let it. That was too much. I couldn't bear it. I didn't know what to do. Or what to think.

The vision pulled me in quickly, before I could put my head down. I felt the rush of air against my skin, but not the impact of the table.

Black mist swirled around me. When it cleared, I was surrounded in inky darkness. But, this black was weird. I couldn't see anything, despite my enhanced vision. I started to panic, wondering what happened. I heard nothing, and saw nothing. Goose bumps rose on my arms. It felt like I was trapped in a coffin, and I almost screamed. But just then—I felt something. A silky thread of the bond licked my stomach.

No. It couldn't be.

I repressed what I thought was a lie, but it wouldn't obey me. The sensation became stronger and I knew it was him. Collin was near. I was afraid to call out, not knowing where I was, and unable to see through the darkness. *Collin?* I silently asked, not expecting anything back. My mind and my senses were at war. My brain was still denying the possibility, but my senses had accepted reality.

Collin's panicked voice reached my mind. *Ivy, run. Get out of here now!*

But, I wasn't really here, so I didn't know why I had to run? I didn't try to wake up. I wanted to find him. A voice in the darkness wasn't enough. I had to see him. Suddenly I felt something, and I could see again. The darkness became thick, as the air dripped with moisture. Flaming eyes, the size of ovens, appeared before me. When the creature opened its mouth to speak, I thought I'd die, the smell was putrid. "Come to me, Ivy Taylor," his voice gurgled like he was choking on rocks. "Let me reclaim what's mine."

I started to walk toward him. He couldn't hurt me. This was a vision. The room felt colder and colder. I stepped nearer and nearer to the demon. "You're Kreturus?"

"I am," it gurgled. As I got closer, I could see faintly. The creature was huge. It spread from one end of the cave to the other. I looked around and noticed it wasn't a cave. I was standing in a pit. Suddenly, the bond raged within me. It wrapped around my core and started to jerk me back into the darkness.

Collin cried out, "You can't have her!" The demon made a horrifying sound. My heart pounded in my chest when I saw that I was right in front of it. I pushed myself away, retreating back into the thick mist, and back into the darkness. The bond pushed me hard, one final time. Then, I woke from the vision sucking in air. My body was ice cold.

"He's alive," the words flew out of my mouth as I sat up. My heart hammered. "And he's with that *thing*."

Al put her hand on my back to steady me. "Tell me what you saw."

I told them everything. No one spoke when I was done. Staring into space, I said, "I know he's there."

Al breathed in a shocked breath. "Kreturus almost took you," she stuttered. "You stopped breathing."

"You went white Ivy. And cold." Shannon sat next to me. Her eyes were wide.

Slightly stunned, I looked at them. I felt it in the vision. It made sense now. "I felt it—the cold, the demon, and the deformed bond. It was weird. I went right up to the demon. I've never been seen in a vision before. How did it see me? It can't kill me in a vision, can it?"

Al shook her head. "Kreturus can't pull Martis in through a vision, but you aren't a pure Martis. The blood that flows through your veins is his blood. While you aren't enslaved like the other Valefar, he can still exert control over you in your visions. And without the ability to conjure light, you will be at his mercy."

"She did conjure light," Shannon said. "I saw it come to her when she healed Collin."

Al regarded me carefully, "If that is true, then you should be able to use it in your visions. But, it's not responding to you as it does to a Martis. And if the light will not protect you when you call it—Ivy, no one has ever gone into that pit and come back out."

A smile spread across my face. A tinge of hope shot through me. "The demons did. Thousands of them almost crawled out of it the other night. But, there was no trace of them in my vision today. They were gone."

Al's voice sounded frantic, "What do you mean, *they were all gone*? The demons should have been trapped in the pit with him. The Martis that captured him made sure that pit was isolated and secure. There was no way in and no way out. The demons who battled with him were trapped down there with him.

"If the demons are able to enter and leave as they wish, then what's holding Kreturus there?" The nun looked sullen.

"I don't know, Al. But, he acted like he was still trapped. He was really pissed off when Collin used the bond to shove me out of the vision. Maybe the demons were able to escape, but not Kreturus. Somehow the demons left the pit, even though they didn't leave through the portal. Al, that means there has to be another way out of Kreturus' pit. And, if they were able to leave, then there's got to be another way in."

Shannon said, "If there is, Julia would know how to find it. She has access to old stuff like that." Shannon's brow was covered in sweat.

"Kreturus," Al said, "is worse than what you faced here, Ivy. Collin knew that when he went it. He knew that when he told you to leave your vision. And, I already know what you're thinking. If you go in after him, you may not come back at all." She smiled at me, "I knew your heart would pave your path."

I looked at her anxious face, and knew she was right. My heart belonged to Collin, and he was alive. There was no way I could possibly leave him there. I risked my life to save him the night he lay bleeding in my arms. There was no way to know back then that we shared the same soul, but we did. He had a piece of me and I had a piece of him. All this time I thought that the Underworld was my destiny, but that wasn't true. Collin was. He was my soul mate, and always would be. Whatever future I had, I knew he had to be in it. Al was right. All this time my heart was paving my path.

I took a breath, "Shannon, you were right."

She looked at me, stunned. "About what?"

I smiled at her. "You told me that the guy in the painting was trouble. That something would make me follow him. Something would make me *want* to be there in Underworld with him. Well, you were right, Shan. I'm going straight to Hell. And I'm not coming back without Collin."

Made in the USA
Lexington, KY
19 April 2011